SMALLPOX ISLAND

G. S. SPOONER

*To all that have served in the military
and to their spouses and families.*

SMALLPOX ISLAND
Copyright © 2022 by G. S. Spooner

All rights reserved. Printed in the United States of America. No part of this book may be used or reproduced in any manner whatsoever without written permission except in the case of brief quotations embodied in critical articles or reviews.
For permissions contact: smallpoxisland@gmail.com

Print ISBN: 979-8-3589386-2-5

First Edition: October 2022

Contents

Prologue	i
Chapter One	1
Chapter Two	21
Chapter Three	43
Chapter Four	66
Chapter Six	103
Chapter Seven	120
Chapter Eight	137
Chapter Nine	154
Chapter Ten	171
Chapter Eleven	186
Chapter Twelve	207
Chapter Thirteen	225

Chapter Fourteen	243
Chapter Fifteen	257
Epilogue	281

Prologue

September 1842

The scene is Sunflower Island, located on the Mississippi River, across from Alton, Illinois. It is a picturesque island with flora that includes numerous patches of flowers (including sunflowers), some thickets of brush, and several large trees. The fauna living on the four-hundred-yard-long by one-hundred-yard-wide island is limited to rodents, squirrels, rabbits, and a few transient deer. The date is Thursday, September 22, 1842, and the time is about 5 p.m.

A large fish jumps out of the river with a great splash, and a small rowboat appears through the mist of a hot, steamy day. The boat approaches Sunflower Island with several formally dressed men on board. Then another similar boat appears nearby. The oarsmen of each boat struggle with the current as they approach a small, sandy beach on the northeastern side of the island facing toward Alton.

The group on the first boat includes James Shields, age thirty-six. Shields is currently the Illinois state auditor. He has an entourage of five men with him on the small boat. The second boat includes a young lawyer named Abraham Lincoln. Lincoln is thirty-three years old and lives in Springfield, Illinois. He has a smaller entourage of three men with him.

Shields challenged Lincoln to a duel after there were several written attacks on him in the local paper. The issue concerned the use of paper money instead of gold and silver. Lincoln's initial provocative writing was written under the fictitious name of Aunt Becca. His fiancée, Mary Todd, then followed up with another Aunt Becca submission without his knowledge. In the article, she called Shields a liar and a fool. After reading it, Shields felt ridiculed by Lincoln, so he sought him out and personally challenged him to a duel. Lincoln accepted, even though he had not actually written the letter. Now, both men have agreed to travel across the Mississippi River to Sunflower Island for their duel because dueling is illegal in the state of Illinois. Since Lincoln was the one who was challenged, he is also allowed to choose the weapon for the contest. He has chosen the heavy cavalry sword instead of the pistol.

The boats pull up onto the sand. While some of the men secure the boats, other men from the groups scramble ahead to set up the scene for a duel near a large tree. They place a plank on the ground as a center and mark out a perimeter with sticks in the surrounding dirt. After a few generally courteous introductions, Shields and Lincoln approach the area near the great tree. Lincoln and Shields both examine the plank on the ground and the lines drawn on the dirt. The duelers are then armed with long, heavy swords. Lincoln grasps his sword, steps back, and begins to swing the sword with long, elliptical motions.

Lincoln, a full seven inches taller than his opponent, then reaches up with his long right arm and whacks off several tree limbs hanging nearly twelve feet above the ground. Upon seeing this, Shields and the encircling support teams begin to chatter immediately regarding the ridiculous nature of the endeavor. James

Smallpox Island

Shields stands strong and wiry, but he looks rather small next to the towering Lincoln. After a brief discussion, the five-foot-nine Shields offers to dismiss the duel, and the six-foot-four Lincoln submits his approval. The two men then exchange a few words of courtesy and the quarrel is ended.

With this, Lincoln states, "Gentlemen, please allow me a brief moment." He quickly pulls out a knife from under his coat. While a few of the men take a step backward, he smiles at them and walks around to the backside of the large tree. The future president takes a knee and carves something into the tree for about five minutes. As he stands up and begins to walk away, he announces to the group, "We don't want anyone to doubt our resolve to be here and to reconcile on this day." As Lincoln walks away, several members of his entourage walk around to the back of the tree. They read the carving that states, "A. L. 1842." It is the only carving on the trunk of the large tree. As both groups walk toward their boats to depart, Lincoln says, "Perhaps a libation from the saloon could mark this adventure as a victory for both parties." The entire group laughs and quickly agrees.

Both groups board their boats and depart the island. The view from the large tree remains with the departing boats and the city of Alton, Illinois in the background. The scene from the tree remains essentially the same as time and life fast forward through the years. Sunflower Island and Alton change very little as the years go forward to 1861. The majestic Mississippi River continues to flow to the south as it has for millennia. It flows past St. Louis, past St. Genevieve, past Cape Girardeau, and past the small river town of New Madrid, Missouri. The quaint yet bustling river town of New Madrid is located in southeastern Missouri's bootheel region.

Chapter One

March 1, 1861

In New Madrid, Missouri, two young men jumped out of a horse-drawn wagon. They quickly entered into a store. It was a cool day, but the sun was shining brightly from a clear, blue sky. The two brothers, William and James Logan (also known as Will and Jimmy), moved rapidly as they walked and jogged through the dirt roads of Main Street in New Madrid. Jimmy was twenty years old and William was eighteen. Jimmy was six feet tall. He was stout and somewhat muscular in stature. Younger brother Will was about two inches taller than Jimmy, but he was slimmer and a bit lanky. They both had brown hair and brown eyes, but Jimmy's hair was straight and Willy's hair was curly, like his mother's. Jimmy had wide cheekbones and strong facial features and Willy's face was a bit longer and thinner. Both Jimmy and Will were handsome young men. They were intelligent, and sharp-witted, and had become immensely strong from years of working on their family's farm.

With abundant energy, they went from store to store, sharing witty and sharply divisive banter as they gathered provisions from a list made by their mother. Will talked to Jimmy as he carried a wooden box of nails to the wagon. He spoke with a slight Southern accent.

"Did you hear? New Madrid's own Captain John McCown is leaning toward the Confederacy."

"Who cares, Will? I need to get some more books to read, so I can stay smarter than him, which really shouldn't be too hard." Strangely, Jimmy didn't have a Southern accent. He spoke with a generally North American accent.

"Caleb Bullman says you're smart enough. Too smart."

"Bullman is a good for nothin' idiot!"

Jimmy entered the town's General Store and went straight for a rack of books and newspapers. Will entered right behind him and started to gather items from the list.

Jimmy took the store owner, Mr. Kimmel, aside and whispered a few words to him. The storekeeper departed only to return a moment later. "Here you are, son, four sets of catgut guitar strings. Just like you ordered." About ten minutes later, both boys exited the store, each carrying a sack of provisions.

"Catgut guitar strings. Really?" said Willy.

"Well, you didn't want me to use your guts, did ya?"

Will playfully shoved Jimmy in the face and quickly moved away. They finished loading all of the supplies in the back of their one-horse wagon and headed for home. The Logan Farm was located on the river, several miles south of New Madrid.

On the twenty-minute ride home, the boys discussed several topics. They talked about ongoing work on the farm, an upcoming dance, and their girlfriends, Patsy and Bonnie Caldwell. Jimmy's girl's name was Patsy and Will's girl was Bonnie. The girls were sisters and were about one year younger than the Logan boys. Even though they had talked about marriage, the brothers had temporarily opted not to marry the girls because of the unexpected death of their father four years before. They felt that it was more important to continue helping their mother out with the family farm. But now, four years had passed since John Logan's death. The delay had started to place an increased strain on the brother's relationships with both Patsy and Bonnie. Recently, and to the sisters' delight, the brothers had both informally promised to marry the girls. But now, just when the time had come to follow through on their promise, a war was brewing. Their plans of life were about to be altered by the times...and by their country.

The wagon approached a large but somewhat modest two-story farmhouse that was tattered white in color. Jimmy and Will Logan were the sons of Irish immigrants John and Martha Logan. John and Martha had come to America in 1831. The home was not a huge plantation-style house, but it did have a good-sized wraparound porch. It was surrounded by several large barns and smaller buildings. The Logans' house and their barns stood about one-half mile from the Mississippi River on several hills nestled around a rocky bluff. The hills had been flattened out to facilitate the buildings, and one of the larger barns had a partially collapsed roof. The Logan family farm stretched across forty acres of semi-wooded farmland located in or near the fertile soil of the mighty Mississippi.

Their mother, Martha Logan, was outside working near the side of the house. Martha was in her fifties but appeared to be slightly older than her actual age. Her brownish gray hair was tied back in a bun, and she was wearing a weathered work dress. Martha was still a handsome woman even though years of hard work on the farm had taken their toll. The Logans had four horses, five cows, ten sheep, and lots of chickens. Their yearly crop routine primarily included corn and one or two other crops (usually beans or potatoes).

About half of the Logans' farmland lay close to the river and was prone to severe flooding about once every five to ten years. Through the years, they had learned not to complain about the intermittent floods because of the rich soil that was usually left behind. Their farmhouse was about twenty feet higher than the flat farm field below and well above any previously known flood level. When John Logan purchased the land and built the house, he paid special attention to assure that the family had a flood-free access from the backside of the Logans' hill. The family worked hard to make ends meet. Since John Logan's murder, two close neighbors, George Cribbon and Tom Machins, had helped tend the crops for a percentage of the profit. The boys also tended to the crops, made repairs, and worked with the larger animals. Their mother Martha and Phyllis Smith, their former slave, tended to the house, the chickens, the sheep, and nearly anything else that came up. It was a busy time and a busy place.

Phyllis Smith was about five foot tall and was somewhere around forty years old. She was thin, strong and wiry. Her customary attire consisted of either a blue or green dress and head scarf. He always wore her favorite accessory, a blue neck scarf. Phyllis had large brown eyes and a quick smile. She was a great worker and an even better person.

The Logans had owned two slaves on their property, Phyllis Smith and Amos Washington. Sadly, about six years earlier, Amos Washington had died in an accident while working on the farm. This single event would ultimately lead to changes in the future of the farm and, more importantly, in the future of the family.

Flashback: March 3, 1857 - Amos Washington Dies

The scene was a patch of tall trees on the Logans' farm with the Mississippi River visible in the distance. The sun was shining through blues skies on a cool yet beautiful day. John Logan and his male slave Amos Washington were clearing forest for more farmland. John Logan was making the final cuts to a large tree that was about to fall. Amos Washington was in his early forties and has a reputation as a strong yet thoughtful man. With the nickname of "Big Man," Amos stood about six-foot-two and weighed over 250 pounds. Amos may have been "all muscle," but he was kind in his demeanor. He stood by with a saw in his hand as the tall tree was about to fall.

Then, with a large "crack," the big tree fell awkwardly off of its stump. It swayed and then unexpectedly started falling the wrong way. "Look out, Amos!! It's comin' your way!!" yelled John Logan. As it fell, Amos yelled, "Yes, sir!!" as he took off running to get out of the way. Suddenly, Amos tripped and with a loud crash, the huge tree landed directly on Amos's lower back, crushing him. Logan ran straight over and frantically tried to move the tree off of him. It wouldn't budge an inch. Amos was such a strong man that he remained alive for a short while. The tree had crushed his midsection but spared his upper body. "Oh no, Amos!! I can't move this. I gotta go get some help!"

Incredibly, as Amos lay dying, he could still speak for a moment or two. He told John Logan, "No!... Oh, no sir...please stay here. I'm sorry, Mr. Logan, I ran the wrong way."

"No, you didn't, Amos. That tree just fell the wrong way."

"Sir, I really don't think I can make it."

John took Amos' hand and held it firmly. Amos squeezed John's hand so firmly as to almost crush it. John started weeping. "You're my man, Amos. I need you here with us. You're part of my family!"

"I know sir. You all mean a lot to me too. But I'm gonna have to see you all in the next place, Mr. Logan sir...that being up there hopefully. Stay with me, sir. Stay here."

"I'm with you, Amos. I'm with you."

Logan fell down aside with his head right next to Amos's. Amos didn't suffer long.

John Logan found himself devastated by the accident. It gave him a sharper perspective on slavery…and on himself.

Flashback: June 17, 1857 - John Logan Is Murdered

After Amos Washington died, while working on the farm, John Logan decided that he would free Phyllis Smith, their one remaining slave. The Logans wanted Phyllis to continue working on their farm, but only if she wanted to.

To make this possible, Logan was traveling back and forth to Cape Girardeau to secure the legal papers. In the New Madrid community, it had become well known that Logan was traveling to the larger city to finalize documents that would free his remaining slave. Some of the New Madrid locals had asked him not to go through with it, but he always brushed the thought aside with a smile. John Logan was intelligent, friendly, and well-liked by nearly everyone in the New Madrid area. He remained well respected in his community regardless of his views on slavery.

Then, at age sixty, while riding his horse back home from Cape Girardeau, John Logan was murdered. No one really knows what happened, but on the day that he was murdered, Logan's body was found on a wooded trail just north of New Madrid. He had apparently been hit in the back of the head and was shot three times. The local marshal investigated the matter, but no one was ever charged or really even suspected of the murder.

But Martha Logan was a strong and resilient woman. Soon after her husband was buried, she pushed her grief aside and moved quickly to finish the legal matter. In a short time, Phyllis Smith was freed. She decided to stay on with the Logans because she (like Amos) felt like she was part of the family. John Logan had even died while trying to free her. Her sense of belonging was intensified as she grieved along with the rest of the family. Martha really missed her husband, Phyllis missed her friend, and the boys missed their father. In the years following his passing, the family often reminisced about their time with him on the farm.

Return to March 1, 1861

Will and Jimmy Logan continued to approach the farmhouse as they rode the wagon up the incline of the hill. Phyllis, the former slave, spryly departed out of the house's front door, quickly waved at them, and passed Martha on her way to one of the outbuildings.

Although small in size, Phyllis was a big presence on the farm. She was always wise as to the needs of the farm and the Logan family. Granted freedom by Martha Logan in 1857, Phyllis decided to stay on and work on the farm. She was a great worker and an even better person. Phyllis was always treated as one of the family, and she drew a salary of four dollars per month, with food and lodging included.

As they approached the house, there was an older lady with gray hair sitting in a chair on the front porch. Their grandmother, Mary Logan, had immigrated to America with her husband Patrick, her sister Catherine, and her sister's husband in 1809. She was thirty years old then and she was eighty-one years old now. When Mary left Ireland in 1809, the trip involved many dangers. Hence, her twelve-year-old son, John Logan, was purposely left behind in Ireland with family members. The plan was for John to join his parents at a later time. Years later, in 1821, a twenty-four-year-old John Logan would bring his new wife Martha to America to also settle in southeast Missouri. He would ultimately purchase the farmland from his parents. Later, he added much more acreage to the farm and build the new house and out structures on the hills that he leveled out around the rocky bluff. John's father, Patrick (the boy's grandpa), died about fifteen years ago in 1846 from natural causes while working in the fields of the Logan farm. Will and Jimmy only have faint memories of their grandpa because they were only three and five years old when he passed away.

As the brothers brought their supplies in through the front door, they chatted back and forth with their grandmother as she sat on the front porch. The family referred to Mary Logan as Granna or Grandma Logan. Mary was a survivor of the Great New Madrid Earthquakes of December 1811. There were four large earthquakes and thousands of lesser aftershocks from December 11, 1811 through February 7, 1812. Even today, fifty years later, Mary still suffered from some psychological problems (later known as PTSD, or post-traumatic stress disorder) from the quakes, which virtually destroyed the entire area. At times, she was still jumpy and could be easily startled. Even today, fifty years later, she didn't sleep well and was constantly on the watch for another big quake. In the past, Granna would never speak of the disaster, but in recent years she slowly started to talk more and more about the earthly catastrophe.

Later in the evening, while sitting on the porch, Mary again started to talk about the quakes to a captive family audience. She still spoke with a thick Irish brogue. "Our house started shaking with a terrible loud cracking. It was like it was being torn apart by a giant. The earth made a great upheaval and commenced to more shakin'. The noise was deafening. Trees were cracking and falling. Houses were breaking up. The Mississippi River left its banks and flowed backwards to the north. They told us later that the big quake even rang church bells way up in Boston, Massachusetts." Mary then looked down and pauses, seemingly ending her descriptive story.

"Tell us more about the big shake, Granna," said Jimmy. Mary sat quietly for about ten seconds and then she looked up directly at Jimmy. "Well, we really thought it was the end of the world! Most houses part collapsed or totally fell down. Ours fell down into a pile of wood. We had to mostly stay outside and sit on the ground for nearly two months because it was hard to stand for any real period of time. Sulfur gas came shooting up out of the ground with a horrible stench! Sometimes the sulfur gas blocked out the sun and it was dark in the middle of the day!"

Then, Grandma Logan's eyes darted wildly as if she is saw the scene again. She started speaking louder and louder. "Giant sand-hills popped up all over and gushed sand way up into the sky. The noise was ear-splitting loud. The people were screaming and the animals were all howling! There were landslides everywhere. The river boiled and had huge waves going in every direction!"

"Are you okay, Granna?" asked Jimmy.

She ignored him and continued, "We thought the quake was everywhere. Around the whole world! We thought that most folks around the world had died. My sister Catherine and her husband were missing after a ten-foot wall of water went over their little farm down near the river!"

Grandma Logan then looked down and spoke quietly. "They were never found. Their farm and house were gone and their land is still underwater. It's part of the river now.... So are they...my sister... my beautiful sister." Mary's face saddens. She quickly starts shaking. Tears immediately flow down her cheeks and she starts to sob. "I don't think I can talk about it anymore right now. I just can't settle down."

Jimmy noticed that she was upset. "That's enough, Granna...it's okay now. Come on, let's go in and get ready for dinner."

The boys helped Grandma Logan stand up, and they walked her into the house.

> *Point of Historical Reference – The Great New Madrid Earthquakes of 1811 and 1812 were amongst the largest earthquakes to ever to hit North America. The four largest quakes were estimated to be between magnitude 7.2 and 8.2 on the Richter scale.*

March 2, 1861

The following day the boys were working in the yard. They were talking about the loss of their father from nearly six years before. On this day, they discussed some of the music that their Irish father had taught them in the good ol' days of playing music while sitting around the fire. They often played music and their father would encourage everyone to contribute.

Flashback: Four Years Earlier—Late April 1857

Not long before John Logan died (and directly before Amos died), he taught the family a well-known Gaelic folk song. He was sure to include the then slaves Phyllis and Amos. "A Ghaoil, Leig Dhachaigh Gum Mhathair Mi (Love, Let Me Go Home to My Mother)" plays in their mind. Sang in their parents' traditional Irish language, the hypnotic song tells the story of a young girl who meets a boy while tending to the family's cattle. Their father worked individually with everyone for several weeks to make the sound just right.

On a magical night after a long practice period, they finally all played together. Amos played the accordion in one haunting low note and Phyllis tapped an intermittent tambourine. Their father played a soft fiddle, while Jimmy played the melodic guitar. Willy tapped a little drum while also playing one soft low note on his harmonica. Their mother sang the song in an unhurried and poignant melody with her beautiful singing voice. When they were finished with the song, they all quietly just looked at each other, stunned with the music that they had just made. Their father had carefully woven all of the individual sounds into a beautiful creation that no one could have ever expected. It was a night to be remembered.

Return to March 2, 1861

Still working in the yard, the brothers discussed the night that they all played together. Jimmy admitted that he actually felt goosebumps while they were playing the tune. They both agree that they'd never felt or heard anything like it before or since. Years later, the brothers still talked of how the tune was imprinted in their minds. It was a great memory from their father that they hoped to never forget.

March 3, 1861

The next day, the boys were working on a door in the barn. Jimmy tossed down the newspaper and said, "You know it's March 3rd. We're gonna have a new president tomorrow."

"Yeah, Lincoln. Who cares?" said Will, as he drove a nail into a door hinge. "I liked John Bell more anyway. Heck, I'd rather just keep James Buchanan than him."

Jimmy added, "Well, I like Abraham Lincoln. I wish I could have voted for him."

Will said, "Well, you and I can't vote cause we ain't twenty-one. Anyway, Bullman says we're gonna land up in a big North-South war 'cause Lincoln won."

"Bullcrap, Will, I told you he's an idiot. We're about to land up in that war anyway and it's not just because of Lincoln. The South wants to secede from the Union for more state rights and the North wants to keep the Union together. Also, the South wants slavery and the North doesn't. It's a big mess. Don't matter who's the president, it's gonna happen anyway."

"You know what's funny, Jimmy?" said Willy.

"What?"

"We can't vote for no president, but we damn sure are supposed to go fight in any war that comes about. That's bullshit."

"You're right there, Willy," said Jimmy. "You're absolutely right."

In the previous November, the 1860 United States presidential election had taken place. In Missouri, Stephen Douglas was the winner by a narrow margin over John Bell. Abraham Lincoln actually came in fourth in Missouri but he won the presidency.

Some of the Logans' neighbors were strong slavery supporters and *did not* like the fact that a freed slave worked on their farm—particularly Caleb Bullman, a pro-slavery advocate with a somewhat checkered past. Most notably, he had served a one-year prison sentence for the assault of his neighbor and his neighbor's son. He was known in the area as a grouchy tough guy and folks generally tried to stay away from him. Except for Willy. Apparently, a few years back, he met Caleb Bullman while he was working in the fields. Bullman was cutting through their property when he got off his horse to help Will pull the old plow out of a mud hole. They chatted and have been friends ever since.

Bullman told Will that he was arrested and jailed because he beat up his neighbor for fooling around with his wife (he's now divorced). He nearly killed the man. Bullman also told him that he beat up his neighbor's twenty-year-old son at the same time. Bullman was a big, tough fellow. Even though he was older and walked with a limp, he was not a person to be trifled with.

"Well, I think you should know, Willy," Jimmy said, "I'm thinkin' about enlisting for the Union Army before it all starts. I told Momma I'm leaving in a couple of weeks. I just can't be for any more slavery. Daddy wasn't either."

Will said, "I know you're joining the North. She told me. Jimmy, I'm enlisting in the Confederate Army." Jimmy sighs. "I just have a feeling that there's more to it and, besides, everyone around here's for the South anyways."

"Not me," Jimmy said.

"Well, they're organizing now and I'm leaving real soon," said Willy. "Bullman told me he contacted a big-shot in the Confederate Army name of Colonel John S. Bowen. So, I'll soon be getting a letter from him and then I'm headin' over to Memphis, Tennessee to meet him and enlist."

Jimmy continued, "You know, Will, I think you should do what you think is right, but I told you a hundred times that Bullman is a scallywag, and he's going to get you hurt one day, or worse. How does that drunk know anybody of any worth anyway?"

"Well, apparently, he wasn't always a drunk," said Willy. "He was a Union soldier. Bullman says about six or seven years ago, he retired out of the Army up in St. Louis at Jefferson Barracks. He says he knew Colonel Bowen up there."

"Really? I never would have thought that he'd done anything good."

"That ain't all!" said Willy. "Like fifteen years ago, he fought for the Union back in the Mexican-American War."

"What?"

"Yes, sir, he was a sergeant. He hurt his leg really bad in some important battle and finally got out in 1855."

"Bullman was a real soldier! Well, I'll be. No wonder he limps around like that," said Jimmy.

"Yep, he says Colonel Bowen was a major back then. That ain't all either! There's more. Bullman says he got some kind of a big-deal medal after the Mexican-American War, from Zachary Taylor!"

"Zachary Taylor?!"

"Yes!"

"The president?!"

"Yes!"

"Are you kidding?"

"No! That's what he says. He lost his left leg after the battle and I'm pretty sure he's not makin' it up."

"Zachary Taylor died like ten years ago!"

"I know! I think Bullman got the medal before Taylor died, when he was still in the Army. He says Colonel Bowen was there when he got it. Because of all that, Bowen thinks mighty highly of Bullman. Now, Colonel Bowen is a big-shot Confederate officer."

"Wow."

"Jimmy, I think that war messed Bullman up, more than just his leg."

"What do ya mean, Will?"

"You know, in the head. Kinda like Granna and her nerves after the big quake. I think that's why lots of folks think he's kinda crazy. Sometimes he's really quiet and then really loud. He hardly ever leaves his house, unless he needs something from town. That's how I met him. Cuttin' through. I don't think folks really know him, what he's done or what he's been through. When you're talking to him, he's really quiet, then he like hears a sudden noise and he nearly jumps outta his skin!"

"Just like Granna does," Jimmy said. "Well, that's all well and fine, but I still think he drinks too much and I just don't trust him. Be real careful around him anyway, Willy."

The boys then sat on the ground next to the barn. They started to chat about many important topics, including their girlfriends, Patsy and Bonnie. Next, they discussed their looming departures. The New Madrid Saturday Night Dance was coming up on the following weekend, so they decided that it would be a good time to let the girls know they were leaving. Then, they discussed the needs of their mother and the family farm.

"Before we go, we need to talk more with the neighbors, Tom Machins and George Cribbon, about tending the crops," said Jimmy. "I want to ask them to try to tend the whole farm while we're gone."

"Yes sir, their wives are also good friends with Momma, so that will help her out."

"Yep, she's gonna need it."

The brothers then talked about the death of their father and how the necessities of life had shaped them for a very long time. But now, history beckoned. They both felt that the time had come to take action as their country began to break apart. "If this war really happens, it's gonna change our lives," said Jimmy. "It could not only destroy our country, it could destroy out family. We could be killed. Even Momma might not survive. Phyliss too. Who knows what could happen?"

"I never thought about all of that," said Willy. "I couldn't imagine us not comin' home to Momma. It would ruin her. After losing Daddy, it would just be too much."

"Right. Another problem is," Jimmy said, "we are both drawn toward opposite sides of the country's fight."

"I know, big brother," said Will. "But that don't change the fact that we're brothers and we're part of this here family. No matter what."

"That's very true," said Jimmy. "I will still be your big brother and I will still try to watch out for you, the best that I can, that is."

"Thanks, Jimmy," said Will. "Just don't shoot me."

"I'll try not to," said Jimmy with a grin.

They both broke out into some needed laughter as Jimmy pushed Will over to the ground and then laid on top of him.

"Get off of me, you damn Yankee!" yelled a laughing Will, shoving Jimmy to the side.

"Anything you say, Reb boy!" answered Jimmy.

The exchange brought some needed levity to an all too serious discussion.

March 5, 1861

A couple of days later, Will and Jimmy were out in the fields preparing the farm for their departure. Today, they were trying to fix an old plow, with the Mississippi River visible in the background. Jimmy had a Colt 45 attached to his belt that he used primarily for critters and coyotes. They were not far from a cut-through path that locals regularly used. Suddenly, a horse with a rider started to approach from a distance.

"Here comes Bullman!" Jimmy proclaimed.

"How can you tell?"

"Easy, he's probably drunk again. See how he rolls to and fro in the saddle. A real gem he is."

"That's probably because of his amputated leg," said Willy. "It makes it hard for him to balance in the saddle.

Caleb Bullman rode up to the boys and started talking loudly. "Hey there, boys!" He did seem to have been drinking. Bullman had mostly gray hair with a moderately trimmed mustache and beard. He looked to be slightly disheveled and appeared to be in his mid-fifties, but he was probably younger. Bullman was a good-sized man with broad shoulders and a bit of a belly. His face was weathered and he had several scars on it, likely from years of fighting. His clothing appeared to be dusty but not tattered, and he wore a flat-brimmed leather hat. Caleb Bullman spoke in a Southern accent.

"You know Abraham Lincoln is come on board as president," said Bullman. "Missouri is supposed to be with the North, and the South is a-gettin' our Army together cause we're gonna break away. Anti-slavery, my ass!" He loudly keeps talking. "Your momma still got that nigra slave up there workin' in the house?"

Jimmy quickly answered, "You know she's free, Bullman!"

"Well, the South is gonna fight and we're gonna win as quick as a wink," said Bullman. "I really should go up there and talk some sense into your momma. If the South wins, she could plain out own that slave. She's a fool."

Jimmy jumped up and nearly flew through the air straight up and onto Bullman's saddle. He instantly put his face directly into Bullman's face and glared directly into Bullman's eyes. With a wild look of craze and confidence, he stated loud and low, "My momma is no fool, Bullman! But you are if you go talk to her. If you do, I'm gonna have a talk with you, and I guarantee you won't like it."

Bullman looked at Jimmy's revolver that was sticking out from his belt, but Jimmy didn't draw it. He was very quiet in his response. "Easy boy. Why don't you go on and fix your plow? I won't have nothin' to say to your momma."

"Good. Keep it that way 'cause I'll rip your stupid head off!"

Jimmy slowly climbed off of Bullman's saddle and backed up to the plow, keeping eye to eye with Bullman the whole time. Bullman was obviously stunned and didn't move. He just sat there, looking at the two boys. Finally, Jimmy called out to him, "Well, what do you want?"

"Nothin' boys. I'll see ya." Bullman sat up straight in his saddle and briskly rode off.

Jimmy yelled out, "Right! Go around next time!"

G. S. Spooner

March 9, 1861

The following week passed quickly, and before the brothers know it the New Madrid Saturday Night Dance had arrived. They got ready for the big evening and hitched up their one-horse wagon for the ride over to Patsy and Bonnie's house. Unfortunately, they arrived to pick up the girls about fifteen minutes late. Their tardiness drew a few sideways glares from Mrs. Caldwell, the mother of the girls. After the exchange of some friendly words, the situation was mended and they were on their way into town. Patsy and Bonnie were attractive young ladies in their late teens. Bonnie's hair was very light brown and Patsy's hair was dark brown. Bonnie had large blue eyes and a slim face with very high cheekbones. Patsy had delicate almond shaped brown eyes and a small chin. Her chin had a very little scar on its left side. They both were wearing fashionable dresses from the period, most likely handmade by their mother.

Jimmy and Patsy sat in the front seat of the flatbed wagon while Will and Bonnie sat in the back on a hay bale. It was a seating arrangement that everyone was familiar with as they had ridden together many times before. "I have something to tell you tonight," Will said to Bonnie.

"What is it? Is it good?"

"Well, not necessarily."

"Can you tell me now?"

The horse-drawn wagon bounced down the dirt road. The noise from the horse and wagon did not allow their conversation to be heard by Jimmy and Patsy. "I guess so. Well, I'm leaving soon to join the Confederate Army."

Bonnie said nothing. She just looked at him. Will looked down and didn't say anything else right away. He knew that Bonnie and he were supposed to get engaged sooner or later. He sadly told her,

"I know that we have plans. We can still go through with our plans, but it may have to wait for just a while."

Bonnie looked away blankly into the distance and didn't speak. After the twenty-minute ride, the couples finally made it to the dance. The main street of New Madrid was abuzz with activity as the local crowd danced to the New Madrid town band. The two couples quickly joined in the enjoyable commotion and blended into the crowd.

After about an hour at the party, Jimmy asked Patsy to come over to their wagon. They went over to the back of the flatbed and he pulled a blanket off of his previously concealed guitar. Jimmy had a Martin brand small guitar that was custom ordered for him in Cape Girardeau about a year earlier. His mother and Phyllis ordered it all of the way from New York for his birthday.

"Are you going to play with the band?"

"No. I'm going to play for you."

"Here?"

"No, I was wondering if you could take a walk with me. Maybe down to the river."

Jimmy and Patsy strolled away from the loud dance and headed toward the river.

"Okay, Jimmy, what's going on?"

"Well, I have something to tell you and I also want to play a little song for you."

After a couple of minutes, the couple was sitting on a quiet wooden dock on the side of the river. They looked at the river by the moonlight as it flowed by. "I can't take it! What are you going to tell me?"

Jimmy noodled at his guitar, and after a long pause he spoke. "I'm sorry, Patsy, but I'm going to be leaving soon to join the Union Army."

"Oh no, Jimmy!" Patsy immediately started to sob.

"It's okay, Patsy, I'm going to come back. Then, we can get engaged and move on with our plans."

"Okay then. So right away, as soon as you get back, we're making our plans to get married?"

"Yes, my dear. That's what I'm talking about. I love you. I don't want to wait long either."

By this time, Patsy had tears rolling down her face. "So, we now have a promise to be firmly engaged to be married?"

Jimmy answered, "Yes, I guess we're engaged to get engaged."

Patsy laughed. "Okay, that sounds funny but I guess I'll accept your offer. We're engaged to get engaged. Look, Jimmy, I don't want to be here without you, so you better come back."

"I may be gone," said Jimmy, "but I'll still be here with you. I'm leaving my heart with you, so I'll be with you even when I'm not here, watching over you."

Patsy frowned and made a noise but remained as stoic as she can. Her face was saddened, but she was no longer sobbing. She still had tears on her face and her lower lip was tightened. Jimmy looked at her silently and tuned his guitar for a moment. Then Patsy asked, "Are you going to play, 'Watching Over You'?"

Jimmy just smiled at her. He didn't answer but started to play the song. Patsy laid her head on his shoulder and a smile slowly appeared on her previously saddened face. He strummed the song and eased her worries with a soothing voice as he played the gentle and rhythmic song for her.

Chapter Two

April 4, 1861

Before the boys departed, they spent a good amount of time talking to George Cribbon and Tom Machins about handling the farm in their absence. Cribbon and Machins had agreed to take over nearly all of the crop duties for a one-half share of any profits. Both men were veterans and had served in the Union Army during the Mexican-American War. While they leaned toward the Confederacy, they were both good friends of John Logan before he was murdered. They promised the boys that they would also keep an eye on the security of the farm while they were gone. Both men were already tending to half of the Logans' crop fields with an agreement of one-third of the profits. They now had agreed to manage nearly all of the crops until the brothers returned.

Both men were hardworking farmers in their mid-fifties. They were strong men, similar in build but quite different in disposition. George liked to laugh and joke around, and Tom was usually soft-spoken and thoughtful. George stood about six feet tall and Tom was about five-foot-ten.

One morning, Will and Jimmy headed across the fields to look for George and Tom. They found their neighbor farmers out in the fields re-shoeing a horse. "Not sure how good of a job we'll do with your farm, or if any of us will make any money with this," said Tom Machins, "but we'll sure try to keep it all going, as best we can." Tom Machins had a thin face that showed the effects of years of sun and wind. He had a medium length gray moustache and he was wearing a large brimmed leather hat. Tom seemed to always have a look of calmness and honesty in his eyes. "Well, boys, I'm gonna give you both a one hundred percent guarantee," said George with a smile. "I guarantee that all of your property will still be here when you get back." George Cribbon had a round face with smaller eyes and a distinct jawline. He had a slight disfigurement on the left side of his face from an explosion during his service in the Union Army during the Mexican-American War.

"Thanks a lot, George," says said Willy. George and Tom's wives were also good friends of Martha Logan, so they planned to help her and Phyllis with some of the other duties around the Logan family farm. They also had connections with other farmers for sporadic help if it was needed.

April 10, 1861
Jimmy Travels to Join the Union Army

Jimmy spent the next week making final preparations and saying goodbye to nearly everyone that he knew. The time passed quickly, and before he knew it he was on a steam-powered paddlewheel boat heading upriver on a two-day trip to St. Louis.

Jimmy had a large leather and canvas bag slung over his shoulder with the top neck of his small guitar sticking out of it. He took special care of his guitar while traveling by wrapping a blanket around it. As the boat slowly moved upriver, he was kind of glad to be in more solid Union territory, considering his plans. Jimmy stared at his surroundings. He was taken in by the peaceful beauty of the river as a large white crane swooped down and landed by the side of the water. He contemplated what the river would look like in six months…or one year. Would it still be so magically beautiful, or would it be ripped apart by war? He whispered to himself as he looked across the river, "Time will tell…. Only time will tell."

It could be dangerous to maneuver large boats at night on the mighty Mississippi. So, the paddlewheel steamboat made an overnight stop in the small town of Wittenberg, Missouri. It was about halfway to St. Louis. Jimmy did not exit the ship. Instead, he played a few tunes on his guitar and later found a place to sleep below deck.

April 12, 1861, 3 p.m.
(1500 hours in military time)

Two days after his departure, Jimmy's paddlewheel finally pulled into the muddy riverbank at St. Louis. As the passengers exited, he immediately noticed a buzz in the air. Everyone seemed to be talking loudly and rushing about. Jimmy asked a passing soldier, "Hey, what's going on? What's happening?"

"Well, don't you know? Fort Sumter is being bombarded by the Confederates. The Civil War has now begun!"

The soldier started to walk away and Jimmy grabbed his shoulder. "Hey, can you tell me where I can enlist in the Union Army?"

The soldier appeared to be indisposed as he turned back to Jimmy. "Yeah, you need to take a wagon to Jefferson Barracks. Enlistments and initial training all take place there. The wagon leaves about every two to three hours from that area right over there." He pointed to a small guard shack.

"Great, thanks a lot!"

Jimmy thought, *I'm pretty sure that I just passed by Jefferson Barracks on the riverboat about half an hour ago.* He started walking toward the Guard Shack as the soldier turned to walk away. A second later, the same soldier called back to him, "Hey! Hey, new guy!"

"Yeah!"

Jimmy looked over and the soldier was pointing over to a large horse-drawn wagon that was just pulling up. "You just got lucky! The Union Wagon is rolling up right now!"

"Wow, that's great! Thanks a lot!"

"You're welcome! Now go and join the Army! We could use the help!"

"Will do!"

Jimmy ran over to the wagon as it pulled up. "Stop! State your business," yelled the soldier at the reins. The sergeant driving the wagon looked like a rough tough grizzled soldier, with many years of service.

"I'm going to Jefferson Barracks to enlist," said Jimmy.

"Okay. After these soldiers get off, you can climb aboard. We leave for JB in about fifteen minutes. It takes us about two hours to get there. Once there, I'll tell you exactly where you'll need to go."

"Thank you, sir."

"Sergeant! I'm a sergeant! I work for a living."

"Okay. Yes, Sergeant!"

"That's better. Now let these soldiers get off and then have a seat."

It was a long and bumpy ride to Jefferson Barracks. Once they arrived, the wagon driver dropped Jimmy off directly in front of the Enlistment Building. "Look here boy, go directly into that building. It's a bit late in the day, so I don't know if they'll enlist you now or just bed you down until tomorrow. Either way, you're at the right place."

"Thanks, Sergeant!"

"That's right, you got it. Sergeant!" said the driver. "You're gonna do just fine. Track me down and say hello once you're in a Union uniform!" The grizzled driver was actually a much nicer fellow than he appeared to be.

"Will do! Thanks again!"

The wagon pulled away and Jimmy entered the building. To his surprise, there were two lines with about ten people in each line. A lieutenant walked directly up to him. "Are you here to enlist?" The lieutenant was an extremely sharp looking officer, with an immaculate uniform.

"Yes, Sergeant!" said Jimmy.

"Lieutenant! I'm a Lieutenant. Either call me Lieutenant or sir."

"Yes, Lieutenant!" said Jimmy.

"That's better. Okay. Stand in that line over there. Once you're enlisted, we'll take you to building number twenty-six. Tonight, you'll be supplied with a uniform and some other equipment. It'll be a late night for you. Your initial training will start tomorrow! In case you haven't heard, there's a war goin' on!"

"Yes, Lieutenant!"

The Lieutenant smiled, nods at him, and points to the line.

April 12, 1861, 2200 hours

On the very official first day of the Civil War, after a long and hectic journey, Jimmy stated the Oath of Enlistment. He raised his right hand, stated the oath, and officially enrolled into the United States Army.

"I, James Daniel Logan, swear to be true to the United States of America, and to serve them honestly and faithfully against all their enemies opposers whatsoever; and to observe and obey the orders of the Continental Congress, and the orders of the Generals and officers set over me by them."

April 20, 1861, 0900 hours

After a week of the initial issue of equipment and some military introduction at Jefferson Barracks, Private Jimmy Logan was sent to another post in St. Louis named Benton Barracks. He and about thirty other new soldiers were to receive more formal military training there. The soldiers were loaded into three different horse-drawn military transport wagons with all of their gear. Then, Jimmy immediately noticed the same grizzled looking driver that had brought him to Jefferson Barracks a week before. "Hey! Good morning, Sergeant! It's me."

"Oh, it's you. Good morning, Private.... What's your name anyway?"

"Private Jimmy Logan, Sergeant."

"Great. We're takin' you to Benton Barracks now, Logan. You're going to get some great military training there."

"Good, I hope so."

"Now sit down, shut up, and enjoy the scenery."

"Yes, Sergeant!" Jimmy yelled loudly.

The driver just smiled at Jimmy and started yelling at another new recruit. "Hurry up, Private! This ain't no Sunday picnic! Let's go!"

"Yes, sir!"

"Sergeant! I'm a sergeant! I work for a living!"

"Yes, Sergeant!"

"That's better." The driver looked over at Jimmy and smiled (as did Jimmy).

The weather was miserable with cool temperatures and rain for the sloppy four-hour ride to Benton Barracks. Much of the day's travel was on a trail that paralleled the Mississippi River. Jimmy thought as he looked at the river, *Everything in my life has involved this river. I grew up next to it, I farm next to it, I travel on it, and today I'm on a wagon looking over at it from a place that is hundreds of miles away from my home. I wonder if I will ever be very far away from it.*

May 10, 1861

Private Jimmy Logan finally completed his third week of military training at Benton Barracks. Just after completing training, he received orders to join the Union Regulars at the same post. He reported to Company D, 5th Regiment, U.S. Reserve Corps, Missouri Infantry.

Just days after reporting, his new unit was sent on an important mission. They successfully attacked a local Confederate Camp that was located right near St. Louis. It was named Camp Jackson and it was an easy victory for the Union. Camp Jackson was manned by a pro-Confederate militia group that was actually formed (mustered) by Missouri's own sitting governor, Claiborne Fox Jackson. Jackson had tricked the voters of Missouri. He was elected as a pro-Union, anti-secessionist, but he was secretly a pro-Confederate. After being voted into office, he actually conspired with Confederate President Jefferson Davis. Then, he started Camp Jackson expressly to capture arms and ammunition from the large St. Louis Military Arsenal.

Just a few weeks before Jimmy's unit defeats Camp Jackson, another pro-Confederate group stole over one thousand rifles from a Union Arsenal in Liberty, Missouri. In Washington, the Union's War Department would have no more of this. So, they ordered Jimmy's Company D, 5th Reg to attack Camp Jackson, in hopes of stopping or at least slowing down the theft of more Union armaments.

During the Battle of Camp Jackson, Jimmy did fire his weapon, but he didn't think that he had hit or killed anyone. After the brief battle, Jimmy took part in the registering and disarming of new prisoners. After that, all of the prisoners were placed into formations. Captain Lyon and his Company D marched the prisoners down to the St. Louis Arsenal. Lyon planned to once again record their names before releasing them. During this two-mile march, a large group of pro-Confederate civilians gathered and started to harass the Union troops. Missouri had a large amount of pro-Confederate civilians, even in the big city of St. Louis. Even though the rebel sympathizers were vastly outnumbered in the city by pro-Union supporters, the pro-Confederates were often louder and more active in their Confederate support.

Many of these civilians considered the two-mile public march of the defeated soldiers humiliating. Then, an angry mob gathered and started to get really worked up. The large commotion finally led to a riot, and the mob started throwing anything they could find at the Union soldiers. Jimmy saw rocks, sticks, and even a lantern flying through the air. During the riot of confusion, a drunken civilian stumbled out of the crowd. He then fired a pistol directly into the Union soldiers, killing a captain whom Jimmy knew and liked. With this, the Union soldiers retaliated by firing into and over the heads of the rioters. In the end, twenty-eight civilians were killed and seventy-five were wounded. The incident became known as the "Camp Jackson Affair." After things calmed down, Jimmy and his Company D, 5th Reg, had to patrol the city for days because of civil unrest that followed.

Jimmy was shaken up by the ordeal but was uninjured. He was just a country boy and he had never before seen so many people that angry before. Angry enough to kill other people. He was beginning to realize the extreme amount of passion that was held by both sides of this Civil War. The fury of the mob made him remember his own rage against Caleb Bullman when he was at home, working in the field. Later, he remembered the rage in their faces and wondered if he looked like that when he became so angry at Caleb Bullman.

July 1861
Jimmy Is Assigned to the "Irish Brigade"

In July 1861, after a short-lived duty with Company D, 5th Reg, Jimmy Logan was reassigned to the 23rd Illinois Infantry Regiment. The 23rd Illinois was also known as the "Irish Brigade." The Irish Brigade was then sent to garrison at a small Union post located in the Missouri River town of Lexington. Lexington was located west of Jefferson City, the state capital, and was right on the Missouri River, just like Jeff City. Assignment to the Irish Brigade didn't bother Jimmy at all since he had a strong Irish heritage. He enjoyed listening to the Irishmen speak because it reminded him of his mother and father's accent.

June 10, 1861
Will Joins the Confederate Army

A full two months after his brother Jimmy's departure, Will finally left New Madrid to join the Confederacy. His later departure allowed him to continue working on the farm while he waited on an acceptance letter from Colonel Bowen. Willy joined a small group of new recruits on a Confederate Wagon traveling directly from New Madrid to Memphis, Tennessee. After the grueling eleven-hour wagon ride, they finally made it to Memphis. Later that evening, Will showed his letter to a sergeant. He told the sergeant that he was told to report directly to Colonel John Bowen (as instructed by Caleb Bullman).

Two guards were standing outside of Bowen's tent and one of them announced Will to the general. Colonel Bowen was pleased to see Willy.

"Son, I'm mighty glad to see ya. So, you know my old friend, Caleb Bullman! You know he's a bona fide war hero. That guy's a bit rough around the edges, but If I had a thousand men like him, I'd win the war in a month."

Colonel Bowen went on to talk about serving with Caleb Bullman while they were both in the Union Army at Jefferson Barracks. "He had a reputation as a perfect soldier, but when he wasn't fighting in a war, he could sometimes get in trouble. Ulysses S. Grant and I both met him up there. Believe it or not, I think we learned a few things from Bullman. There's a brutal and an empathetic component to war and a soldier really needs to try to have both to succeed. You can't just have one or the other. Sergeant Caleb Bullman knew this and that made him an exemplary soldier."

The next day, Colonel Bowen enlisted Will at the advanced rank of corporal for just two reasons; because he was short on leaders who were not officers and because he was referred by Caleb Bullman. Bowen himself conducts Will's Oath of Enlistment into the Confederate Army in front of about thirty Confederate soldiers.

"I, William Logan, do solemnly swear, that I will bear true faith and allegiance to the Confederate States of America, and that I will serve them honestly and faithfully against all their enemies or opposers whomsoever; and that I will observe and obey the orders of the President of the Confederate States, and the orders of the officers appointed over me, according to the Rules and Articles of War." Will was not promoted to the rank of corporal, but he was enlisted at the rank on his official enlistment papers.

The following day, Will was assigned to the Confederate Unit, the 1st Missouri Infantry, Company I. The 1st Missouri was the very first Midwestern unit to muster for the Southern cause. Will then traveled to Portland, Tennessee and received some robust military training at a place called Camp Trousdale. After a few short weeks, Will became a soldier and his unit was prepared to engage with the Union enemy.

After his initial training, Will was assigned to several garrison duties at Camp Trousdale. One of which included duty as a carpenter. In July 1861, Will assisted in the hasty construction of a much-needed military hospital at Camp Trousdale. Much like his brother, Willy was pretty good with a hammer. Although diseases and sickness were widespread in the camp, Willy made sure that he did have some fun. In a letter to his mother, Will wrote that the Army work was really hard, the hours were long, and the food was only fair. However, he also mentioned that there were dances on a regular basis with the local folks from Portland, Tennessee.

September 13-20, 1861
The Siege of Lexington

Private Jimmy Logan's next battle for the Union Army was on September 13, 1861, in the Siege of Lexington, Missouri. Jimmy's Irish Brigade was caught up in brutal action when they were surprise-attacked by the Confederate Missouri State Guard (MSG). The MSG was led by Major General Sterling Price. Price was a successful Confederate general who had previously gained notoriety as the governor of Missouri from 1853 to 1857. In the future, General Price would become the commander of Jimmy's brother, Will.

During the Siege of Lexington, Jimmy received a minor shoulder injury from an exploding cannon shell fragment. When the shell exploded, the blast was so loud that he could hear nothing but a mid-toned buzz for about ten minutes. Jimmy saw several Union troops die in the battle and he was fairly certain that he shot and possibly killed several Rebel soldiers.

Near the battle's end, the Confederates amassed a huge armada of giant hemp bales and soaked them with water. They then rolled the soaked hemp bales between them and the Union forces. They even rolled them directly at the Union soldiers. Jimmy fired directly into the rolling bales, but his rounds could not breach them. This ingenious tactic not only protected the Confederate soldiers, it also prevented the bales from catching fire from the Union's red-hot rounds. Years later, the former Confederate President Jefferson Davis, compared the deployment of the hemp bales to other brilliant and resourceful tactics, such as those used by ancient Arab warriors hundreds of years in the past.

Just as the end of the battle was near, the Union commander, Colonel Mulligan, knew that his Irish Brigade was massively outnumbered by the Confederate force. In order to prevent the slaughter of his men, he began to negotiate terms of surrender with Major General Price. As this happened, Mulligan dispatched Private Jimmy Logan and another soldier to escape in a small skiff. They were instructed to head downriver to Jefferson City and to alert Union leaders that the battle had been lost. This quirk of luck prevented Jimmy from becoming a prisoner of war (POW) and allowed his military journey to continue.

October 5, 1861
Jimmy's Returns to Benton Barracks

After the Siege of Lexington, the Union needed to reorganize assets in the area. The brutal battle had decimated the Irish Brigade, so the unit was temporarily mustered out (discharged from service). Jimmy received new orders to return to Benton Barracks in St. Louis, where he was assigned to Garrison Support as a carpenter. A huge influx of hundreds of injured Union soldiers increased the need for medical support, so Jimmy was quickly put to work constructing several new hospital buildings.

November 15, 1861
Jimmy's Military Journey—Home for Christmas

After seven months of active duty that included garrison work and several brutal battles, Private Jimmy Logan received an unexpected surprise. He was temporarily allowed to muster out and to head home. But, before his departure, Jimmy was given official orders that required him to report back to St. Louis on January 12, 1862. Jimmy was to report to a newly forming unit called the "Army of the Mississippi." The new unit was being organized to stand up in February 1862, with overall mission operations in and near the Mississippi River. Before Jimmy departed, he asked the lieutenant why he was being excused from duty for such a long time. The officer told him, "Well, we have big plans and important missions not only for you, but for many thousands of other soldiers. We've also looked at your record, Logan. So, we know that you'll report back for this duty on time."

"Oh, okay. Thank you, Sir."

Jimmy turned to walk away and the lieutenant added, "Hey, Logan! This next mission is really important and we don't want you all to die before we get started."

"Oh, that makes me feel better… I guess," said Jimmy with an uneasy smile on his face.

Jimmy packed up and started his return home to New Madrid.

Once again, he found himself on the Mississippi River, but he was heading south this time. To his surprise, he was on the very same paddlewheel boat that had brought him up the river. Just as before, the 160-mile river trip from St. Louis to New Madrid took two days. This time, the paddlewheel boat had two Union guards on it and it would be making an evening stopover in Cape Girardeau. As always, Jimmy traveled with his leather and canvas bag with the neck of his guitar poking out the top of it. During the journey, Jimmy pulled out his guitar and went to the back of the ship, by the paddlewheels. He listened to the *blop, plop, blop* of the paddlewheels hitting the water and started playing his guitar to the beat of the sound. After constructing a small tune, he pulled out his notebook and recorded the notes so he could remember them later.

The next day the captain pulled the boat ashore about a mile north of New Madrid, "... 'cause the Rebs are thick as a thicket up ahead. They have the entire river shut down to traffic." Jimmy disembarked and as he approached the town on foot, he noticed a strong Confederate presence, so he quickly found some bushes and put on his civilian clothes. Unfortunately, the Logan farm was south of town, so he had to walk through the outskirts of New Madrid as he went home.

Jimmy finally made it to the Logan farmhouse and walked through the front door. Seeing no one, he walked around the house...still no one. Then, he walked upstairs and found Granna Logan sleeping in her room. Finally, Jimmy went out the backdoor and after a brief search, he found his mom and Phyllis feeding the small animals in the barn. As Jimmy walked into the barn, Phyllis yelled, "Hey now!" Then his mother exclaimed, "What?! Who?! What are you doing here?"

"Well, I'll leave if you want me to." They all laughed and hugged in their happy and unexpected reunion.

Then, Mary ushered everyone into the main house, warning

Jimmy that Confederate troops were in the area and had visited the farm several times. He quickly asked her if they had bothered her or the farm. She said, "No. Not really. They were all really nice. They simply asked for water and seemed to cause no problems." With this, Jimmy said, "Good. That's a real relief." He hugged his mom again and smiled at Phyllis while grabbing her hand. Then, he went upstairs to wake up Granna Logan, unpack, and hide his Union uniform. Later, Mary and Phyllis cooked up a great "Welcome Home" dinner. That evening, Jimmy even walked the property before he went to bed, just to survey its condition. He arose early the following day and went straight back to his usual farm duties, much as if he had never left.

November 16, 1861
Will's Military Journey—Camp Trousdale Is Abandoned

In November 1861, Corporal Will Logan and his unit were abruptly ordered to stop the construction of the Military Hospital they'd been working on. The very next morning, they were ordered to quickly move out of Camp Trousdale. The word spread that the camp was being abandoned because large numbers of Union troops were moving into middle Tennessee. Most of the departing Confederate units were repositioned into the surrounding area, which was generally very friendly to the Southern cause and their soldiers.

Will's unit was repositioned toward the Missouri/Tennessee border, to be promptly available for Rebel operations in Missouri. Will and his 1st Missouri Infantry, Company I, eventually established a temporary camp right on the Mississippi River near Port of Cates Landing, Tennessee. To Will's delight, the new camp was only about ten miles from New Madrid. It was even closer to his family's farm, which was about five miles away, just on the other side of the river.

December 1861
Will Comes Home for Christmas

Will's officer in charge (OIC) knew that he and several other soldiers lived within a day's walk from their camp. In Will's case, he lived just on the Missouri side of the Mississippi. On December 11, 1861, Will was allowed a pass to return home for Christmas. He was also ordered to report back to the Port of Cates Landing camp on January 1, 1862, or sooner if notified.

"If I send a messenger to your home to get your ass, you better be there and ready!"

"I'll be there and ready, sir!" yelled Willy. He crossed the river on a small ferry with another soldier on Christmas pass in the area. Not long after crossing the river, the other soldier headed south and Will headed north toward New Madrid and his home.

"See you in three weeks, Corporal Logan."

"Yup. See ya later, Seth."

Since Will approached the farm from the south, he did not see the town of New Madrid, which was several miles to the north.

Willy walked in the front door only to hear Mary Logan let out a surprised little scream. Phyllis also let out a bit of a yelp. He hugged them both at the same time. "What are you doing here, Will?" his mother said loudly. "Did you desert your unit?"

"Ha!! No, Momma, not yet. I'm on a pass. I gotta go back in a few weeks."

"Oh my, that's so good! Guess what?"

"What, Mamma?"

"Your brother's here!"

Smallpox Island

"Did he desert his unit?"

His mother broke into laughter, with Phyllis joining in. "No! He's here on Army leave from St. Louis."

Willy was beyond surprised to find that his brother Jimmy was already there. "Where is he?"

"He's out workin' on that same old plow in the south fields. It's broke again."

"Wait a minute. I just walked through there, and I didn't see him."

Right then, Jimmy walked around the corner, having just entered the house. "You didn't see me because I saw you first." They both smiled and grabbed each other for a brief hug. "I saw a Confederate soldier uniform, so I softly sashayed over into the wood line. Just as not to create any kind of commotion. Been doing it since I got home."

"Well, I'm glad to see ya, Jimmy."

"Me too, little brother."

"Seen any action?" said Willy. "Not too much. We attacked a little place named Camp Jackson in Saint Louis. They pretty much just surrendered. Not many were killed, but we had some civilian rioting in the aftermath. Twenty-eight civilians were killed, but none of them were by me. Not a real big battle." Jimmy tried his best to downplay his war experience. "Then, I got sent up to Lexington, Missouri. We were outnumbered and overwhelmed by our old Governor Sterling Price. Lost the battle, but, right at the end, I was on messenger duty, so I wasn't made a prisoner." Jimmy didn't mention that he had likely killed five to ten Confederate soldiers during the battle. He continued, "All I got was a cut on my upper arm and some bad ringin' ears. How about you?"

"Nope, not that much. I've mainly been at Camp Trousdale for about six months. They say we are gonna be ramping up for some big missions coming up, but I sure don't know what they are."

"Same here, but I don't know either."

"Well, in this case, ignorance is bliss!"

"Agreed!"

"Well, brother, can you change clothes and come out here and help me with this stupid plow."

"I'd love to do nothing more."

"Well, hurry up!"

Willy shoved him with a grin on his face, grabbed his bag, and ran upstairs to change.

December 12, 1861
Back on the Farm

As the cool days of their military leave passed by, the weather was relatively mild. It allowed Jimmy and Will Logan to get back into the groove of working at the farm. They completed many important tasks and reconnected with both of their girlfriends. On an unusually warm day and evening, they took the sisters to a bonfire dance on the outskirts of town. Jimmy was still somewhat incognito concerning his Union soldier status, but most local folks knew about it anyway.

While at the gathering, Jimmy felt somewhat awkward because there were several Confederate soldiers (in uniform) at the dance. He knew most of the soldiers. The Logans' family friends, George Cribbon and Tom Machins, were also at the dance. Tom chatted with Jimmy. "Well, neither side is fighting around here. Missouri is a Union state anyways, so hopefully they'll just leave well enough alone. The damn war will sure enough rear its ugly head 'round here soon enough. I'm just glad you guys are back for a while, for your momma's sake."

"Me too, Tom. Me too."

Smallpox Island

Suddenly, Caleb Bullman came walking through the party, having just been to the General Store. He had a sack of provisions slung over his shoulder. Bullman steered clear of Jimmy but walked straight up to Will with his noticeable limp. Bullman slapped him on the shoulder and said, "I got a letter from Colonel Bowen. Good work, Willy. Keep it up!" He leaned in and said a few words in Will's ear and then walked on. As he departed, he tipped his hat toward Jimmy. Jimmy smirked at him and turned to talk to his girlfriend, Patsy. "Sometimes I just wanna kick that son of a bitch's ass. I hope to get a chance someday."

"Oh, Jimmy, he's just a crippled ol' man. It wouldn't even be a fair fight."

"Maybe so. I guess I should let it go, but it ain't easy." He then walked over and asked his brother, "Hey, Will, what did Bullman say into your ear?"

"Oh, nothing bad, Jimmy. I'll tell you later."

For the rest of the evening, Jimmy and Patsy talked, laughed, and danced a lot. Will and Bonnie did have some fun, but they ended up spending much of the evening separated while talking to other friends. The bonfire dance was generally a success with no real incidents. While no harsh words were spoken between Jimmy and the many Confederate soldiers, at times you could feel the tension in the air.

December 25, 1861
Christmas Day

On Christmas Day, 1861, the family got up at around 5 a.m. and started their chores, much like any other day before the war started. There was always work to do and there were several rooms with fireplaces that needed to be supplied with plenty of chopped-up wood. The brothers both woke up early to place wood in and near the fireplace in the great room and the kitchen. Jimmy and Will had been chopping and stacking wood outside the house for the last couple of weeks. They were trying to cut enough wood to last the entire winter since they probably would not be home.

The brothers were sitting down outside taking a break when suddenly there was a loud shriek from inside the house. It sounded like their momma. They looked at each other and raced inside only to find a racoon running through the living room. Phyliss was right behind it swinging a large broom. Their momma yelled to them, "There's a big raccoon in the house! It scared me half to death!!"

Jimmy quickly grabbed a rifle and Will armed himself with two pieces of wood. "Prop the front door open!" said Phyliss.

The animal became cornered while it showed its teeth and hissed at its attackers. After about ten minutes of raccoon related confusion, the varmint ran out of the front door. Jimmy ran out right behind the critter and leveled his rifle to shoot at it. "No!" his momma yelled.

"What?!"

"No! Don't shoot it! It's one of God's creatures!"

"Momma, it's in my sights. I've got a clear shot!"

"Jimmy, it's Christmas… let the raccoon live."

"Really Momma? Okay… Merry Christmas varmint!" yelled Jimmy as he broke into laughter.

After a good half an hour of laughter and reminiscing of the *Raccoon Incident*, the family finally calmed down and got back on track toward their Christmas Day.

Martha, started to decorate the little Christmas tree sitting upon a small table in the great room. Reluctantly, Martha had decided not to travel to church on Christmas Day as to not draw any more unnecessary attention to their situation (two soldiers in the house from opposing sides). She also didn't want to have to tell friends that the boys were both getting ready to leave again.

After a memorable breakfast, Phyllis, Martha, and Grandma Logan worked all day preparing for their special Christmas dinner. Will and Jimmy spent a good part of their day keeping the fireplaces going and firing up the cooking stoves. The day passed quickly and before they knew it, everyone was sitting down to Christmas dinner. The menu included turkey, bread with cranberry jam, corn, beans, and apple pie.

Martha said a special prayer. "Dear Lord, thank you for this food. If it is your will, please keep my sons alive and safe through the upcoming days and years." The entire table quickly united to say, "Amen!" As expected, the Christmas dinner feast was delicious and memorable. Their mother and Phyllis had planned it that way because soon, both of the boys would be heading back to their units and back to the uncertainties of war.

After the meal, the family sipped warm apple cider and exchanged a few gifts. Jimmy gave his momma a small jar of cinnamon, which he had bought at the General Store. Will gave her a twelve-month calendar for the upcoming year 1862. Both brothers teamed up to give Phyllis a special cookbook (also from the General Store). They had both heard Phyllis tell their momma in the past that she wished that she had a real cookbook. Phyllis was delighted (to put it mildly) after she received it. The boys also gave Grandma Logan a pair of spectacles since she often mentioned that it was hard to read at her age. Phyllis gave both boys a small Bible, and each received a shirt that she had sown herself.

Later, to bring the mood up a bit, the whole family joined in for an upbeat version of a relatively new song, called "Jingle Bells." By evening's end, a smile was to be found on every single person's face. Finally, they wrapped up the evening by singing "O Come, All Ye Faithful."

G. S. Spooner

O Come, All Ye Faithful – 1751 – Wade

Oh, come, all ye faithful, Joyful and triumphant!
Oh, come ye, oh come ye to Bethlehem.
Come and behold him, Born the King of angels;
Oh, come, let us adore him; Oh, come, let us adore him;
Oh, come, let us adore him, Christ, the Lord.

During both songs, Jimmy strummed his guitar and his mother played along, lightly tapping a tambourine. It was a joyous Christmas that really was not expected only a few weeks earlier. It was a Christmas that the Logan family would never forget. Primarily because the brothers had come home from the war and also because of the notorious Raccoon Incident.

Chapter Three

January 1862
Back to Military Duty

Jimmy and Will completed a lot of productive work on the family farm while they were home for the holiday, but duty beckoned. Willy had to report back to his unit on January 3, and Jimmy had to report on January 12. Both men left several tearful goodbyes behind them, followed orders, and returned to duty. Willy was kind of happy that on the 3rd, he simply had to walk back to his camp. On the other hand, Jimmy had to take a two-day paddlewheel trip back to St. Louis.

Once again, Private Jimmy Logan found himself back on the very same paddlewheel boat as before, headed back up to St. Louis. It was cold and Jimmy was stuck on the boat. His military orders were in his pocket, instructing him to report back to St. Louis. Jimmy's newly forming unit was named the "Army of the Mississippi." He still has his standard leather and canvas bag with him and, of course, he had his guitar in tow.

Jimmy sat below deck in a cold and barren little room with only a cot in it. It was too cold to play guitar, so Jimmy had time to ponder his future as he tried to stay warm. He thought about the lieutenant telling him that the "Army of the Mississippi" would operate in missions in and near the Mississippi River. Jimmy wondered if his duties could soon bring him right back down the very same river toward his hometown of New Madrid. He would find out only too soon.

After arriving at Benton Barracks in St. Louis, Jimmy had barely signed into his new unit when he started hearing talk of an important mission back down by New Madrid. With this, Jimmy quickly sent a letter to his momma alerting her that there might be some kind of military action in her area. This probably would come as no surprise to her since the entire New Madrid area was chock full of Confederate soldiers.

Jimmy also noticed a great number of soldiers in his new unit. There were far more soldiers than in any of his previous outfits. The Army of the Mississippi was formally activated on February 23, 1862, at a special ceremony with thousands of soldiers standing in an inaugural formation. Two days later, Jimmy and many hundreds, indeed thousands, of other soldiers were loaded into a flotilla of transport boats. Then, the massive armada started heading south down the Mississippi River right toward the city of New Madrid. Boats in the flotilla consisted of gunboats, mortar rafts, armed ships, engineer boats with cranes, paddlewheel steamers, and many other support ships packed with cannons, arms, munitions, rations, and supplies. *Holy crap,* Jimmy thought. *It looks like we're going to take on the entire Reb Army.*

Jimmy played his guitar sporadically on the boat trip, but he spent a lot more time receiving instructions on military tactics and maneuvers from his platoon leaders. All of the sergeants and officers were very enthusiastic. They all had a positive attitude when addressing the troops. This seemed to come down from their bosses because nearly all of the unit's leaders had it. They radiated a constructive, can-do atmosphere. The positive attitude was contagious and it seemed to spread throughout the troops. Jimmy thought to himself, *We'll be able to do nearly anything with this many troops and this much enthusiasm.*

February 28 – March 12, 1862
Landing at New Madrid

Under the command of Brigadier General John Pope, the Army of the Mississippi arrived at their destination just north of New Madrid, Missouri. When the boats arrived at their destination, Jimmy's transport landed at the same riverbank he had embarked and disembarked from on his three previous paddlewheel trips. "Here I am again," Jimmy whispered to himself. For the next several days, a great number of Union soldiers kept arriving in the area by land and by the river. The huge group of soldiers "mustered in" (signed in), and the bulk of the enormous unit was organized into companies and platoons. General Pope organized the massive group in an area just north of the big "N" in the river. The "N" caused the Mississippi to go from north to south, then from south to north, and then again from north to south.

Several days later, all of the soldiers had arrived and organized platoons were assembled. Jimmy and hundreds of other soldiers were then tasked to travel overland to the west with massive amounts of horses, wagons, cannons, and military equipment. The sergeants informed some of the troops that General Pope had sent for four 128-pound siege cannons. These huge canons could lob a shell for nearly a mile. The sergeants also mentioned that the big cannons had yet to arrive. The men trekked across the top of the "N" toward New Madrid for about one day. Then to Jimmy's horror, his unit started setting up cannons, mortars, and artillery to shell the city of New Madrid. When Jimmy questioned this action, he was told, "Aw, hell, son. Don't you know that town is chock full of Confederate soldiers or Confederate sympathizers?" Jimmy thought to himself, *This is the nightmare that I feared from the moment we left St. Louis.*

On March 12, the big siege cannons that Pope had sent for had arrived, and final preparations were made for the bombardment of New Madrid. Jimmy's unit had hastily set up a massive military encampment about a mile outside of town. The encampment had a lot more than just sleeping tents. It had everything that could be found in a well-running unit: supply tents, mess tents, medical tents, sleeping tents, and, of course, ammunition tents. Jimmy asked a fellow soldier, "What the hell's going on here? Are we going to live out here for a couple of years or what?"

"Yeah, I think General Pope wants us to be well fed and well supplied because he's planning to work our asses off."

March 13, 1862
The Bombardment of New Madrid

After the strategic positioning of horses, heavy cannons, armaments, and soldiers, the Army of the Mississippi was ready to rain fire upon the city of New Madrid, Missouri. Jimmy's battery team included eight men to manage their twenty-pounder Parrott rifle (a cannon). Not surprisingly, the cannon fired a twenty-pound shell. They also had six horses to pull the cannon and six to pull the *caisson* (ammunition wagon). Each man had a specific duty. Jimmy's job was to quickly pack the shell to the back of the tube.

Suddenly, the word had been given. "Open fire!" echoed off of the surrounding hills.

With the very first cannon blast, several horses broke their leather straps and ran off. The shell blasted through the air and flew toward Jimmy's hometown of New Madrid. He stood there in awe and watched the cannon shell fly off into the distance as a cold chill rushed through his body. His mouth fell open and he stood there staring into the distance, nearly dumbfounded. His trance was quickly broken when the sergeant yelled, "Load the cannon! Let's go!"

For the entire day, Jimmy found himself loading and packing cannon shells into their Parrott rifle. During each blast, the soldiers would move away and try to place their hands over their ears. A great many shells malfunctioned. Some spun off in crazy directions and others exploded just after they left the cannon. At first, this caught the firing team by surprise and they would all hit the deck with their hands over their heads. Later in the day, the team started to ignore these close explosions and just kept on working. Jimmy thought that this was dangerous. These exploding shells were only fifty to one hundred feet in front of them, so he kept dropping to the ground with his hands over his head. The sergeant noticed this and allowed it, saying, "That's right, Logan! You're smart! Don't get killed by our own shells!"

During the assault, Jimmy tried hard to hide his emotions, but he found himself tearing up throughout this long, long day. Whenever possible, he would kick the cannon wheel just a bit, hoping to make it miss its target. At one point, Private Jimmy Logan had to walk over into the woods to vomit. The sergeant in charge was the cannon gunner. He looked over at Jimmy, somewhat puzzled. "Are you okay, Private Logan?"

"Yes, Sergeant. Some of that last chow must have disagreed with me."

"Ha! It probably had some rebel blood in it! You'll be okay. Now pack that cannon, Private. Let's get busy!"

"Yes, Sergeant!"

Later in the day, designated soldiers provided scouting reports to all of the battery teams. They reported that there appeared to be very few casualties in the town. The scouts also reported that it appeared that the rebel soldiers were bugging out and they could not see any civilians in the town. The officers in charge (OICs) now believed that most of the civilians must have evacuated the town prior to the shelling. This information spread throughout the battery teams and it made Jimmy feel much better. He looked to the sky and let off a sigh of relief, saying to himself, *Thank you, God.*

That evening, a very heavy thunderstorm hit the area. The sergeants and the officers told most of the troops to go to their tents and bunk down for the night. With lightning crashing and thunder pounding, Jimmy lay there in the tent. He whispered as he prayed, "Please, Lord, please allow any people still in New Madrid to leave the town. It's storming so hard right now that no one could ever see them as they go." Jimmy slept off and on through the night. His sleep was sporadic at best, not only because of the storms, but also because of his unbelievable situation.

March 14, 1862
The Miraculous Bypass Plan

Early the following day, the rain had finally stopped and the sergeants rousted up the troops at the first peak of daybreak. Jimmy and a few others were sitting on an old log eating a breakfast of dried pork and hardtack with some coffee. Then suddenly, two Union scouts came walking up through the woods with their rifles leveled at two captured Rebel soldiers. The Confederate soldiers apparently had surrendered and one was carrying a white flag on a long stick. The group of four walked right past Jimmy and reported to his OIC. Within earshot of Jimmy, the scouts and the rebel soldiers reported that the town of New Madrid was deserted. With this, the OIC immediately sent a messenger to forward the information to General Pope. Shortly after that, and to Jimmy's delight, the platoon sergeants announced that the shelling of New Madrid would be halted.

Later that morning, Private Jimmy Logan and his fellow soldiers started breaking down their cannon positions and then their entire encampment. By mid-afternoon, Jimmy and his platoon were headed back to their original position near the river. As they were marching back, Jimmy overheard two officers saying that the total number of Union troops in the area was now more than 23,000 strong.

After they arrived, the word came down from the OICs and the sergeants. The entire Army of the Mississippi would be massed together into a colossal division formation. The following day, they were assembled into the massive formation in a nearby clearing that had previously been a large farm field. A large six-foot-tall platform was built solely for General Pope to address the troops. Pope appeared on the tall platform and started explaining their next big mission. He was a bearded man with a sharp looking uniform and a loud voice. But, Jimmy and most of the soldiers nearby could not really hear the general very well, even though he was standing on a tall platform. They were just too far away. Jimmy did hear a few words that included: digging, bypass, and dynamite. Although he heard those words several times, he still had no idea what the general was talking about.

Soon after the general spoke, dozens of his leaders descended on the troops to explain the overall plan. Platoon sergeants, OICs, executive officers, and officer engineers used cone-shaped megaphones and diagrams to define and describe the mission. It seems the Confederates had effectively closed the river to all traffic. The leaders detailed and clarified the mission, which appeared to include a nearly impossible task. It appeared that the Army of the Mississippi was going to attempt to dig a twelve-mile canal across land. It would go right through the land and marshes just north of New Madrid. Once finished, this canal would allow a massive Union flotilla to bypass the Confederate strongpoint that was just south of New Madrid at Island #10. The leaders reiterated that the Confederate Army had entirely closed the river and would allow no Union troops or supplies to get through.

The primary Confederate position was at Island #10. The island was located right at the bottom of the "N," just before the river turned back toward the north and to New Madrid. The sergeants and officers repeatedly emphasized that the mission was sorely needed because the Confederates had effectively closed the river to all traffic.

The sergeants and officers went on to describe the seemingly impossible mission. When the Mississippi River approached New Madrid, it zigzagged from heading south to heading north and then back to heading south again, much like the letter "N." The officers further explained that the Army of the Mississippi would dig a canal across the top of the "N" and bypass the rebels at the bottom of the "N." After this, the Union Army would come out downstream and behind the enemy to conduct a surprise attack.

The engineers explained that they needed a considerable amount of manpower to cut the bypass canal through land, forest, rock, and marshes. They would use saws, shovels, dynamite, horses, and pure manpower. They further explained that the canal would bend through the existing terrain through the lowest points and ultimately link up with St. James Bayou, northeast of New Madrid. They would then clear the St. James Bayou, which led straight into the Mississippi. In many areas, there were trees in deep standing water. For these areas, the engineers had designed and would build two submerged saw rafts. These highly specialized boats could cut through trees well below water level, so they could be removed.

While their colossal group of soldiers worked on the bypass, the Union's Mississippi River Squadron would constantly bombard the Rebels' position at Island #10. This would help to mask the sound of exploding dynamite as the Army of the Mississippi cleared the bypass canal. The plan was for the Union's gunboats and Ironclads to continue hammering the Confederate positions day and night until the bypass was finished.

After all of the troops were briefed, the rumor mill started churning. The scuttlebutt was everywhere, and the tension was palpable. The general consensus among the troops was that the entire plan sounded more than a bit sensational. Especially the part about digging a twelve-mile overland river bypass. The mission sounded like it was an impossibility. But they were Union soldiers… they were the Army of the Mississippi…they had taken an oath. If it were humanly possible, they would do it. If it were humanly possible, they would complete their mission. Jimmy started to wonder if his new unit's positive can-do attitude might allow this miraculous plan to actually succeed. He thought to himself, *Well, I thought this enthusiasm might allow us to do just about anything. I think this crazy bypass canal mission might really test that theory.*

March 15, 1862
Digging the Bypass

After a sporadic night's sleep (due to the constant shelling of Confederate positions from Union gunboats), Private Jimmy Logan's thirty-man platoon was fed, equipped, and assembled. Then, they were quickly dispatched inland to work on the twelve-mile canal route, but they weren't alone. They were accompanied by approximately twenty thousand other soldiers. The twenty thousand soldiers marched into and through the woods carrying shovels and picks. They were accompanied by several hundred horse-drawn wagons carrying supplies and dynamite. Each of the over six hundred platoons was sent to a specific area along the path of the yet-to-be-dug canal route. The officer engineers had already placed stretched-out ropes to show the soldiers exactly where the canal was to be dug.

Within a few hours, the Army of the Mississippi had started cutting, digging, blasting, and sawing. All of the canal work was done under the watchful eyes of the lieutenants, sergeants, and Union engineers and their survey teams. Jimmy immediately noticed that much of the ground was actually kind of easy to dig because it was primarily sand. Some areas required a lot of digging and clearing, while others required very little. Jimmy's platoon was part of a group placed in the latter half of the forest. They had joined several other platoons with a mission to cut channel nearly all the way to St. James Bayou (about one-third of a mile away). Many other platoons were placed in front of them and behind them to clear the canal channel.

In some of the swampier areas, trees had to be cut through at a level at least four and one-half feet below the water level. This was the level of the draft that the engineers needed for the passage of the Union ships. The engineers had the troops assemble the submerged saw rafts in these areas. These engineering marvels could cut the trees well below the water level. It was becoming clear that the level of ingenuity and pure manpower used to dig the bypass was beyond the pale.

After about two days of effort, it became apparent that much of the work was extremely taxing. Many soldiers were not used to this level of intense physical labor. Jimmy, however, was used to extremely hard work because of his duties on the family farm.

He was also accustomed to working long hours. Because of this, it didn't take long for the platoon sergeants to zero in on Jimmy (and several others) for the lifting and clearing of the heavier objects.

Every so often, a dynamite team would come in and blow apart large portions of the land, rock, and forest. Often, there were large boulders and trees laying directly in the canal's path. During one of these dynamite blasts, Jimmy received a cut from a large tree splinter in the same shoulder he had previously injured in Lexington, Missouri. "Geesh, what's the deal with this shoulder," Jimmy said to himself. Because of the heavy bleeding, he was sent to the doctor. The doctor cleaned the wound, wrapped it up, and told him to let it heal. Jimmy was told to rest for one evening and he was ordered back to full duty the very next day. Two days later, a different soldier received a nasty cut across his face during another huge dynamite explosion. After that accident, the engineers made everyone move back to one hundred yards away every time they detonated dynamite.

March 20, 1862
Working on the Bypass Canal

The days were long and the work was hard. At one point, when the dynamite teams were otherwise occupied, one of the lieutenants placed long leather straps around a boulder that needed to be moved. Unfortunately, several soldiers had teamed up but had tried and failed to move the rock.

After quietly watching on the side, Jimmy said, "All right, that's enough." He walked up and said, "Please move back, fellas. I'm gonna try to show you the smart way to do this if I can.... That's if I'm smart enough." The soldiers all stood back. They knew Private Logan was not one to boast. Jimmy arranged the straps in a particular manner. He then wrapped them around a tree and pulled them around his shoulders.

Jimmy then backed up to pull the straps tight. He bent his knees and then backed up a little more. Jimmy leaned back so far that he was nearly parallel with the ground. Then with a deep guttural sound, he pushed off and twisted his body as he leaned back. The leather straps twisted as he straightened his knees. Jimmy then let out a hard growl and just as one of the straps broke, the large stone popping out of the earth. The soldiers, sergeants, and lieutenants all let out a huge roar and yelled, "Horaahh!!" They ran up to Jimmy, slapping him on the back as they congratulated him for the mammoth deed. Jimmy had used the same method many times back at the family farm while clearing trees and boulders for farming. Breathing heavily, he stated proudly, "It's not in how strong you are. It's the way that you do it." The platoon sergeant yelled, "Ha! I think it's how strong you are!" and the entire group all laughed.

After that, Jimmy became known simply as "The Big Man." This was a confusing nickname since Jimmy (although very strong) was not a really large man. He was just a bit larger than average. Also, "Big Man" was a moniker that Jimmy preferred not to have because that was also the nickname of Amos Washington. Jimmy had spent most of his time in the military doing the best job that he could while trying not being noticed. He tried to blend in when he could. Now, several times each day, you could hear the calls from his fellow soldiers, echoing off the surrounding hills, "Hey, Big Man! Give us a hand with this tree stump." With time, he didn't mind the nickname too much because he still deeply believed in the Union cause. As the days passed, Jimmy became known as one of the hardest working soldiers in his unit. He was all in and his cohorts knew it. He was truly dedicated to service to his country and was ready to sacrifice himself for the mission if it were necessary.

One day, another platoon was having difficulty clearing a large boulder that was stuck between two trees. Their sergeant called over to Jimmy's lieutenant, "Hey, sir, can we borrow the Big Man!" After arriving at the site, Jimmy stood there for a moment, surveying the situation. He then started giving instructions to the group. "Okay, listen up. I need someone to throw a rope over that tree and tie it to that horse." The men jumped into action. "Now, I need two leather straps wrapped around the rock. Pull the straps over that way."

"That way?" said the sergeant. "But it needs to go the other way."

"I know it does, Sergeant, just trust me."

Jimmy had the horse pull the tree back in what was apparently the wrong direction. "Now everyone pull on the straps! Pull hard!!" The men grabbed the straps and had just begun to pull when they all fell flat on their backs. The boulder just popped right out of its hole. "Just like we did it back on the farm," said Jimmy. "Thanks, guys."

"Thanks, Big Man!" said the sergeant. The soldiers all stood there with puzzled looks on their faces. The sergeant tapped on his right temple and proclaimed, "I think the Big Man is an even better engineer than he is a soldier!"

As Jimmy walked away, he smiled and proudly answered, "I'm a farmer!"

April 4, 1862
The Bypass Is Completed / Ships Travel Through

After only nineteen days, the new canal was completed. The entire channel was cut and it was now full of water. Union transports were then dispatched to test the operation of the new Bypass Canal. As the ships floated into the canal, thousands of proud soldiers cheered from both sides of the new waterway. The nearly inconceivable accomplishment was more than good news to General Pope and his team of officer engineers. It was great news.

Later, while testing the canal, they found that the heavy Ironclad gunships drafted a bit too deep and couldn't get all of the way through the bypass. But fortunately, the large Union transports drafted shallow. As a result, they made it all of the way through the canal. With this, General Pope quickly sent for several more of the shallow drafting transport ships, which for the most part were paddlewheel steamships.

On the same day, April 4, 1862, thousands of Union soldiers (including Jimmy) began traveling through the newly opened bypass canal. To his dismay, the transports kept going right past the abandoned city of New Madrid. Jimmy gazed over toward the town through the darkness and could only make out a few Union scouts standing guard on the shoreline.

The transports quickly turned to the right and headed south down the Mississippi River. The massive armada was totally out of the vision of the besieged Confederates at Island #10, so they passed unchallenged.

As the transports traveled south under the cover of darkness, Jimmy couldn't believe what was happening. A thunderstorm had just passed and the night sky had suddenly cleared. Jimmy could see pretty good because of the ambient light from the moon and the stars. Suddenly, he found himself looking over at his family's farm field. He looked at the same ol' plow that was still sitting in the field, right where he and his brother had left it. Jimmy then gazed upon the trees and fields of the Logan farm on the Missouri side of the river. About one minute later, he found himself looking directly at the house that he was born and raised in, with his mother inside of it. As he looked over, he noticed that one small lamp was lit inside the house. "Hi, Momma," Jimmy whispered to himself as his ship passed on by.

Smallpox Island

> *Point of Historical Reference – The little-known New Madrid Bypass Canal would later be heralded as a modern military miracle. It was truly a remarkable feat and it was a testimonial to the intelligence, the raw power, and the will of man.*

April 4-6, 1862
The Ironclads Maneuver

In the darkness of night, at about the same time that Jimmy was looking at his family farm, important maneuvers were taking place back in the main Mississippi channel, near the bottom of the "N." First, on April 4, the Ironclad USS *Carondelet* slipped past Island #10 under the cover of the night thunderstorm. Then two nights later, on April 6, the Ironclad USS *Pittsburg* also slipped past Island #10 under the cover of night. These ships would continue to provide protection for the Union troops traveling not only through the Bypass Canal but also up and down the Mississippi. While all this was happening, Jimmy and thousands of other Union troops were being repositioned on the Tennessee side of the river, just a few miles behind the Confederate troops.

Meanwhile, the Mississippi River Squadron (aka the Western Gunboat Flotilla) continued to relentlessly shell the Confederates' position on Island #10. The rival troops had no idea that they were about to be trapped. To General Pope's delight, there was only one road going in and out from the Rebels' position at Island #10.

To assure victory, Pope kept adding more and more troops to the massive numbers that were already gathered directly behind the Confederates. The soul route of escape was right near a town named Tiptonville, Tennessee.

G. S. Spooner

April 7, 1862
Victory Over Island #10

By April 7, the Union Ironclads had pounded the Confederate troops on Island #10 to the extent that they could no longer resupply their ammunition or provisions. Finally, the leadership was forced to pull their soldiers back. The order was given to retreat and escape to the south, but the Rebel troops had no idea they were about to walk into a trap. The Confederates quickly found that Jimmy and many thousands of other Union troops were strategically positioned directly behind them. General Pope's immense number of troops stood directly in front of the Confederates and on the only escape route that they had. As they moved farther down the little road near Tiptonville, Tennessee, the Confederates, about five thousand in number, became completely overwhelmed by the massive Army of the Mississippi. Outnumbered at nearly four to one, they looked out and slowly scanned across the thousands of Union soldiers before them. Awestruck, most of the men didn't even raise their weapons.

The proud but exhausted Confederate soldiers had to surrender with hardly a shot fired. The Battle for New Madrid and Island #10 was finally over and the Mississippi River would once again open to Union and civilian ships. Jimmy pondered how quickly it had all ended. Especially after such an extensive period of intense work. He and his fellow soldiers still could hardly believe what they had accomplished. They were all very proud to have been a part of building the Bypass Canal to New Madrid. The entire Union Army, and indeed the whole world, might someday come to know of the building of the twelve-mile Bypass Canal in only nineteen days. Just maybe, people might someday talk about this nearly indescribable feat and their incredible display of human fortitude.

After the surrender, Jimmy once again found himself disarming and registering prisoners, much like he did in St. Louis after the *Camp Jackson* Affair during the previous year. But this time, there were thousands of them. He found that many of the rebel soldiers seemed to be glad that it was over. Many of their soldiers were weak and hungry because they were running seriously low on supplies.

Little did Jimmy know that on this very same day (April 7, 1862), his little brother Will was in his first real battle of the war. While Jimmy's unit was wrapping up with an important victory, Willy was knee-deep in the Battle of Shiloh, about 160 miles to the southeast in Hardin County, Tennessee.

But Jimmy was getting ready to head north. Directly after the New Madrid and Island #10 victories, he received orders to immediately return to garrison duties back at Camp Benton in St. Louis. His company commander told him that he (and indeed many others) had only been on loan to the Army of the Mississippi. Jimmy was now needed back at his previous unit. General Pope had asked for (and received) massive numbers of troops to succeed in the New Madrid and Island #10 missions. The Union had to reopen the Mississippi River. So, Pope had to cut a deal with Camp Benton's commander, Brigadier General William Tecumseh Sherman. The borrowed troops were to return to their prior duty stations immediately after the primary mission was completed.

Thus, Private Jimmy Logan was quickly ordered back to duty at Camp Benton in St. Louis, Missouri. He was still needed there for his carpentry duties, which included the construction of more instructional barracks for the training of Union troops. During his absence, Benton Barracks had become a much busier place. In addition, the hospital at Benton was steadily becoming the busiest Union hospital in the West.

G. S. Spooner

April 6-7, 1862
The Battle of Shiloh

Will Logan and his unit, the 1st Missouri Infantry, had been added to the South's Army of the Mississippi. They saw their first real action on April 6 and 7, 1862, at the Battle of Shiloh. This famous and brutal battle happened near a place called Pittsburg Landing in southwestern Tennessee. Confederate General Albert Johnston was defeated by Union General Ulysses S. Grant and his Army of the West Tennessee. During the battle, Will's platoon was tasked with resupplying of munitions, food, and water. Although he did experience some action, Will was fortunate enough to be spared from some of the worst of it. The deadly and two-day-long Battle of Shiloh caused nearly 20,000 soldiers to be either killed or wounded from both sides.

After losing the advantage, Will's 1st Missouri Infantry retreated south and headed to Corinth, Mississippi to reconsolidate. Will found himself shaken up by the brutality and the raw savagery of war. While resupplying the troops with ammunition, he had to run by (and jump over) the bodies of possibly hundreds of dead Confederate soldiers. He had never seen (or even dreamed) of anything like this. Some of the dead were soldiers that Willy knew or had met. He thought to himself, *There may be great gallantry here, but there is no honor in this. This is just the bloody butchery of a lot of brave, brave men...from both sides.*

September 19, 1862
The Battle of Iuka—Willy Is Captured

Later that same year, after several small local missions and more reconsolidation, Major General Price directed Will's unit, the Army of the Mississippi, to join the Confederate's Army of the West. The Army of the West was then deployed by train to Iuka, Mississippi, and on September 19, 1862, the Battle of Iuka ensued. Once again, they were matched up against Ulysses S. Grant. This time, Grant brought two massive Union armies with him, the Union's Army of the Tennessee and the Army of the Mississippi. The Army of the Mississippi was Jimmy's previous unit. They had shelled the Logans' hometown of New Madrid, Missouri and had gained notoriety by digging the amazing New Madrid Bypass Canal.

At the Battle of Iuka, Will was on one of the primary attack lines. He moved forward, fired his Springfield Model 1861 rifle, fell back, reloaded, moved forward, and fired again. Some of the soldiers had help with reloading and alternating rifles, but Willy was not that lucky. It was an active and chaotic battle. The noise, the smoke, and the fog of war clouded Willy's mind. Even though he aimed his rifle directly at the enemy, it was hard to determine whether or not he had killed or even hit an enemy soldier. He thought that he might have hit someone, but he really wasn't sure.

Will had only fired about ten times when an exploding cannon shell hit a giant oak tree limb far above him. The limb fell directly onto Willy's head, dazing him and knocking him to the ground. Ears ringing and in a stunned daze, he lay on the ground in a trance, barely able to move. He kept trying to open his eyes only to see spinning and blurry scenes of war. Then, two soldiers nearby him were shot and hit the ground right near him. One of the soldiers was shot in the neck. This mortally wounded soldier landed one foot in front of Will's face and splattered blood across Will.

Willy tried hard to sit up, but his head injury incapacitated him for another five to ten minutes. Right before he ultimately passed out, he tried hard to push himself up and focus. When he finally did, he saw Major General Sterling Price looking down at him from a large horse. With his sword drawn, the general turned and yelled orders to advance. After staring at Will for a few more seconds, the famous general then ignored him and rode toward the enemy. At that very moment, Willy passed out.

September 20, 1862

When Willy came to and started opening his eyes, it was the next day, although he didn't know it yet. He found it hard to focus, so he closed his eyes again. With his eyes closed, Will could hear people talking. Then he heard birds chirping and singing. Willy thought to himself, *Well, either I'm dead or the battle's over, or maybe both.* He slowly tried to open his eyes again and the first thing that he could focus on was a Union soldier. He then looked around and tried to move. Will quickly realized that he had been tied up. He also noticed that he was leaning against a tree and apparently was in a prisoner's holding area. Will sat there. He moved his arms and legs as much as he could. He now had a clearer head and was starting to realize that maybe he was not too seriously injured.

Will looked around and saw ten armed Union soldiers guarding himself and about forty other POWs. He watched as two of the Union soldiers untied the captured Confederate soldiers one at a time. Once untied, they would then point them toward another Union soldier sitting at a field desk. Next to the desk were a few buckets filled with water and several blankets on the ground, which appeared to be covered with biscuits and hardtack.

One of the Union guards walked straight up to Will. He took a knee and then smiled and spoke to him. "Hey there, soldier! You're finally awake! You took a bad hit to the head. We wrapped it up for you while you were still passed out. The doc says you're going to be okay."

Will asked the Union soldier, "Are you going to kill us?"

"Awe, heck no, Corporal," he said, seeing the corporal stripes on Will's arm." He started to untie Will. "Right now, we're untying you so you can get up and go to that field desk over there. First, you need to log your name on the register as a prisoner. Then, you can go get yourself some food and water off of those blankets over there. After that, they say you're all heading up north to take the rest of the war off. Heck of a deal if you ask me!"

"I wonder," Willy muttered.

The Battle of Iuka was another major win for the Union. The Confederates lost nearly three hundred soldiers with seven hundred more wounded. They also had over five hundred troops either missing or captured and imprisoned. Corporal Willy Logan was now one of these casualties of war. Now captured, Willy was about to be sent north to wait out the war as a prisoner. Little did he know that he would end up in Alton, Illinois, at the Alton Federal Prison. Willy had never heard of the small island located in the river, directly across from the prison. He had never heard of Smallpox Island…but he would.

September 21, 1862
Prisoners Marched North

Willy and most of the Confederate prisoners were marched north for one day.

Somewhere near Savannah, Tennessee, the captured troops were then loaded onto trains that were headed for Memphis, Tennessee. Just three months earlier, the city of Memphis had been captured by the north in the famous Battle of Memphis. Thanks to the Battles of Memphis and Island #10, the Mississippi River was now open all of the way to Minnesota. Even though Willy was a prisoner, he was somewhat happy today because the Union troops were loading the prisoners onto trains. He had acquired several painful blisters on both of his feet from the long road march from Iuka and he was looking forward to sitting down—even if he was sitting down on a train, in a cattle car, as a prisoner of war.

September 22-24, 1862

On September 22, the large group of prisoners reached Memphis. After some coordination by the Union leadership, the prisoners were broken up into several groups. The first group continued to move north by train in cattle cars. The second group continued marching north. The final group was boarded onto a giant paddle-wheel troop carrier named the *Continental*. Will was placed in the last group and he found himself loading onto the *Continental* that evening. He overheard one of the Union soldiers stating that the ship was nearly three hundred feet long. As the prisoners started walking up a steep ramp onto the vessel, Will looked around at the layout of the massive ship. "Dang, this is a mighty big target," Will said to a fellow prisoner.

"Yeah, I hope we don't get shelled by our own side."

"Me too!"

Willy was placed on the boat's top deck and was told to sit down. Then all of the prisoners, more than two hundred of them, were rearranged into long rows along the deck.

The prisoners' hands were tied in front of them. Within a half-hour, the massive transport disembarked. Will calculated that in twelve to fifteen hours, the *Continental* would be passing by his family farm on the west side of the river. Hours later, Will sat there, considering his options. He thought about escaping somehow and swimming over to see his momma at the farm. He closed his eyes and leaned his head against the wall behind him. Then, Willy formulated and fantasized the detailed plans of execution for his grand escape.

First, I can get untied by the soldier if I ask to use "the street" (the latrine). After I use the facilities, I'll just make a mad dash and leap over the railing. Then, I'll swim underwater to escape the bullets. Once I make it to shore, I'll move inland to find cover and carefully make my way over to the farm...keeping off the beaten path, taking the back way. I'll lay low and sneak along carefully all the way home. When the coast is clear, I'll walk right in through the front door and Momma will scream with joy. Phyllis, too. I'll get a big hug from Momma and she'll cook me up some supper. Right after that, we'll hear that the war is over and the South has won! I'll go into town just in time to see a big victory parade starting. They will all proclaim me as a big hero. Jimmy will come home soon after that and everything will be made right. Then, we'll be back in the field working on that same stupid ol' plow. Jimmy will mess and joke with me all the time about my side winning the war.

Just then, Will was jolted back into reality as he was accidentally pushed by a fellow Confederate prisoner sitting next to him. It was already the next morning. Will had fallen asleep and had been dreaming of his grand escape.

"Wow, that was great," he said.

"What was?"

"Oh, nothin'. I just dreamed I escaped and was back home."

"Sounds like a real good one, Corporal."

"It was.... It really was."

Just then Willy looked over at the shoreline. Then, he quickly spun his head around and realized that they were already passing New Madrid. He had been asleep for hours and, sadly, the giant paddlewheel boat was miles past his family farm.

Chapter Four

September 25, 1862

Two days later, on the morning of the 25th, the *Continental* transport pulled up to the big city of St. Louis. "Welcome to Mound City!" yelled one of the Union guards. All of the old riverboat captains had given St. Louis the nickname of "Mound City" because of the many Indian mounds that could be seen from the river. The two hundred-plus men were hustled up and taken off the ship onto the shore. They were placed into formations and marched toward the west, away from the river. After about a fifteen-minute march, they were all standing in front of the Gratiot Street Prison. For several hours, the men were signed in and processed into the prison. Gratiot Street Prison had previously been a medical school called McDowell's College. The new prisoners were fed and were provided with prison garb. They were then placed back into their platoons and were assembled into a large formation. The colonel in charge came out and gave a short briefing. The only part that Will remembered was, "Do not stand in or near my windows. If you do, you will be shot!"

After the briefing, the prisoners were quickly placed into their cell rooms. The current inmates and even the guards chatted with the new guest. They all repeatedly warned the newcomers not to stand in or near the windows unless they wanted to be shot. Indeed, a guard had shot a man for this just a few days earlier. Apparently, there was a reason for this rule. The prison's windows had been retro-fitted with bars since the college was turned into a prison. These bars were notoriously weak and many of them were loose.

The very next day, seventy-five of the new inmates were brought out of the barracks. Will was not one of these. He peeked out of his window and then listened to the Union captain address the seventy-five inmates as he sat by the window of his cell. The captain told the Confederate prisoners that they would be traveling upstream on the Continental transport to an old prison in "the beautiful city of Alton, Illinois." Will realized that he was going to now live at the Gratiot Street Prison for at least a short period of time. Little did he know that his brother Jimmy was stationed only a few miles away at the Benton Army Barracks.

March 28, 1863 and Forward

Will Logan had made it through the first six months of his captivity in the Gratiot Street Prison. He gazed carefully through his second-floor window (standing off to the side) and noticed two Union guards walking by. One of the guards looked like a boy and the other guard looked like a very old man. The current guards at Gratiot Street Prison were known as the infamous Greybeards. The Greybeards were the 37th Iowa Volunteers. They were a very large Union unit that was composed of (for the most part) very old men.

Their commander, Colonel George Kincaid, recruited soldiers that were older than and even younger than the generally accepted age restrictions. This led to guards who were not the picture of your typical soldier. Many, save most, were older than fifty and a few were even older than seventy years old. Indeed, a handful of the Greybeard guards were over eighty and had even fought in the War of 1812. On the other end of the spectrum, a few dozen soldiers in the 37th Iowa were only sixteen years old.

Will had mentioned to some of the Greybeard guards that his brother was a Union soldier, but none had taken the time to correlate this information with local Union troops. If they had, they would have found that Will's brother, Private Jimmy Logan, was working about four miles away as a carpenter at Benton Barracks. Benton Barracks was also the location of the Headquarters building for the 37th Iowa Volunteers in St. Louis.

Time passed by for Willy as if it were water flowing down the great Mississippi River. After six months in the Gratiot Street Prison, he had started to succumb to the wretched life that prison had become. Illness was everywhere, with smallpox, typhoid, and pneumonia among the worst of these. Willy did the best that he could to try to stay healthy. He paid close attention to his surroundings and tried to stay away from people who looked like they were ill. He also did his best to eat and drink as well as he could.

One day, Will told the guard that he had been feeling really bad. Worse than usual. The guard found that Will had come down with a fever. He reported it to his sergeant of the guard and the lead sergeant decided to have Willy sent to the Benton Barracks Hospital. Unfortunately, many of the prisoners did not receive this kind of positive attention. But Willy was well-liked by most of the prison guards because of his kind and cooperative demeanor. Many of his fellow prisoners looked upon their captures with a great amount of contempt, but Willy had a different viewpoint of the Union soldiers. Probably because his brother was one of them.

Will was then taken by military escort to the Benton Barracks Hospital. Within a few hours, he was diagnosed to have a fever and mild pneumonia. His treatment for pneumonia included routine care, quinine, muster plasters, and small doses of opium. After four days at the hospital, Will's eyes started to clear and his fever started to break. Will thought about how amazing it was to receive good care, good food, clean water, and fresh air. He noticed that his primary nurse, named Arabella, seemed to go above and beyond in regards to his care. He also thought that she was very pretty, but he wouldn't dream of telling her so. After all, he was a prisoner. Arabella was tall for a woman and she wore a gray dress past her knees. She had brown hair that held a small white nurse's cap. Most noticeably to Will, she had the most caring brown eyes that he had ever seen. When she looked at him, he felt as though he could see into her gentle and kind soul. Will noticed that she seemed to take care of him emotionally as well as physically. Her kindness made him feel special and important. She seemed to always be cheerful and that made Will feel the same way. The care that he received almost made him feel as though he was not a prisoner. "Arabella, why do you take such good care of me?"

"Well, Mr. Logan, I try to give exceptional care to everyone I treat. As a nurse and a ward matron here, it's my job to comfort patients spiritually as well as physically. My supervisor is in charge of this entire hospital and she makes sure that I do just that. Her name is Emily Elizabeth Parsons. She truly cares about people to an extent that I have never seen. I hope that someday I can be even one half of the nurse that she is."

"Well, thank you for the special care. I really like you," said Willy.

"Well, I really like you too, Mr. Logan. You seem to be a very nice gentleman and I'm a pretty good judge of character."

"Please call me Willy, Arabella."

"Okay, Willy. You can call me Belle."

"Well, Belle, you sure have taken good care of this farm boy from southern Missouri. Thank you."

"It's my pleasure and you're very welcome, Willy. It's not every day that a patient thanks me for my work."

"Well, they should, Belle…they really should."

The very next day, Belle was working at Will's bedside when a woman approached. Belle's eyes widened and she looked directly at Will. "Mr. Logan, this is our hospital administrator, Emily Elizabeth Parsons." Belle winked at Willy as she walked away. Ms. Parsons often took the time to meet with the patients at Benton Barracks Hospital. Parsons walked with a limp. She was a short woman with brown hair, but her sharp attire and professional mannerisms distinguished her as a formidable leader at her hospital.

"Hello! It looks like you're doing much better, Mr. Logan. When I visited you a few days ago, you didn't even know I was here." Parsons looked at Will's paperwork at the foot of his bed. She then noticed Will's name on the paperwork and mentioned, "One of my best carpenters has the last name of "Logan."

Will asked her, "Really? Is he from New Madrid and is his name Jimmy Logan?"

"I don't know, but I can check for you." Parsons then smiled at Will and told him to keep getting better before moving on to the next patient's bed.

The following day Will was feeling even better. He was about to be checked out of the hospital and ushered back to Gratiot Street Prison. Just as he and his Greybeard guard were preparing to leave, Emily Parsons came running into his hospital dorm with a broad smile on her face. She ran straight up to Willy. "Yes!!" she said excitedly. "One of my carpenters *is* from New Madrid and *is* named Jimmy Logan!! I just spoke to his platoon sergeant and he's on the way over right now!"

Will's guard then told Emily Parsons that they really had to go. Ms. Parsons sternly told him, "Really? Well, as you were, soldier! I am the director and the administrator of this facility! If you don't stand fast, I'll need to have a talk with your unit commander. I guarantee to you that I not only know him, but I also know the general he works for!"

"Yes, ma'am!" said the guard as he stepped back.

A moment later, Private Jimmy Logan walked through the door of the hospital ward with a hammer in his hand. Dropping his hammer, he yelled, "What the...! Holy crap!!" as he rushed over to his brother.

Will said, "I can't believe it," as the brothers grabbed each other with a tight hug. The two soldiers from opposing armies had tears rolling down their faces. With this, the Greybeard walked away and departed out of the dorm.

"What are you doing here?!"

"I work here! What are *you* doing here?"

"I'm a prisoner over at Gratiot Street Prison. I wrote Mom and told her. Didn't she tell you?"

"No. She wrote that you were in some prison but never told me where. Honestly, I've been so busy, I haven't written her back in several months and I never thought of looking for you here or anywhere else. I also didn't know if my bosses would take kindly to it."

Ms. Parsons smiled and walked away as the boys sat down on the bed. They talked and they kept on talking for a long while. About home, Momma, their girlfriends, and even the old plow. The one thing that they really didn't talk much about was the war. Finally, after about ten minutes, the guard came back and quietly stood to the side. It was time for Will to go. The harsh reality of confinement was waiting for him back in his cell at Gratiot Street.

"Now that I know that you're here, I'll try to come over if I can," said Jimmy.

"Okay, but please write Momma and tell her that you saw me. They don't let me send out mail as often as I would like."

"Will do!"

As Jimmy walked out of the hospital dorm, he shook his head in pure astonishment. Will picked up his personal bag. He then looked over his shoulder at his brother and yelled loudly, "Unbelievable!!"

"I know little, brother, I know!" answered Jimmy.

March – September 1863
Serving in St. Louis

For the next six months, Jimmy primarily had the same job. While the war raged on, he was a soldier carpenter. His work was noticed, and he was promoted to second squad leader in the Maintenance Platoon. Their mission was the construction and repairing of buildings at Benton Barracks. Jimmy's work was also noticed by a few of the higher-ups. When the unit's leaders also realized that Private Jimmy Logan was a great carpenter, not only did they keep him on the job, they even promoted him to corporal.

Jimmy had a way of teaching the newer soldiers and could simplify difficult tasks. He was always quick to give credit to his dad for teaching him how to fix things. Jimmy's father had taught him how to use a hammer and about thirty other tools. His new corporal rank made it a little easier for him to move about the post and get things done. There were not a lot of corporals and sergeants on the post. The corporal rank even made it a little easier to visit his brother at the Gratiot Street Prison. He tried to go over to Gratiot Street about once a week, depending on what was going on.

Unfortunately, in July 1863, the Greybeards from the 37th Iowa Volunteers had received a new mission and were now gone. They had been reassigned to the Alton Prison about twenty miles away. Jimmy frequently talked with Will's new guards in hopes that it would help out his brother with his confinement. Unfortunately, even though the guards did what they could, it did little to change the overall conditions of Will's captivity.

About two months later, on Friday, September 25, 1863, it was the one-year anniversary of Willy's arrival. He was informed on that very day that he and ninety-nine other soldier prisoners had been reassigned to the Alton Military Prison. The move had apparently been planned for a long time by higher-ups along with other realignments of resources. With little or no warning, the one hundred were told to gather their few valuables quickly. In about five minutes, they were all standing outside in formation. Minutes later, they were all marching down toward the river. The one hundred were swiftly loaded onto a transport boat and within a few more minutes, the paddlewheel was headed for Alton.

On the very next day, Jimmy came over to visit his brother only to be told by the guard that Will was gone. He told Jimmy that his brother had been reassigned to the Alton Prison.

"What?! Son of a bitch!" Jimmy hollered.

"Sorry, Corporal," said the guard. "Even us guards didn't know about the move until right before it happened."

"Oh, I know it's not your fault. I'm just pissed off because it just got a lot harder to visit my brother."

"Understood, Corporal. I lost my brother in the war about a year and a half ago. The Rebs killed him down at the Battle of Shiloh."

After a short pause, Jimmy spoke. "Sorry about that, Private. I guess I'm lucky that at least my brother is still alive." Jimmy patted the guard on the shoulder and departed.

September 28, 1863 and Forward

On the following Monday (three days later), Jimmy went to the Post Headquarters. His buddy, Private Moore, was the lead clerk for the commander. Moore knew a lot about most of the military activity in the area, so Jimmy asked him, "What unit is running the Alton Prison?"

"Oh, it's the ragtag Greybeards from our own Gratiot Street Prison. They transferred there about two months ago."

"Can I transfer there, too?"

"I doubt it, Logan. Our commander, Colonel Densmore, thinks you're toeing the mark. I don't think he'll let you go anywhere."

Nonetheless, Jimmy made a formal request to be transferred to the Alton Prison. One week later, he received return paperwork stating that Headquarters had disapproved his request. However, Moore told him that if he wished, he could resubmit a new transfer request after three months.

A couple days later, Jimmy was up on a ladder. He contemplated his future while hammering a piece of fascia board onto the roofline of a hospital building. "They think I'm too good to let me go anywhere, eh?" Suddenly, the far side of the two-by-six-inch board fell down and was hanging in the air. In his mind, Jimmy thought, *So, the Commander thinks I'm toeing the mark, eh?* Jimmy climbed down off the ladder and looked at the board. *Let's go ahead let 'em all get a good look at this shabby work. After a few weeks of this kind of work, they'll be glad to get rid of me.* He smiled, grabbed his ladder, and walked off.

About forty feet away, Jimmy stopped and turned around. He gazed at the hanging board, still contemplating his future. He looked and looked at the board. Suddenly, he hurriedly started walking back. "I can't do it. I just can't do it," he muttered. He quickly went back to the building, set up his ladder, climbed up, and hammered the board until it was secure. Jimmy jumped down, grabbed his ladder, and walked away, thinking to himself, *Crappy work is just not my style. It's just not in me. I can't do it.*

In the approaching days, weeks, and months, Corporal Jimmy

Logan continued his carpentry duties. Although it had become much more difficult, he continued to find a way to visit his brother in Alton about once a month. Several of the Greybeard soldiers (now at the Alton Prison) immediately recognized Jimmy and were glad to see him whenever he visited. Although Willy was surviving, he was starting to look weaker and weaker with every visit. He complained to Jimmy that prisoners were being moved around a lot from cell to cell. When Jimmy mentioned this to the Greybeards, they told him that all of the moving around was because of "the smallpox." Smartly, they were trying to isolate the smallpox prisoners away from the others to protect them.

Even though Will looked weak, he actually was not one of the sick inmates. Will told Jimmy that he almost liked his most recent cell. He could reach through the bars and open the window. The cell was way up high on the fourth floor. It allowed for decent outside air movement from the prevailing breezes. Willy felt healthier there because he could open the window enough to get that breeze of fresh, clean air into the cell. His cellmates didn't always like outside air, but Willy did. Jimmy was sure to add this positive news (if only slightly) in his next letter to his mother. Will and Jimmy had both been writing their mother, so between the two groups of letters, Martha was somewhat well informed on both of their circumstances.

February 1864 – February 1865

As time moved forward, the days, weeks, and months passed by like water flowing down the river, and the war continued to rage on. In January 1864, the Greybeards from the 37th Iowa were reassigned and no longer running the Alton Prison. In late February 1864, Jimmy decided to resubmit another transfer request to be reassigned to the Alton Prison. Once again, his request was denied.

Things had been changing at the Alton Prison, but not for the better. Diminishing health conditions at the prison had caused it to be closed to all outside visitors. Jimmy's buddy, Corporal Moore (now promoted) from the Unit Headquarters, informed him of the new policy. Now, he would not be allowed to visit his brother, even though he was only twenty miles away. Moore told Jimmy that the guards would more than likely stop him before he could even enter the prison grounds. Jimmy didn't want to wait for the policy to be changed, so he decided to try to visit Will anyway.

While in uniform, Jimmy took a transport to Alton. He walked straight up to the prison just like he had before. Upon arriving, he was met by an armed guard and some new fencing around the prison. The Union guard was a sergeant, and he was standing at a checkpoint gate that wasn't there on his previous visits. Jimmy thought to himself, *Hell, I'm a corporal. I'll just walk right past him like I own the place.*

"Halt!" said the guard.

"Yes?"

"Sorry, Corporal, this is a quarantine zone. By order of the prison commander, you have to be a prisoner, a guard, or work here at the prison to pass, and I don't think you work here. I don't know you."

"That's bullcrap! What if I need to see someone?"

"I'm sorry, Corporal, but if you really need to enter, you'll need to get a gate pass from the commander. You'll have to go to Unit Headquarters. Just go straight up that hill and then go to the left. Honestly, Corporal, I don't think you really want to go in there anyway. It's a bad place. There's a lot of smallpox and other sicknesses. Every day, we are losing a lot of people in there, and it's affecting a lot more than just the prisoners."

Jimmy stood there and looked at the gate guard. He then looked at the massive prison. Then he looked over at the hill that led up to the Headquarters. "Do they ever give a pass to someone that doesn't work here?"

"Honestly, no. A few times, a prisoner's momma has convinced the commander to let a pastor or a priest in to see her son. That's the only people that I've seen them let in…and that was just to give prayers or last rites."

"Okay, thanks."

"Sorry, Corporal. Really. Do you need me to give a message to anyone?"

"Well, since you asked, yes. That would be good."

The guard fished through his pockets and offered Jimmy a paper and pencil.

"No. No writing is needed. Just tell Willy Logan in 423W that his brother came by and is trying to find a way to visit him."

"Brother? You have a brother that's a Confederate prisoner in here?"

"Yes, Sergeant."

"Well, I'll tell ya, I can't tell him myself, but I *can* have my runner deliver a message to him through his guard."

The gate guard waved a few other prison guards past the checkpoint. He then took the paper and wrote the following message on it: "Willy Logan 423W. Your brother came by. He's trying to find a way to visit you. Take care." He then showed it to Jimmy and said, "Is this, okay?"

After reading it, Jimmy said, "Yes, that's great." The sergeant took the paper and signed his name at the bottom."

"Runner!" he yelled.

A Union private appeared seemingly out of nowhere. "Private! Take this message to prisoner Will Logan on the fourth floor, pronto! Cell 423W!"

"Yes, Sergeant!" The runner took the message and took off running toward the prison.

"Wow! Thanks, Sergeant."

"You're welcome, Corporal. I've lost two brothers in this awful war, and I'm real glad that you still have one to visit. I can't visit my brothers...except at a cemetery. I'm impressed that you are willing to enter a dangerous place like this just to see him. It's commendable."

Jimmy shook the sergeant's hand and smiled at him. He then departed. On the short boat trip back to St. Louis, he pondered his future, the future of his brother, and the future of the country.

Weeks later, Jimmy finally received a long-awaited letter from his brother. Willy wrote that he had received his message from the Guard Station. Jimmy quickly wrote back to him, and the brothers continued to write to each other. Will's letters spoke primarily of poor food and decrepit conditions. Jimmy's letters spoke about his everyday duties and his repeated request to transfer to the Alton Prison. In a letter Willy had received from his momma, she revealed that Bonnie (Will's girl) had married and moved away. He quickly responded to her with a letter declaring that he didn't really expect her to wait for him that long. Especially since it had been nearly three years since he had left.

As time passed, Jimmy continued to request a transfer to the Alton Prison. The requests were usually returned to him with these words attached: "Conditions at the Alton Prison are not amiable to the allowance of voluntary transfers at this time." Jimmy asked his sergeant what exactly that statement meant. Jimmy's sergeant looked to be over six feet tall. He was a slightly unkempt with a big belly, but he was highly respected because of his many years of service. "I'll check into it, Corporal, but don't be getting me into trouble."

The next day the sergeant found Corporal Logan working on

a ladder up on the side of a building. He yelled loudly, "Corporal Logan, report!!" Jimmy quickly jumped off the ladder, falling a bit as he hit the ground. He shuffled to his feet and went to perfect attention three feet in front of the sergeant.

"Yes, Sergeant!" Jimmy yelled.

"Maybe you could report a little faster next time, Corporal." Jimmy smiled.

"I asked for you regarding transfers to the Alton Prison. This is what they gave me." The sergeant handed him a small piece of paper on which the following statement was written: "Voluntary personnel transfers to Alton Prison are currently prohibited due to exceptionally high levels of the following; smallpox, dysentery, measles, typhoid, diphtheria, pneumonia, and other infectious conditions."

After reading this, Jimmy asked the sergeant, "Oh, heck, Sergeant. We have half of those sicknesses right around here."

"Not like they do there, Logan. Why in damnation do you want to go there anyway?"

"My brother is a prisoner there, Sergeant."

"Your brother is a Rebel prisoner? Well, I'll be. You're a good man, Logan. Keep putting your transfer request in and I'll do what I can, but don't expect much."

"Thank you, Sergeant."

February 28, 1865

Jimmy continued to work hard at his carpentry mission at Benton Barracks and submitted several more requests to be reassigned to the Alton Federal Prison. In late February 1885, he had submitted another one. On a frigid day, he was working on a chimney on top of a hospital building when his sergeant yelled up to him, "Corporal

Logan, report!!" Jimmy said to himself, *"What now?"* He jumped up and ran down to the end of the roofline. Just as he reached the gutter, he dropped down low, threw his hands down, and hurled his legs over the edge. Jimmy jumped off the roof. He flew through the air with a spinning motion, and as he hit the ground, he rolled about one and a half times (apparently on purpose). Jimmy then quickly sprung to his feet uninjured and sprinted over to his sergeant. Once again, he went to perfect attention about three feet in front of his sergeant.

"Corporal Logan, reporting as ordered, Sergeant!"

"I told you, Logan! You need to try to report a little faster."

Jimmy smiled as he tried to catch his breath. "Yes, Sergeant!"

"Well, that was definitely faster. Good job."

"Thank you, Sergeant!"

"Just don't accidentally kill yourself reporting. No more jumping off of the roofs. How the hell did you do that anyway?"

"I practiced, Sergeant. I saw one of the civilian roofers do it, so I thought I'd give it a try."

"Okay, that's fine, but I still don't want you jumping off any more damn roofs."

"Understood, Sergeant!" answered Jimmy.

"Logan, you have repeatedly requested reassignment to the Alton Federal Prison."

"Yes, Sergeant." He handed Jimmy a piece of paper. "Well, it's been approved! You have just a few days to report." Jimmy smiled from ear to ear. "Thank you, Sergeant!!"

"I hope you can help out your brother, and I hope you can stay alive and safe. Good luck, Logan." He smiled, grabbed Jimmy (still at attention) by his shoulders, and gave him a brief shake. "Now go finish that chimney, Corporal, and no more jumping off the damn roof!"

"Yes, Sergeant!!" yelled Jimmy at the top of his lungs. "Now as you were. Get back to work!"

"Yes, Sergeant!!" yelled Jimmy as he immediately ran back to his ladder and scampered up to the roof, going straight back to work.

Finally, Corporal Jimmy Logan had received official orders to report to the Alton Illinois Federal Prison. The orders stated that he was to report to the prison commander from the 144th Illinois Volunteers, Colonel John H. Kahn. The duty description on the orders stated that Jimmy had been assigned as the NCOIC (non-commissioned officer in charge) of the Maintenance Platoon. He had apparently been chosen to lead the repairs of the gigantic prison. Jimmy was to report to his new duty station at the Alton Federal Prison in four short days. He was not only excited about his new duty closer to his brother, but also because he was apparently now going to be promoted. Nearly all Union Army NCOICs were sergeants because they needed the rank to do their job properly.

Chapter Five

March 4, 1865 Day One at the Alton Prison

On March 4, 1865, Jimmy found himself headed to Alton on the same familiar paddlewheel transport on which he had traveled several times. It was the *Continental*. Today was a special day for the Union because Abraham Lincoln was going to be inaugurated for his second term as president. He walked up to the *Continental*'s captain's bridge to take a look around. The captain of the *Continental* recognized Jimmy and he spoke freely with him. He was obviously well-spoken and was very diplomatic with his casual speech. The captain spoke to Jimmy only briefly about the president's second inauguration. This made Jimmy consider that the captain probably tried to stay somewhat apolitical, since he often traveled through areas controlled by Southern factors. Instead of talking a lot about the inauguration, the captain turned Jimmy's attention toward the Mississippi. He spoke with great admiration for the river as if it were his bride.

The captain was a good-sized man with peppered white hair and beard, both cut short. His eyes seemed to glow with admiration as he scanned the river. "See there, Corporal?" The captain pointed toward the massive expanse of water where the Missouri River joined with the Mississippi. The distance from one bank to the other looked as though it was more than a mile.

"It's sure is a long way from shore to shore," said Jimmy.

"That's the great confluence of the Missouri and Mississippi Rivers," said the captain. "It's known as the greatest river confluence in the world. Even the famous French explorer Pierre Francois de Charlevoix called it "the finest confluence in the world."

Jimmy looked out at the massive expanse of water. Indeed, the area at the joining of the two rivers was very large, very awe-inspiring, and very beautiful. The captain gazed out at the remarkable confluence and continued, "See the Missouri River? It's a fast river. Difficult for boats to navigate. Nothing like this lazy ol' Mississippi. As a boy, I was schooled about twelve miles up that river on the right side. At a city called Saint Charles. My school was The Academy of the Sacred Heart. My teacher's name was Sister Rose Philippine Duchesne. She taught me how to read and write—and love nature. She showed the students faith, courage, and humility. Things that we could use a little more of these days." He then paused for a moment.

Jimmy remained silent as he looked at both of the rivers and their banks. Then, the captain continued, "When Sister Rose Philippine Duchesne was older, she even went further up that same river to teach to the Potawatomi Indians. Unfortunately, I heard she died back in 1852, about thirteen years ago. There was something about Sister Rose...she was special. She touched a lot of people in a special way. I'll never forget her. I can see them making a saint out of her someday."

Jimmy looked at the captain and saw the seriousness in his face and a slight wetness in his eyes. Although Jimmy was raised with religion and was somewhat well-read, stories like this made him realize that he was a novice to the amazing stories of the West... and of the world.

G. S. Spooner

> *Point of Historical Reference – Sister Rose Philippine Duchesne was canonized by the Roman Catholic Church on July 3, 1988 by Pope John Paul II.*
>
> *There is a shrine dedicated to her in St. Charles, Missouri.*

After a short three-hour trip, Jimmy found himself in the bustling river city of Alton, Illinois. As he walked through the dirt streets, Jimmy noticed how the townspeople hustled around with seemingly no notice of the war. He thought to himself, *Thousands of soldiers dying in the war, and these people just go about with their lives as if nothing of consequence was happening. Well, Jimmy, what do you want 'em to do? Run around in circles, panicking? They all have to move on with life as best they can. Just like they are probably doing down home in New Madrid.*

Corporal Jimmy Logan looked around as he walked up to the gigantic four-story-high Alton Prison. It was hard to miss. The huge brick and stone building must have been the biggest building in the city. On his arrival, he once again approached the quarantine fencing around the prison. The Union guard stopped him, "State your business."

"I've been assigned here by the Army. Here are my official orders."

"Okay," said the guard as he looked at Jimmy's orders. "Corporal Logan, be aware that this is a quarantine zone with area restrictions. You'll need to report to the Unit Headquarters. You have to go way up that hill and then to the left. You'll see the flag in front of the building, Corporal."

"Thanks. I remember that." Jimmy walked up the hill and found the Headquarters building quickly. After he signed in, the clerk asked him to stand fast. He told Jimmy, "The old man has been waiting for you." Jimmy thought to himself, *I can't possibly be in trouble. I just got here.*

The clerk went into the commander's office and then quickly returned. "Corporal, please report to Colonel John H. Kahn, the unit commander of the 144th Illinois Volunteers."

Jimmy straightened his jacket and he quickly entered the commander's office. He stood at attention and saluted. "Corporal Logan, reporting, sir!"

"At ease, Corporal! Relax." The colonel stood up and shook Jimmy's hand. Kahn was a tall, imposing man. He was a sharp-looking officer with blue eyes and an impressive mustache. "Damn good to see you, boy! This place is falling apart, and I've been asking Washington for a top-notch carpenter for months. I also heard through the grapevine that you were requesting to be assigned here. So welcome!"

"Thank you, sir."

"Well, son, it can be really tough duty here, but you'll be okay. Let me know if you need anything. My clerk will direct you from here and my deputy commander will get with you soon with paperwork concerning your mission."

"Great. Thank you, sir!" said Jimmy.

As Jimmy departed, the clerk assigned a young private to show him around the general prison area and take him to his bunk in the soldier's barracks. The soldier's barracks, the officer's barracks, and the Headquarters building all sat atop a steep hill overlooking the prison area. While Jimmy was settling into his bunk area, another soldier saw him unpacking. "Howdy there. How'd you get so unlucky as to get stationed here, Corporal?"

"Hello. Well, I actually asked to be stationed here."

"What?! Okay. Well, to each his own. Welcome to the Alton Federal Prison."

"Thanks."

The next day Jimmy found the Carpenter/Maintenance Shop. Once there, he met and was briefed by the shop's acting NCOIC, Corporal Helms. Helms was a clean-shaven, squared-away soldier. He looked to be about five-foot-nine inches tall. He had a noticeably great attitude and a keen sense of the needs of his soldiers and their missions. What Corporal Helms wasn't was a carpenter. He provided his new boss with details regarding the team's ongoing missions. The colossal building was made of brick, stone, and wood, and it was in a state of constant disrepair. Helms and Jimmy talked for a long time. He told Jimmy that their team of soldier carpenters was fighting a losing battle with the decrepit building. He also told him that the pitiful health conditions made life very difficult not only for the Confederate prisoners but also for the Union soldiers. This made their battle with the building's maintenance even more difficult.

March 5, 1865
Day Two at the Alton Prison

The next day, Corporal Jimmy Logan woke up at 0530 hours (5:30 a.m.). Shortly after rising, he was met by a messenger with three envelopes from the prison's deputy commander. The envelopes were clearly marked with large circled numbers of one, two, and three. Although he wanted to see his brother right away, duty called. So, Jimmy said to himself, "Well, I'd better open these up in order, or I might get in big trouble."

The first envelope contained a list with the names of twenty-nine soldiers who would be standing in the Maintenance Platoon formation at 0700 hours. By each man's name was their rank and their job description. All of the men (except himself and Corporal

Helms) were privates and all of their job descriptions were listed as "Carpenter/Soldier." Corporal Helms was listed as "Assistant Platoon Leader" and Jimmy's name was at the top of the list. He was listed as "Sergeant Logan." His position was noted as "Platoon Leader." Jimmy said to himself, "Ha! Look at that. They got my rank wrong. I'm not a sergeant. At least not yet."

The second envelope had a congratulatory note from the unit commander stating that he would be promoted to sergeant at the morning formation. "All right!" said Jimmy with a broad smile on his face. "This gives me some more rank to help me get things done, and I'm also goin' to make at least five more bucks a month! Yes!!"

The third envelope contained a long four-page list of repairs that were needed at the Alton Federal Prison. The list indicated the location and the severity of each issue. Most of the repairs had stars next to them, indicating the urgency of the needed repair. One star meant "Delayed," two stars meant "Urgent," and three stars meant "Immediate." Jimmy noticed that several of the repair annotations were listed with the location of "Smallpox Island."

"Smallpox Island?" said Jimmy. "What the hell does that mean?"

After completing his morning routine, Jimmy went straight to the Maintenance Shop. At the morning's 0700 formation, Corporal Jimmy Logan stood in front of the Maintenance Platoon and introduced himself. He had four squads (in four rows) with seven men in each. Each squad had a squad leader. The squad leader of Squad One was also his assistant platoon leader, Corporal Helms. Helms looked at Jimmy and then quickly looked over to the side where the unit's first sergeant, First Sergeant Foreman, and unit clerk were standing. Helms had told Jimmy that the first sergeant was fifty percent American Indian. Foreman was short, stocky and tough looking but he had a reputation as a soldier's soldier. Foreman had obviously been in the military for a very long time..

Jimmy nodded and the first sergeant quickly walked up. He

stood directly in front of Jimmy. After Jimmy saluted him, First Sergeant Foreman returned the salute and Jimmy promptly moved over to the side of the formation. First Sergeant Foreman was the top NCO in the 144th Illinois and he was ultimately in charge of everything. Corporal Helms had also told Jimmy that even though Foreman was greatly feared, he was actually a really nice fellow with a great sense of humor. Helms had told Jimmy, "If you're squared away, you have nothing to fear from the first sergeant."

Then, out of the silence, Foreman yelled, "Corporal Logan, report!"

Jimmy yelled, "Here, First Sergeant!!" and ran in a full sprint until he stopped directly in front of the first sergeant. Immediately he saluted and yelled, "Corporal Logan, reporting, First Sergeant!"

After a return salute, the unit clerk then read the promotion orders and Corporal Jimmy Logan was promoted to sergeant right in front of his new platoon. Jimmy smiled and beamed with pride as he realized that he was now a sergeant. Very few soldiers in the Union Army ever made it to the rank of sergeant.

After the formation, everyone relaxed for a moment. The Maintenance Platoon shook Jimmy's hand and patted him on the back with their congratulations. After a short period, each squad was dispatched by Corporal Helms to tackle one of the "Immediate" three-star issues from the maintenance list. The four teams (squads) meant that four maintenance problems could be taken on simultaneously. At least two men on each team were armed with either pistols or rifles at all times. The Maintenance Platoon had two workshops, both located on the north end of the hospital. Those being the large main Maintenance Shop and another smaller room full of equipment and supplies. After the squads departed on the day's repairs, Corporal Helms met with his new leader, Sergeant Jimmy Logan.

Helms explained that he and the squad leaders would typically spend a good part of each day updating the repair list and helping the men acquire the materials and supplies needed to complete their repairs. "Don't worry about knowing everything right away, Sergeant. You can ease your way into it all because I'm here. I'm glad you're here because we truly need a real carpenter. Maybe you can teach us better ways to do things, so we can fix this place up. Hell, most of the time, we're just winging it. I've got your back on the organizational stuff. These are good men working in a hell hole, Sergeant. They just need some guidance."

Jimmy answered, "I'll do my best. But, I gotta tell you that it really feels weird when you call me "Sergeant." Helms cracked a quick smile and they both laughed.

Jimmy and Corporal Helms then talked for a while about the urgency of some of the repairs from the maintenance list. Jimmy asked, "What can you tell me about Smallpox Island? I saw that location on the list and wondered what it meant and where it was located."

"Well, Sergeant," said Helms, "Smallpox Island is a little island straight across the river from here. It's close to the Missouri side and they tell me its real name is "Sunflower Island."

"Okay, I get it," said Jimmy. "They're sending the prisoners with smallpox there to isolate them."

"You got it, Sergeant. But, in reality, the prisoners are sent out there to die. They have a makeshift hospital over there with a couple of wooden buildings and two large tents. Our team conducts maintenance over there on the buildings and the river dock. We get in and we get out."

"Understood. Thanks, Corporal."

Corporal Helms then took his new boss on a tour of the entire prison. During the tour, Jimmy told Helms, "Geeshh, this place is falling apart."

"Yeah, just like the prisoners. Sergeant, I'll tell you the same thing that I tell our soldiers every single day. Try to stay away from the inmates if you can. Try to keep fresh air around you wherever you are. Open the doors, open the windows. Whatever you can do to keep the air moving. The main thing is staying away from the prisoners as best you can. There are a lot of diseases here, and we're all pretty sure that they can't be seen and they're floating around in the air."

"Agreed and understood. Will do!"

At the end of the long first day, Jimmy sat on his bunk and pulled out the most recent letter from his brother Will. The envelope had a return address that simply stated, "Alton Federal Prison," but his brother signed his name at the end of the letter and added his cell number. Will was in cell 423W. Each of the four stories of the prison had around sixty cells. Each floor had about thirty cells on the east side and thirty on the west side. Will's cell number indicated that he was on the fourth floor in cell 423W. The "W" meant that the cell was on the west side of the prison. Jimmy gathered some biscuits and bacon that he had saved from his breakfast and put into a bag. He then picked up a leather flask filled with water and headed down the hill toward the prison. He planned to hopefully give some food and drink to his imprisoned brother.

Jimmy entered the building with his new sergeant's rank on his sleeves and walked right by the two guards at the entrance. He thought to himself with a nervous smile, *I'll just walk around like I know what I'm doing and where I'm going. A private wouldn't be able to walk past those guards.* He found the stairs and headed up to the prison's fourth floor. As he approached the top of the stairs, he heard people moaning and smelled a musty stench. He was familiar with the sounds and smells of the prison because he had walked through the building earlier in the day. But his duties had not yet taken him to the fourth floor of the prison, and right now the fourth floor was his destination.

At the top of the stairs, Sergeant Logan was met by two armed soldiers. "Can I help you, Sergeant?"

"Yes, I need cell 423W."

"Yes, Sergeant. Please check your sidearm here and follow me."

Jimmy regularly wore a .44 caliber Colt sidearm, but only guards could carry weapons on the prison floor. He checked his .44 with a guard sitting at a desk and started following the other guard as he headed down the hall to the cell. Jimmy was surprised that the guard hadn't asked him what his business was. He then walked seven cells down the hall and looked to the right at the door of cell 423W.

The guard unlocked the barred cell door and pulled it open. "I'll be standing right here at the door, Sergeant."

"Thank you."

Jimmy walked into the small eight-by-twelve-foot cell only to see four people lying on small wooden cots with blankets pulled over their heads. "Corporal Will Logan?" stated Jimmy. All of the prisoners moved, but only one pulled back his blanket. It was Will. He began to sit up as Jimmy went to his side. As Jimmy sat down on the cot with Will, he immediately noticed a very thin and emaciated brother, who had managed to put a smile on his face.

"Are you really here... or am I dreaming?" said Willy.

"I'm here, little brother. I'm really here." Jimmy tried to stop his tears, but his eyes watered up and a tear streaked down his left cheek. Willy sat up straight and Jimmy put his arm over Will's shoulder. "I made it. I've been trying to get here to see you for a year and a half."

"I know you have. Well, what are you gonna do now, brother?"

"Heck, I don't know. I've been transferred here. I work for the maintenance team and there's plenty of work around this place."

"Yep, I figured that. This building is falling apart."

They sat silently and somewhat awkwardly, both trying to take in the moment. Jimmy reached in his side pocket and pulled out the bag with biscuits and bacon in it. He handed the food over to Will and then he handed him the flask filled with water. Will devoured the biscuits and bacon as he talked to Jimmy. "Thanks for this, brother. But listen, Jim, you got to be really careful around here. Everybody's sick with one thing or another. There's a lot of smallpox here." He started drinking water from the flask. "You gotta keep yourself away from people that look sick and try to stay out of stagnant air. I'm lucky, my cell is on the top floor and we get more air movement here from the breeze. All winter long, it's been more closed up in here, but I've been keeping our window open as much as I could."

"I understand," said Jimmy. "Will, like I said, I'm on the maintenance team here now. I have work to do all over this place, so I'll be around. I'm gonna try to see you at least twice a week if I can."

"Look, Jimmy. You don't need to put yourself in danger just to see me. I'll be okay."

"Well, I'm gonna be working all around this prison, so I'm going to see you one way or the other."

"Make it the other then. Stay off of these floors as much as you can. I got me some built-up immunities that will protect me. I was vaccinated for smallpox during my training at Camp Trousdale. I was sick for a couple days, but I think it took. Were you vaccinated?"

"Nope, but I heard about it. I think it was available if I wanted it."

"Look, you can still catch it even if you are vaccinated and there's a lot of other diseases here, so be careful. We go outside to the yard for about one hour two times a day, weather permitting. See me out there. There's more clean air out there. We also go down to the end of the hall to eat crappy food twice a day. Don't come to see me there. It's too crowded."

After another moment of sitting in silence, Jimmy said, "I'll write Momma and tell her that I saw you."

"So will I, but I bet your letter gets there first."

"Ha, funny. Listen, I gotta go. I'll see you in a couple days, inside or out. I'll figure this joint out and we'll get through it."

"Okay, brother. See you soon."

Jimmy added, "I'll tell the guards that I'm your brother."

"I already told them. Why do you think I'm in such good shape?" said Willy with a big smile on his face. Jimmy knocked on the door and the guard opened it. The cell door had not been locked while he was inside.

As they walked down the hallway, Jimmy told the guard that Corporal Will Logan was his brother. "Well, I figured as much. I heard you fellows talking. Look, Sergeant. I'll give you the same advice I give everybody else. Do your time here and try to make it out alive."

"Okay, thank you for the tip."

Just then, Will yelled down the hall through his cell bars, "Hey!! Did you bring your guitar?!"

"Yep!" With this, Sergeant Logan went to the guard's desk, picked up his pistol, opened the door, and scampered down the stairs.

March 12, 1865
Day Nine at the Alton Prison

One week later, Sergeant Jimmy Logan and some of his soldiers were working outside in the prison yard. The first maintenance squad was fixing a wooden fence that was falling apart. Two prisoners had climbed through it and had escaped the week before, only to be quickly recaptured. It was a cold and dreary day with off-and-on rain. Two men of the seven-man carpenter squad stood by with rifles while the others worked on the fence. Jimmy and another soldier were heading back to the maintenance shop to pick up some wooden planks when he saw Will standing in the corner of the yard. Will had just looked around and flipped a blanket over his head and shoulders. "Hang on a minute, Private," Jimmy told his soldier as he walked over to Will. "What's up, brother?"

"Well, you might want to come up to the cell later and I'll tell you."

"Why? Tell me right here, stupid." Will pulled open the blanket to show a large area of reddened blisters wrapping around his torso and over his shoulder. "Holy shit!" said Jimmy, holding his voice down. "That's not smallpox, is it?"

"No, I don't think so. I think it's that crap I had a few years ago. Remember? The town doc called it zoster shingles," said Willy.

"Yep, I remember."

"He said it can be brought on by stress. Imagine that."

"You're funny. Does it hurt?" said Jimmy.

"Hell yeah, it hurts. I remember this crap from the last time. Same blisters, same pain, and it hurts like hell. Last time, it didn't go away for over a month."

"I remember. You had trouble working in the fields." Jimmy moved Will's blanket a bit. "Will, it's almost on your neck and face."

"I know it. That's why I'm wearing this damn blanket. I don't want them to send me to Smallpox Island."

"Right. If they do, you might catch the real smallpox. Look, try to lay low and hang in there. I'll bring some food up to your cell tonight and we'll talk more."

"We can't talk about this crap," said Willy. "My cellmates will hear."

"Oh, that's right. We'll just have to talk out here then. Look, I'm gonna bring some food up anyways. I might have an idea. Maybe we'll go ahead and talk about the zoster. We can tell them the truth. You know, we'll tell them that it's zoster and not really smallpox."

"Well, I don't know. Maybe it's worth a try. But I'm screwed if they tell the guards on me, 'cause this shit looks a lot like smallpox."

At that moment, the maintenance soldier who was waiting on Jimmy walked over. "Hey, Sergeant, the guys are a waitin' on those planks."

"Right! We gotta go now! See ya, Willy."

That evening, Sergeant Jimmy Logan went up to his brother's cell. This time he made a point to bring extra biscuits and water to share with Will's cellmates. He took time to chat not only with Will, but also with the other three prisoners. Jimmy thought to himself, *If these guys like Will a little more, maybe they'll cut him some slack and not turn him in when they see those damn blisters on his body.* During the visit, Jimmy and Will talked openly about Will's zoster blisters in front of his cellmates. Jimmy told them, "He's had this before. The doctor says it's not smallpox, even though it does look a little like it. It's *not* smallpox!" The cellmates just ate the biscuits and looked at Jimmy. They nodded their heads but didn't really talk. Will kept the blanket partially covering his head and trunk during the entire visit, trying to hide the blisters on the side of his face and neck.

March 19, 1865
Day Sixteen at the Alton Prison

After another week, Will's zoster blisters hadn't gotten any worse, but they also hadn't gotten any better. Will was declining to go to the outside prison yard very often because he didn't want the guards (or the inmates) to discover his condition. Then, on an unusually nice day, Jimmy's second squad of carpenters was again repairing the same area of fencing because another prisoner had escaped. Jimmy looked around and saw Will once again standing in the same area, in the corner of the yard. This time he didn't have a blanket over his head. Jimmy walked over to him. "Hey, Will, why aren't you covered up? Somebody's going to see your blisters."

"I don't care. I'm tired of trying to hide. It's such a sunny day and it feels good on my skin. This zoster shingle crap hurts and I don't care if they find out. I'm just gettin' tired of it all, Jimmy. I know you're helping out as much as you can, but sooner or later, somebody's going to see this crap. One of my cellmates will tell the guards if that doesn't happen. They've seen it several times. It's bad and it hurts."

Jimmy answered, "Okay, okay! I understand. I'm gonna figure this out. Tonight, I'm bringing up some ham slices and water to your cell. I'll talk to them and explain once again that it's not smallpox. Now be careful and I'll see you tonight...and write Momma. She wrote me and said you're not writin'."

"I don't want to give the letter to the guard. I'm trying not to be noticed, and what am I gonna tell her anyway? Hi, Momma, I'm having a great time in prison, and I'm miserable with shingles and off-and-on diarrhea?"

Jimmy quietly laughed as he grinned at his brother. "You know, you're a pretty funny guy."

"Thanks."

As Jimmy walked away, he spoke over his shoulder, "Funny-lookin', that is."

Willy smirked. "I knew that was coming."

That night at about 7 p.m., Jimmy went up to the cell with a bunch of ham slices and a water flask in his side bag. He sat on Will's bunk and chatted with Will and his cellmates. While he handed out the food, Jimmy told them once again that Will had zoster shingles and that he had had it before. He explained, "This stuff does not kill you like smallpox does and it's really not catching. So, you can't give it to someone else like you can with smallpox." They all ate the ham and gulped the water down. The cellmates all seemed to understand and once again didn't really have much to say about the condition.

One of the three cellmates was named Richie. Suddenly he said, "I know about shingles. My grandma had it and she had a whole lot of pain with it. It looked like that. It went away after a month or two."

"Did anyone else catch it?" said Jimmy.

"Nope, she just had a lot of pain and blisters, then it went away. Nobody else got it."

"Exactly, that's what Will has."

Jimmy then asked for their help concealing the condition and said he would thank them by bringing up some food and water to them whenever he could. He also told them that the guards had warned him not to come up to visit more than two or three times a week.

March 26, 1865
Day Twenty-Three at the Alton Prison

After seeing his brother only twice in the previous week, Jimmy had been preparing for his next visit. He gathered some biscuits, cheese, and water for his side bag and he headed up the stairwell to cell 423W. It had been a stormy day and no prisoners had been going outside. When he arrived on the fourth floor, the guard talked to Jimmy. "Good evening, Sergeant."

"Good evening, Private." Jimmy laid down his sidearm pistol and signed the ledger.

"Where are you going?" said the guard.

"What do you mean, where am I going?"

Jimmy started walking down the hall and the guard said, "But Sergeant!"

"Come on, stupid, let me in the damn cell. You're not funny."

"Whatever," said the guard. They arrived at the cell and Jimmy looked through the door. There were only three people in it. Willy was gone.

"Where's Will?! Where's his bunk?!"

"They most likely burned his bunk, Sergeant," said the guard.

"What? Burned his bunk? What are you talking about? Where the hell is he?!"

"Sergeant, I tried to tell you. They took him over to isolation on Smallpox Island."

Jimmy looked straight at the guard. He then straightened his jacket and stood up straight, taking a deep breath. He then looked in on the three men left in the cell and asked the guard to let him in. "What the hell happened?" said Jimmy. Two of the cellmates pointed at Richie. One said, "Richie was mad at Will 'cause he kept opening the window. He was holding the shingles thing over him for leverage, and food and such. Finally, Will had enough and said something like, "Screw you, Richie!" and then he opened the window."

The other cellmate then jumped in with more details. "Right then, Richie jumped up and yelled something like, 'Guard! Guard! This guy Logan's got the smallpox!!' He screamed it to the whole floor. The guards came and then left. Then, some other special guards came back. They took Will away. Then, they came back and took away his bunk and all of his personal stuff."

Richie sat there silently, looking at the ground. Jimmy reached in his bag and tossed a piece of ham at him. "Really, Richie? After all the food and stuff I brought you? After I explained everything?" Richie looked up. He looked bad. He had a black eye with some dried blood on his nose.

"I'm sorry, I was cold...real cold. I'm sorry. I don't know what came over me. I'm sick."

"What happened to your face?"

"These guys hit me after I told."

"Just once," the first cellmate added. "I only hit him once."

"Well, I hit him twice," the other one said, "but that's all."

The first cellmate added, "Will didn't deserve that. He was trying to give us fresh air so we wouldn't get sick, that's all. Not only that, but now we ain't gonna get no extra food or water because of dumbass here."

"Okay, boys. I gotta go. But I *will* still see you later." Will walked down the hall with the armed guard and yelled loudly, "Son of a bitch!!" Jimmy grabbed his pistol. He ran down the stairs, past all the guards, and straight outside to the street. It was raining again. Jimmy stood there in the rain and looked off into space. He had tears running down his face, but they became hidden by the rain. The rain suddenly intensified and lightning struck in the distance as it started to pour down.

March 27, 1865
Day Twenty-Four at the Alton Prison

Sergeant Jimmy Logan muddled through the next day. At one point he was showing Corporal Helms and the first squad how to properly stabilize a thick door jamb. But his mind was in a different place. Jimmy took Helms to the side and told him that his brother had been taken to Smallpox Island even though he didn't have smallpox. After the door jamb was almost completed, Helms saw that his sergeant was not in the best of moods, so he then took Jimmy to the side. "I got this, boss. You've taught us well. We know how to finish this up and we'll also know what to do next time. I'm sure you have other more important stuff to do." He looked at Jimmy and quietly gestured for him to go.

"Thanks, Corporal."

Jimmy went back to the Maintenance Shop. Then, one of his men asked for his help moving a large board. As he helped the soldier with the board, he tried to reconcile his situation. Jimmy felt more than a little bit mixed up. He felt confused. He thought to himself, *What the hell was I going to do anyway? I've been here for weeks. All that I've really done is talk to him and give him food. What did I hope to do for Will by being here anyway?* He kept thinking to himself concerning his next actions while he was walking around the Maintenance Shop. *I need to make a plan. I need to make several plans and pick the best one.*

Jimmy deliberated on his situation. He thought to himself, *Okay, so I have to do something. Should I go to Smallpox Island, break Will out, and help him escape? No, no way. I don't want to go to prison, too. Should I go to the prison physician and explain the situation? Maybe.* He thought more and more about the situation. He had to figure out what to do. He had to actually do something. *Should I go to the commander, Colonel Kahn, at the unit headquarters? He told me to let him know if I needed anything. Well, now I need something. I could tell him the truth. I could tell him that Will doesn't have smallpox. I could tell him that he's had this before and it isn't smallpox. Sounds farfetched, but Momma always said, "Tell the truth, boys. The truth will set you free." That's what I need. I need the truth to set Willy free.*

The rest of Jimmy's workday was a blur after that. Jimmy was so deep in thought that he suddenly found himself sitting at his bunk, still contemplating all of his possible actions. Finally, he looked around and realized that it was still raining. Jimmy could hear the rain pelting off the walls and windows of the barracks. *Geesh, when is this crap going to stop?* he said to himself.

Smallpox Island

March 28, 1865
Day Twenty-Five at the Alton Prison

The next day was a busy one. Jimmy was helping the third squad today. He showed the soldiers how to place proper supports on a porch overhang that was falling down. Several prisoners were shuffling by and, of course, it was still raining. He automatically taught his soldiers the proper technique to shore up the overhang without really thinking about it. His mind was somewhere else. Jimmy had decided on what he had to do about Willy, but he also felt like he had some other unfinished business. Unfinished business was with Will's former cellmates.

After evening chow, Jimmy gathered some cheese, biscuits, and water. He then headed up to his brother's old cell. Upon reaching the top of the stairs, Jimmy laid his pistol on the table. The Union guard, a corporal, greeted him. "Evening, Sergeant. What are you doing here? You know your brother's gone, right?"

"Yeah, I know. I'm just keeping a promise. Can I go to his cell?"

"Of course. Private, take the sergeant to 423W."

"Yes, Corporal." On arriving at the cell, Jimmy noticed that another bunk was gone. It was Richie's. "Now what happened!" The two remaining prisoners looked up at Jimmy from their bunks. "Richie came up with smallpox," the first cellmate said, "It didn't look anything like the stuff Willy had. It looked bad and he looked sick. They took him and his bunk away. I guess they'll burn his bunk and send him to Smallpox Island."

The other cellmate chimed in, "Yeah, ain't that poetic justice? Richie rats out Will for having smallpox that he doesn't even have and then Richie actually gets it. God sometimes works in mysterious ways, doesn't he?"

"He does," said Jimmy. "But I hope Richie makes it out alive just the same."

"Yeah, us too, Sergeant…us too."

"Well, I brought some grub up for you guys. I told you I'd see you again. Open the door, Private," he told the guard. After entering the cell, he opened up his side bag and sat on the nearest cot. "Okay, boys. Here's some biscuits, cheese, and water." After some small talk, Jimmy stood up. "Well, stay healthy and try to make it out of here alive, boys."

"Thanks, Sergeant, you too. Make it out of here alive with Willy."

Jimmy looked right at the cellmate and paused. He didn't want to say too much and he hadn't told anyone what he had planned to do. "Thank you. May God help us all."

As Jimmy stepped out, he looked up and noticed that the window to Will's old cell was still open. "Boys, keep that window open as much as you can."

"Oh, don't worry. We will, Sergeant. We will."

Chapter Six

March 29, 1865
Day Twenty-Six at the Alton Prison

Sergeant Jimmy Logan had started to formulate a plan, but before he vested too much into it, he needed to go up the hill to see Colonel Kahn at the Headquarters building.

As a sergeant and a non-commissioned officer in charge of the Maintenance Platoon, Jimmy was allowed to take important issues directly to the commander if necessary. He also knew that Colonel Kahn had an open-door policy. Today, Jimmy needed to use it. So, after the morning Maintenance Platoon formation, he and Corporal Helms deployed their squads to their various assignments. At about 0900 hours, Jimmy told Corporal Helms that he would be out for a short period and he headed up the hill in the pouring rain to the Headquarters building. Once he arrived, the lead clerk told him that the colonel was out, but he gave Sergeant Logan an appointment for later the same day at 1400 hours.

Jimmy went back down the hill in the drenching rain. Once back in the Maintenance Shop, he attentively went over the daily list of needed repairs. He particularly focused in on three repair items…located on Smallpox Island.

Later, Sergeant Jimmy Logan reported on time for his appointment with Colonel John H. Kahn at 1400 hours. There were several clerks working in the Headquarters and an armed guard stood by the door to the commander's office. "You can go in," the clerk said. "The old man's expecting you."

Jimmy knocked on the door and quickly heard the words, "Come in!" He walked into the room, stood at attention, and saluted. "Sergeant Logan, reporting, sir!"

"At ease, at ease! Come on in, boy! It's damn good to see ya. I hear you're doing some fine work with my Maintenance Platoon. Mighty good job of fixing that fence in the prison yard. What's on your mind today?"

"Well sir, it's complicated."

"Okay then, you might as well have a seat, Sergeant."

Jimmy awkwardly sat down in a plush chair that was in front of the commander's desk. He then began to explain to the colonel that his brother was a Confederate prisoner in their Alton Prison. He told him that his brother, Willy, had been a prisoner since the September 18, 1862 Battle of Iuka. "Holy Mississippi, son! That was over two and a half years ago! It's a wonder that he's still alive!"

"I know, sir. Well, there's more."

Jimmy went on to explain to the colonel that his brother had a condition called varicella zoster shingles. He told him that Willy had struggled with the ailment once before. "Sir, the condition isn't fatal and it's not even contagious, but it does slightly resemble smallpox. The blisters wrap around his trunk and even go up onto his neck. But sir, it generally clears up in about a month or two."

"Well, I appreciate that information, Sergeant, but I need you to tell me why you're here."

"Yes, sir. He's now on Smallpox Island."

"Holy shit!" the colonel said."

Smallpox Island

Jimmy continued, "Sir, they think he's infected with smallpox, but he isn't. I saw it. He just has the zoster shingles! Can we do something to get him back before he actually does get smallpox?"

"Well, son, I've got news for you. I just got back from Washington and this war is about to go into its final throes. Both sides are tired and the president is done with it all. I happen to know from very reliable sources that we are preparing to move massive forces into Virginia to overwhelm Confederate General Robert E. Lee. General Grant is involved and *that* son of a bitch cannot be stopped. I received a telegram just today from Edwin Stanton, the secretary of war. In it, he informed me and all of the Union commanders that yesterday, President Lincoln met with Generals Sherman, Porter, and Grant. They are making plans for the Confederate surrender and the Reconstruction of the South."

The colonel stood and walked across the room, looking directly at Jimmy. "The word is that the South is on the ropes and they can no longer adequately resupply their troops or supplies. It's over, Sergeant. It's just a matter of time."

Jimmy was shocked. He stiffened up and sat at attention. "What's that got to do with my brother and Smallpox Island, sir?"

"Well, I'll tell you what it has to do with it, Sergeant!" the colonel said. "I'm a full bird colonel in the United States Army and I'm also the commander of a federal prison that's very overcrowded. Washington has greatly restricted it, but I still can parole inmates that I deem to be worthy and are not a risk to re-engage in the battle. Of course, anyone that I parole has to give his word not to take up arms against the Union."

Jimmy stared at the colonel with a stunned look on his face.

"Logan, give me your brother's name and I'll have my clerk check into his record."

"William Lawrence Logan, sir!" said Jimmy, "He was in cell 423W, but he's on Smallpox Island now."

The colonel wrote down the name and continued, "If your brother has a good record of discipline with no escape attempts, I can submit for orders to parole him and send him home." Jimmy still sat there with a look of astonishment on his face. His mouth had dropped slightly open. "Now get the hell out of here and report back here in a couple of hours, Sergeant. I'll let you know if we can parole him. We'll just have to see."

"Yes, sir! Thank you, sir," Jimmy shouted as he jumped up, stood at attention, saluted, and swiftly left the room.

Sergeant Jimmy Logan once again found himself walking down the hill in the heavy rain. There was even some thunder and lightning, but Jimmy barely noticed it. He was numb to it all and he couldn't believe it. "I'll believe all of this if it actually happens," he spoke out loud to no one. Jimmy went straight to the Maintenance Shop. His assistant platoon leader, Corporal Helms, was there. Jimmy told Helms everything about his visit with the colonel. "Well, Sergeant. We do have some work to do over there on Smallpox Island."

"I know."

"Well, if you have to go over there, let me know. We'll go with you."

"Helms, I know how good a man you are, but right now, I'd rather not send you or any of our guys over there unless we have to."

"Agreed, Sergeant. We will conduct our maintenance repairs properly and accordingly."

At 1545 hours, Jimmy was once again walking up the hill in the rain. As soon as he walked past the guard and into the Headquarters, the clerk smiled at him. "I've been working on your issue, Sergeant. Colonel Kahn wants to see you right away. Go straight in."

Jimmy walked in and stood at attention. "At ease, Sergeant. Let's talk."

The Colonel's voice started out with a normal tone, but he became louder and louder as he spoke. "Your brother is eligible for parole by my strong standards. I have 749 inmates in my prison and I want to have 748. In about a month or so, I want zero! My clerk is working on two sets of orders, Sergeant. The first is for your brother, Corporal William Lawrence Logan." He looked at a piece of paper in his hand. "After he swears to a non-commissioned officer (you) or an officer not to rejoin the Confederates, he will be paroled to return to his home of record."

"The second set of orders is for you, Sergeant James Daniel Logan." He looked at the same piece of paper. "You will be put on orders to ensure that Corporal William Logan returns to his home of record. Corporal Helms, your assistant platoon leader, is more than competent. Besides, your Maintenance Platoon has done a bang-up job. I don't need maintenance repairs as much as I used to. All repairs that are not 'Urgent' or 'Immediate' are now hereby deemed 'Non-urgent.' Listen. You've done a great job and this prison should be shutting down before too long."

The colonel then yelled loudly as he slammed his hand on his desk, looking intensely at Sergeant Logan, "Once this terrible war ends, I will recommend that this prison gets torn down!"

"Yes, sir!! What do I need to do, sir?"

"Tomorrow, I need you to go to the Smallpox Island in the early morning and find your brother."

The colonel then handed Jimmy a leather folder and Jimmy looked at it. "Sergeant Logan, I need you to ask him to read that paper out loud and to sign it. Then, I need you to sign it and return it to me." Jimmy opened the leather folder and looked inside. In it was one piece of paper with the following annotation:

I do hereby solemnly swear and pledge my most sacred word of honor that I will not during the existing war between the Confederate States and the United States of America bear arms for or aid and abet the enemies of the United States of America, said Confederate States or their friends, either directly or indirectly in any form whatsoever. Signed

_____

Witnessed

_____

"After this is signed, you need to return it to me immediately. By the close of business tomorrow, my clerk should have both of your official orders completed. These orders will suffice for your mission needs. They will be sanctioned, with U.S. Army letterhead and signed by me."

"Yes, sir!"

The colonel then continued, "If everything goes just like I've stated, both of your orders will be dated for the day after tomorrow, March 31, 1865. On that day, you can go to get your brother and then get the hell out of here. Once you get him home, you will return here to duty, but that's only if the war is still going on. If the war has ended, we will send your discharge orders to your home of record in the U.S. mail. What are your questions?"

"I don't have any questions, sir."

"Good, then see my clerk, Private Brockman, on the way out and get the hell out of my Headquarters building!"

"Yes, sir!!" Jimmy jumped up, saluted the colonel, and departed the room.

Brockman, the lead clerk, told Jimmy that he was working on the orders, but everything needed to happen exactly like the colonel had stated. "Any changes and we will have to start the process all over again, making it all take longer." He gave Jimmy a special quill pen for the signing. Jimmy took it and said, "Don't worry, Brockman. I'll make it happen."

Jimmy departed and once again headed down the hill in the

rain. He didn't notice the rain at all this time. It had become a regular part of his day. Under his arm, he had the leather folder wrapped up in another small leather bag. His mind was reeling from what had just happened. Then, he went straight to the Maintenance Shop and found that no one was there. So, he looked at the mission board and went out to find his squads. As he walked through the prison, Jimmy saw the misery. He saw the pitiful conditions, and now he even saw a way out for his brother...and possibly even for himself.

The day had gone by very quickly and Jimmy found himself at dinner contemplating the next two days. He thought to himself, *Man, I need to go to Smallpox Island twice in the next two days and I've never even been there once. The first time I need to find Willy to have him sign the official paper. Then the next day, I have to get our orders and go back to get him so we can get the hell out of here. It will be a miracle if this all goes off without a hitch. I wonder if it's ever going to stop raining. I'm not sure how we'll get home, so I'd better grab some more food to take with me on the trip.*

March 30, 1865
Day Twenty-Seven at the Alton Prison

The following morning, Jimmy completed his usual routine and then went to chow. Once again, he tried to grab food that wouldn't spoil for his anticipated travels. He then went to the Maintenance Platoon's usual morning formation and spoke to his troops. Jimmy explained the colonel's plan for him and his imprisoned brother. Most of the soldiers from Jimmy's platoon had already heard by word of mouth about Jimmy's brother. They knew that he was a prisoner there and that he had been improperly sent to Smallpox

Island. The Maintenance Platoon was a small and tight-knit group and they all tried to watch out for each other.

Jimmy also told them about the news that the colonel had relayed to him concerning the likely end of the war. This made the entire team look surprised, happy, and somewhat shocked. All twenty-nine men in the platoon looked around at each other with big smiles on their faces. Jimmy also told the men that the colonel had expressed great thanks to the entire Maintenance Platoon because they had all done a "bang-up job!" He added that the colonel no longer needed repairs that were not deemed "Urgent" or "Immediate," because he anticipated that the Alton Prison would be torn down soon after the war.

"This morning, I'm heading to Smallpox Island to find my brother. After he signs a pledge not to fight against the Union, I'll deliver it back to the unit commander. Then, hopefully, my brother and I will depart tomorrow with orders in hand. After I escort my brother home, I'll return here if the war hasn't ended."

Corporal Helms added, "Look, Sergeant, we still work for you. In four short weeks, you've taught us a lot. The seven soldiers of the third squad have been to Smallpox Island several times to make different repairs. They all know how to safely deal with the hazards of the island. I'll have them accompany you today and then again tomorrow to the island. I don't recommend that you go there alone. Besides, you have an armed Maintenance Platoon at your disposal. Like I said, we all work for you. While they're there, I'll have them fix something," he added with a smile on his face.

Within an hour, morning assignments were completed for the first, second, and fourth squads. Jimmy and the third squad were also ready to go. They had carpentry tools and some wooden planks and were wearing their rain gear. Sergeant Jimmy Logan grabbed his official leather folder and announced, "Let's go, third squad!" They all headed down toward the river with Corporal Helms in tow.

Smallpox Island

Once they were all outside, Corporal Helms marched the squad over to the dock. It had stopped raining, but the ground between the prison and the shoreline was still a muddy mess. It was well known that the prison had been built far too close to the river. The wet and humid conditions were thought to have contributed to the many illnesses found there. As they marched through the mud, Jimmy talked to Corporal Helms, "Listen, Helms. I really appreciate this, but tomorrow I want to go to Smallpox Island by myself, without the third squad. I don't want to jeopardize the men for two days in a row just to rescue my brother."

"Understood, Sergeant!"

They finally made it through the mud and water to the flatbed ferry that was tied up to a small dock. The small steam-powered ferry was used to usher people and supplies over to Smallpox Island. The ferry had two small boats tied to its side for emergencies or other needed duties. It was named *The Wiggins*. As soon as Jimmy and his men arrived, the captain of *The Wiggins* walked out. He quickly told them that the ferry was temporarily out of service. The captain of the ferry was an older civilian of medium build. He wore a captain's hat and he had gray hair and a short gray beard. The ferry captain appeared to be a competent seaman with many years of experience.

"Why is that?" asked Corporal Helms.

"Well, the river is just too high. There's a lot of trees and debris passing by out there. It's very dangerous."

Corporal Helms then spoke up. "Well, that's all well and good, but I'm in charge of the Maintenance Platoon and the prison commander has sent us on an important mission over there. We have to get there today and we have to get back. It's really not an option. We have to go."

Jimmy was proud that Corporal Helms had stood up for the mission and had introduced himself as "In charge" of the Maintenance

Platoon. *He's truly ready,* Jimmy thought to himself.

The captain stood there looking at Corporal Helms with his hands on his hips. Finally, after about thirty seconds, he spoke. "Well, as long as I'm not responsible if we get rammed, destroyed, and sunk by a floating tree."

"You are not, sir."

"Okay then, load up, boys."

The captain signaled to his two workers and they started to prepare the ferry for departure. He then fired up the steam engine of the rugged ferry while Jimmy, Helms, and the third squad quickly loaded onto the boat. Two soldiers from the third squad were armed and the others were carrying wood and assorted tools.

Within about five minutes, the boat disembarked from the shore and moved into the rapidly moving river. About thirty feet from shore (and to everyone's surprise), they all heard the ship captain yell loudly, "Here comes one!"

"Jeeesh, already?" Corporal Helms said quietly. A large tree was approaching the boat from upstream at a steady pace. The ship's captain and his two men quickly took action. The workers grabbed two long poles and tried to push the uprooted tree to the side as the captain took evasive maneuvers with *The Wiggins.* Their actions worked as the enormous tree glanced off the side of the ship.

Everyone breathed a sigh of relief. It quickly became apparent that the captain and his crew had made the trip through the dangerously flooded waters before. "That was a little one," said the captain.

"Little one?" said Jimmy.

"Yep. We can't do much with the big ones other than try to avoid them. So, listen up! The flooding has caused a lot of junk to be in the water! So, please help us out with eyes upstream for logs and debris! Some of those big sons a bitches can sink us, so pay attention!"

"Yes, sir!" yelled Jimmy. "Third squad! Pay attention for crap coming at us from upstream!"

"Yes, Sergeant!" all of the soldiers yelled simultaneously.

After that, the ferry cruised across the flooded river with little difficulty, save for the captain slowing down twice to let debris go by. Because of the extremely swift current, the captain had to aim the craft upstream toward the northwest end of the island to avoid missing the island entirely. The boat's captain advised the maintenance team, "Look, boys, I'm not going back and forth. I'll be here until you're done. Hopefully, that'll be one or two hours at the most."

As they slowly pulled into the dock, two armed Union guards from the shore met them and assisted in tying off the ship. The island's guards advised the maintenance team that they were at Smallpox Island and asked their business there. Corporal Helms explained to them that they had maintenance duties to perform as well as other duties at the request of the prison commander. After a head nod from the guards, the team disembarked with their gear and supplies. Corporal Helms sent the third squad to work on two broken doorways, then he and Jimmy went off in search of Corporal Willy Logan. At that very moment, it started to rain again.

Jimmy and Helms found a passing Union soldier and asked him who was in charge of the island. The soldier guided them to a small building that housed the NCO who was currently in command of the island, Sergeant Lancaster. "Hello, Sergeant," said Jimmy. "We are on a mission from Colonel Kahn. We need to locate a prisoner named Corporal William Logan."

"Okay, stand by and let me check." Lancaster looked at his prisoner roster. "Yep, I have him. He's still alive and he's one of eighty-eight living inmates that I have right now. He's probably in Bunkhouse Number Two right over there...or he could be walking around outside. But be careful while you are here, gentlemen. We've had two deaths today already. My men and some inmates are in the process of removing the bodies."

"Yes, Sergeant," said Jimmy. "We understand and thank you."

Jimmy and Corporal Helms went over to the bunkhouse that was full of Confederate soldiers infected with smallpox. Standing in the door, Jimmy announced, "Corporal William Logan!"

One soldier popped up from his cot. "He's outside toward the backside of the island. He sits out there with a tarp over his head... says he doesn't have smallpox."

"Okay, thanks. Which way is the back of the island?"

The inmate pointed toward the Missouri side of the river. Logan and Helms headed toward the island's backside just as four soldiers walked by carrying a stretcher with a deceased inmate on it. They were heading to the downstream end of the island. They both stood quietly in the light rain and watched the stretcher go by. When they reached the back of the island, they saw a large tree, a lot of bushes, and some other smaller trees. They didn't see Willy or anyone else.

"Corporal William Logan!" Jimmy yelled out.

Slowly and from behind a group of bushes, Willy walked out with a tarp over his shoulders. "Here!" he called. "Who is it? Is it Jimmy?"

"No, it's Sergeant Jimmy Logan. I have something for you."

Will walked up to Jimmy and Corporal Helms. "I thought that sounded like you." The brothers stood several feet from each other. They looked each other straight in the eye and smiled precisely at the same time. They didn't touch or hug. Will was wearing a tattered and torn gray Confederate uniform. He had an old, misshaped, large brimmed hat and some leather boots that Jimmy had brought to him when he was back at the Gratiot in St. Louis.

"Where the hell did you get these clothes, Willy?"

"Well, they burned my clothes and told me to put this crappy stuff on."

"I'm thinking that when they bury me, they want me to already be in the proper uniform."

Smallpox Island

"Wow. Okay then," said Jimmy. "Well, the guys back in your prison cell told me what happened. How's the zoster, Will?"

"It still hurts like hell and looks like shit. But hey, guess what?" said Willy.

"What?"

"That asshole, Richie, who turned me in is here and he really does have smallpox."

"I heard," Jimmy answered.

"Well, I still wish he didn't," said Willy. "I went to him and we talked for a bit. I'm pretty sure that he's probably gonna die. He said that he was sorry and I told him that it was okay. You know what? I wouldn't wish that smallpox crap on him or on anybody else. Not even on my worst enemy."

"Right. I agree. Now, listen up, Willy. I told the prison commander that you're here with zoster shingles and not smallpox. He listened and he understands. I have some paperwork from him that I need to show you. It's a non-battle pledge. If you say the pledge and sign the paperwork, the commander will parole you to home. If you sign, I'll take the paperwork to Headquarters. Then tomorrow, I'll pick up official orders for your parole."

"What! Are you kidding! Hell yes, I'll sign!"

They walked over to the side under the big tree where it wasn't raining as much. "Do you know that this tree is called the Lincoln Tree?" said Will.

"Why's that?" said Jimmy.

"I'll tell you later. Let's finish this pledge thing that you've brought me. It sounds kind of important."

"Right, that's a good idea, brother."

Then, Corporal Helms held out his jacket over the paperwork so it wouldn't get so wet. "Read this out loud, Willy," said Jimmy.

Will spoke the words out loud and clear. *"I do hereby solemnly swear and pledge my most sacred word of honor that I will not during the existing war between the Confederate States and the United States of America bear arms or aid and abet the enemies of the United States of America, said Confederate States or their friends, either directly or indirectly in any form whatsoever."*

"Great, sign here." Jimmy laid the paper on the inside of the leather folder. Then, he pulled out the special ink pen that the clerk had given him just for this mission. After Will signed the oath, Jimmy also signed it before promptly placing the paper back into the leather folder.

"Okay, Will. Now I have to leave and take this back to Colonel Kahn. If everything goes right, I will be back tomorrow with your pardon orders and also my orders to escort you home."

"What?! Your what?!"

"Right!" said Jimmy. "He's cutting me official orders to escort you home because of your condition and because of the circumstances. That being that the war's approaching its end."

Will laughed. "Really? I don't get it."

"You heard it right. The commander says he has inside information that this war is ending real soon with a Union victory."

"Good, I hope so," said Will. "This bullshit has to come to an end."

They stood there and talked for a moment under the big tree. The very same tree that had some of its branches whacked off by Abe Lincoln nearly thirty years before. Then suddenly, four soldiers went by carrying another stretcher with a deceased smallpox victim on it. The three men watched them as they headed toward the downstream end of the island.

"What do they do with them, Will?"

"They got a big deep trench over there. The soldiers dig it out as they go. As it gets filled in with bodies, word is about every eight or so, they cover them up with dirt. After that, they just keep on going down the trench as more people die. They keep digging trench to the front while covering trench to the rear. A soldier told me that they have three major trench rows about ten feet apart. They dig 'em as they go. When it's raining, they cover the hole with tents and tarps. Word is, they have two trenches filled with around one hundred dead people per trench. They are on their third trench right now."

"Well, may God help them," Jimmy said.

"May God help which ones, Jimmy? The Yanks or the Rebs?"

After a short pause, Jimmy answered, "All of them, Willy…all of them and all of us."

In what was now a steady light rain, Sergeant Logan and Corporal Helms gathered the third squad to get ready to depart. The Maintenance Team then boarded the transport to head back to the mainland of Alton, Illinois. On this trip, the ship's captain again dodged several trees, but this time without much difficulty. As they docked, Sergeant Logan advised the captain that they would need to do this all over again the next day, by order of the commander.

"Oh great…that's just great!" the captain said loudly. "I received a telegram this morning from my friend docked up in Hannibal, Missouri, one hundred miles north. The weather is not changing and he said there's now major flooding up there. That same major flooding is coming this way. It's worse than this. So, what I'm telling you, Sergeant, is that we may not have it so easy tomorrow."

"Understood, sir. We'll make it happen as quickly as possible."

The team disembarked and Jimmy quickly took the leather folder directly back to the Headquarters building. It was approximately 1430 hours. As Jimmy walked in, Private Brockman said immediately, "Good afternoon, Sergeant. Can I have my quill pen back?"

"Certainly. Here you go." Jimmy pulled the special pen from his top pocket and handed it to the lead clerk.

"Okay, do you have the pledge from Corporal Logan, Sergeant?"

"Yes, right here." Jimmy pulled up the leather bag, fished out the folder, and handed it to Private Brockman. The lead clerk then reviewed the paper closely.

"Well, it all looks good to me, but I have some bad news for you. We will not have your orders ready until approximately 1000 hours tomorrow morning. We had some serious issues today and your orders had to go to the back burner."

Jimmy's heart dropped. "So, am I still good to go?"

"Yes, you are. The colonel will have my ass if I don't cut you and your brother free by tomorrow. We're good. I have the pledge and I have my orders from Colonel Kahn. Report here at 1000 hours tomorrow, Sergeant, and I'll have both sets of your orders. I will have them dated for tomorrow, 31 March, 1865."

"Okay. Thanks, Brockman. I'll be here." With that, Jimmy departed and headed down the hill.

Later, at the evening meal, Jimmy once again tried to gather as much non-perishable food as he could. He felt lucky because he had acquired a bunch of cooked, dried, and salty pork belly from one of the cooks, Private Wriggs. Wriggs was a black Union soldier. He and Jimmy had become friends as Jimmy chatted with him daily while walking through the food line. He basically knew nearly everything about Jimmy's situation.

"Thanks, Wriggs. I don't know exactly how we're getting home, but I know we won't get hungry," said Jimmy, shoving the paper-wrapped pork belly into his side bag. "I'll remember you, buddy."

"That's good, Sergeant Logan. Now you go and get your brother tomorrow and you get the hell outta here. Remember me, but try to forget this place."

"Okey-dokey. Will do. Thanks again, Wriggs."

With that, Jimmy went back to his quarters and packed up his personal effects.

Smallpox Island

He sat on his bunk and worked through his plan for the following day. First, he would go to breakfast. Next, he would go to the Maintenance Platoon formation. Then, he had to go to Supply to turn in his bed linens. Finally, he would go to Headquarters at 1000 hours for two sets of orders. One set was for Willy to be pardoned and the other was for him to escort Willy home.

Once he had orders in hand, he was off to Smallpox Island again. But this time, it would be without the third squad. Jimmy wondered how it would go without Helms and his soldiers with him. Once he left the island with his brother, he really didn't have a solid plan for his next actions. He guessed that his only real option was to bring him back to Alton and wait for a transport boat heading south, or maybe a train. But, in reality, Jimmy wasn't sure how that part would all go. He really hadn't thought that far ahead.

Chapter Seven

March 31, 1865
Day Twenty-Eight at the Alton Prison

The following day it was not raining, but it was still cloudy. Sergeant Logan had a busy morning planned, so he went straight to it. First, he went to breakfast and then hurried down the hill to the 0700 Maintenance Platoon formation. After the formation, he visited with his men as he wrapped up some issues in the shop. Then, after many good wishes to and from his men, Jimmy went back up the hill. First, he went to Supply to turn in his linen and then to Headquarters to get his orders. The second that he entered the Headquarters building, Private Brockman walked straight up to him and handed him the two official orders.

"I've been waiting for you, Sergeant. Here are your orders. All done. Did you strip your bunk and clear at Supply?"

"Yes, I did."

"Well, the colonel is out, but he told me to tell you 'God speed.' If the war don't end in the next few weeks, we'll see you back here again. If it does, I'll send discharge orders to your home of record."

"Understood...and thank you." Private Brockman put the orders in the same leather folder and document sack that they had used before.

Jimmy set out and headed back down the hill to the shoreline to find the steam-powered flatbed ferry, *The Wiggins*. While on his way, he immediately noticed that the river water was much higher than it was the day before. It was nearly halfway across the street that was right in front of the prison. He found the ship and as he approached, he was beyond surprised. There, at the floating dock standing at attention was Corporal Helms and the entire third squad. They all had rain gear on and were ready to go.

Corporal Helms spoke loudly, "Third squad assembled, Sergeant Logan!"

"What the heck are you guys doing here?"

"Well, Sergeant, we have work to do at the island."

"Really?"

"Yes, Sergeant," said Helms with a smile on his face. "We didn't finish yesterday and besides, we want to make sure you complete your mission as well. We're with you, Sergeant."

Just then, it started to rain. Jimmy was tearing up and again, but the rain hid his tears. The transport's captain was waiting as the group loaded onto *The Wiggins*. He spoke loudly in his usual manner, "Morning, boys. Listen up! We are in full-blown flood stage today. It's up more than a foot from yesterday. I suspect your Smallpox Island is about to be submerged! We have to be more vigilant than ever in regards to watching for debris from upstream. You are my eyes! Speak up with extreme prejudice if you see anything and we will hopefully make it over there alive! Anybody have any questions?" No one spoke, but they could feel the tension in the air. "Okay then, let's go fight God's raging river!"

The captain and his crew negotiated the tie ropes and *The Wiggins* disembarked. Less than twenty yards from shore, once again, a large tree was headed directly at them. The captain saw it and yelled, "Tree starboard, thirty yards!!" The crew grabbed long polls and managed to steer it aside as the captain gunned the ship to get out of the way. *Jeesh*, Jimmy thought, *Here we go again*. About halfway across the river, the captain was maneuvering to get out of the way of another large tree when the ship was slammed by a small floating building. The building hit the side of the boat with a loud crash. Two of the men were knocked to the ground as *The Wiggins* shook with the impact.

The flatbed ferry was now being awkwardly shoved sideways and downstream. "Son of a bitch!!" the captain yelled. "Boys, get ready to swim if we have to!" The men tried to remained calm but you could see panic in their eyes. Jimmy and Corporal Helms both looked at one of the two small boats tied to the side of the ship. All of the soldiers instinctively squatted down to get close to the deck.

The captain revved up the engine of *The Wiggins* as it listed heavily to the starboard side. He turned and worked the boat to such an angle that he could make slow forward progress even with the building stuck to the side of his ship. Jimmy looked at his soldiers and then at everyone on the ferry. Even though just minutes earlier they were near panic, they now had determinate and serious looks on their faces. Especially the captain. He would not surrender to the river. Not on this day.

The crew shoved off several other trees as *The Wiggins* limped up to the Smallpox Island shoreline, listing badly to the right. The captain had pulled off what seemed to be impossible. His expert seamanship had saved the ship and everyone on board. Everyone was a bit shaken upon arrival and had very little to say. The captain's crew jumped off, tied off the ship, and placed the exit plank. As they all disembarked, the captain yelled, "Look here, boys! We are going to try to get this building off of the ship! This island is starting to flood, so get your missions done and let's get the hell out of here!! I wish I had some whiskey, and I don't even drink!"

Once on shore, they all noticed that water was pooling everywhere, even though it was raining only lightly. They could hear yelling and commotion coming from all over the island. Also, there were no dock guards there to greet them. Corporal Helms quickly sent the third squad off to finish the work they had started the day before. "Listen, third squad! Check back with me every ten minutes. We may have to pull the plug on our repairs if this water keeps coming up." After that, Helms stuck close to Sergeant Logan as he looked for his brother. It didn't take long. They went out to find Willy, and in less than five minutes, Willy had found them. "Jimmy, did you hear?"

"Hear what?"

"The island is going under. The upstream side is already one foot under, and before long the whole island will be underwater."

"That's just great. Well, I have our orders. Let's go before something else happens."

With that, Corporal Helms nodded and peeled off to gather the third squad while Jimmy found the NCO in charge of the island, Sergeant Lancaster. Lancaster quickly looked at Will's orders and said, "Look, fellas, we are in the middle of an emergency. I'll mark him off of my ledger when I can, but right now, the OIC (officer in charge) just told me that he is thinking about evacuating the island. If he does evacuate, we are going to have to remove everyone to another island just downstream. All of the walking sick and all of the bedridden. I have to go and talk to my soldiers right now. This is going to be a mess."

"What can we do to help you?" said Jimmy.

"Nothing, Sergeant." Lancaster then looked at Willy, "Follow this order and get this William Logan fellow and all of your other people the hell off of my island. I should have enough help and I don't want your people exposed to the Smallpox during all of the upcoming craziness. Also, I have the walking sick Rebel soldiers. They are all good workers and they're usually ready to help."

Jimmy and Will quickly headed toward *The Wiggins*. Once they arrived at the boat, Jimmy immediately noticed that the crew had removed the small building that had struck the side of the vessel. The boat was no longer listing and it appeared that they were good to go. Corporal Helms quickly showed up with the third squad and they all started to board. As they boarded, a Union lieutenant came from below deck and quickly exited the ship. Jimmy, Corporal Helms, and the third squad all saluted the lieutenant, but he walked by and didn't even notice them.

The captain of *The Wiggins* then popped up from below deck and spoke. "Hey, boys, I have good news and bad news! The good news is that *The Wiggins* is seaworthy. The bad news is that my boat has now been confiscated for the flood emergency. Per the officer in charge, Lieutenant Friendly there, we are about to start evacuating this island! We're going to another island called Ellis and it's less than half a mile downstream. We don't have any choice. We're going to get everyone off of this island because it just isn't safe anymore. She's slowly going under and by this time tomorrow, there will be at least twelve inches of water in all of the buildings."

Jimmy called everyone together to evaluate their next options. They could all hear yelling coming from the entire island as the Union soldiers and Confederate inmates dealt with the flooding. There was an empty guard shack nearby, so they all went into it to get out of the rain for a moment. Nine soldiers were standing in the small building. Jimmy said, "Okay, listen up. We may have to evacuate with the prisoners to Ellis Island. After that, we will just have to wait it out until we can get back to Alton."

Corporal Helms then spoke up. "That's all well and good, but what if we get flooded at the next island? What if we get smallpox from being so close to all of the infected prisoners? We have a mission and we have to figure out the best path in which to complete it. That means both our mission as Maintenance Platoon and Sergeant Logan's mission, which is to get the hell outta here." With that, Corporal Helms turned and walked out of the guard shack.

"Where is he going?"

"Heck, if I know."

They all stood in the shack for a few moments discussing everything. The muddy mess, the hurried evacuation, the flood, and how not to get smallpox. One of the third squad soldiers added, "I really don't swim very well."

About five minutes later, Corporal Helms returned and said, "Sergeant Logan, could you and your brother please follow me?" It had again stopped raining. They followed Helms outside as he quickly walked back toward *The Wiggins*. Jimmy immediately spoke up. "Helms, the captain said that we couldn't use his ship to return to Alton."

"Yes, I'm well aware. Follow me." They walked up to the riverbank about thirty feet downstream from *The Wiggins*. On the bank sat one of the side boats of *The Wiggins* with two oars in it. They looked over to *The Wiggins* and noticed that the boat now had only one side boat and not two. "I spoke to the captain. He is aware of your mission. He gladly authorized me to procure this boat for you. It has two oars, some drinking water, and provisions in it as well. The captain said that *The Wiggins* is stalwart enough and he's tired of dragging both of those side boats along anyway."

Right then, the captain walked up, obviously having been listening to their discussion. "Hey, boys, those side rafts just give the upstream trees something more to grab on to anyway. I don't need them. Besides, they are emergency craft, and this is an emergency, right? I'm glad to offer them to you to fulfill your mission, Sergeant Logan. Your corporal explained everything.

God willing, you will complete your mission, and God willing, I will complete mine. I have people to save, and you are included in that statement. Look here. There's a compass, a water jug, some jerky, and dried-out bread in a box under the seat of both emergency boats, including yours. If you really want to leave now, I suggest you take that boat and get the hell outta here. I've seen bad flooding like this happen before. The river could be closed to all traffic for up to a week at the very least. If you wanna go, move out now before something else happens."

"Thanks, Captain."

"You're welcome. If you do go, be careful. I shouldn't have to tell you, but watch out for debris in the river." He put his hand on Jimmy's shoulder and looked him in the eye, "I have work to do." With that, the captain turned and hurriedly walked back toward *The Wiggins*.

Jimmy looked at Corporal Helms. "You didn't have to do all of this. You didn't have to come out to this hellish nightmare to help me today. And you didn't have to find me a boat to take my brother out of here."

Corporal Helms answered, "I'm still your assistant platoon leader. Until the minute you're gone, I still work for you. Your mission is my mission. This is a noble cause and I'm proud to help you with it. So is the whole platoon and especially the third squad. I have a feeling that your adventure is only just beginning.

Jimmy and Willy looked at each other and they both nodded simultaneously. Then, as the floodwater continued to rise, Jimmy suddenly said, "I'll be right back," and he took off running toward *The Wiggins*. He quickly grabbed his leather and canvas bags and then returned. Willy then spoke, "I don't have any gear. They burned all of my stuff." Jimmy took his bag and sat it into the skiff. The top neck of his guitar was still sticking out of it. "Look here, Willy, I've already signed out from the unit, so this is all that I have.

It has my clothes, my guitar, and some provisions that I've been gathering before our departure."

"Good. At least we have something to take with us other than just the boat."

They climbed into the small skiff at 1230 hours and settled in as Corporal Helms walked out into the water to shove them off. The area that they departed from had been far above the water level just the day before. As they started to float away, Corporal Helms snapped to attention while standing knee-deep in the water. "Carry on, Corporal Helms!" Jimmy yelled, "... and thank you!!"

As they departed, Jimmy and Will looked over at Smallpox Island. They both saw the Lincoln Tree, which was now standing in about six inches of water. They heard a commotion and noticed that soldiers had already begun loading prisoners onto *The Wiggins*. They could hear the captain yelling to the inmates and soldiers, "Careful on my ramp, boys. It's very slippery!" As the brothers slowly rowed past the downstream end of the island, they looked over and saw four soldiers hurriedly filling in the open section of the Smallpox Island burial trench.

As they continued to row, they quickly noticed the dark and muddy river water. Its current was tremendous and treacherous. Within five minutes, they were rowing past Ellis Island, the destination for all of the inhabitants of Smallpox Island. There was already one transport boat there that looked to be departing back upstream to Smallpox Island. "It definitely looks like it's higher out of the water than the other one," said Jimmy as they floated by the island. "I wonder if they'll change the name of this island to Smallpox Island Number Two?"

"Probably," Will said.

> *Point of Historical Reference – Smallpox Island, (previously known as Sunflower Island), was prone to flooding. It was used to quarantine smallpox infected prisoners from the Alton Prison from August 1863 until July 1865 (after the end of the Civil War). Approximately three hundred or more Confederate prisoners died on the island.*

Just at that moment, there was a loud crash! Their boat had become entrapped by a huge tree that was largely underwater. The brothers quickly tried to push it off with their oars, but they couldn't. "Son of a bitch!!" Jimmy yelled. Slowly, the colossal tree started turning the little boat sideways. Then, the boat began to list and water started splashing up over the side. Willy started to panic. He hurriedly moved around and yelled, "What do we do!" Several people on Ellis Island noticed the commotion and looked over. The tree limbs had now intertwined with their boat and were stopping them from breaking free. They both fought to push off the tree for about a minute when Jimmy yelled, "I'm done!" He stood up, leaped out of the boat, and attacked the tree. At one point, he was standing on the tree, jumping up and down. Suddenly, Jimmy slipped down into the water, but he had been holding onto the boat and he popped right back up. The jumping and bouncing finally made the tree move just enough to loosen most of its grip on their little boat. Jimmy climbed back onto the boat and with brute strength, he broke off a crooked limb that was still clinging to their boat. Their skiff was finally free. Willy was shaking. He paddled away from the tree as fast as he could, while Jimmy took a knee, trying to catch his breath.

"Look here, Jimmy, I'm going to move as close to the shore as I can," Will said as he vigorously rowed. "If something else like that happens, we gotta be able to swim to shore."

"I agree. Good idea, said Jimmy, "Let's paddle toward the Missouri side, the right side of the river. We have to make a plan on how to deal with this river." It was then that Jimmy noticed Willy. He was on guard at a high level, moving fast, and constantly assessing their danger. Willy was jumpy. His head was turning 360 degrees and he was near panic. "Agreed!" yelled Willy. Jimmy studied his brother as they moved toward the Missouri side of the river. They quickly noticed that the water was over the bank in many places, but not everywhere. Many areas were still above the floodwater.

After about thirty minutes, they started to slow down a bit and Willy seemed to be a little calmer. One would row while the other one watched for river debris. The brothers were getting weary of fighting the river and the constant watch for debris. They had been running on adrenaline and now they wanted to rest. It had stopped raining, so Jimmy decided to find a good place to pull over so they could eat something, rest, and survey their new situation. "This looks like a great area. Nice and high with lots of woods for cover."

Willy pulled his hat down tight. "Okay, let's dock this skiff and take a break!" They found an area of sandy mud to pull up the skiff. After stopping, they proceeded to pull the little boat up onto the shore. Together, they grabbed the skiff and pulled it up farther into the wood line so it could not be seen from the river. Just as they finished, a large transport steamship came around the river bend, paddling straight up the center of the river. They watched as it plowed into a rather large tree. Although it seemed to slow down a bit, the big ship just shoved the tree to the side and kept on going. Jimmy looked around. He then found a small clearing and started setting up a place to rest. He also wanted to take inventory of all of their food and provisions.

Will and Jimmy went back to the boat and unloaded all of their supplies, including the emergency box, from under the boat's seat. First, they laid all of their provisions out in a straight line along with Jimmy's large bag (still with the top of his guitar sticking out). Next to that, Jimmy laid his small leather bag with their official orders and his other side bag. Then, they opened the lid of the box from the boat and stood back, looking at their provisions. Next, they opened things up a little more to see precisely what they actually had. Jimmy's bags contained: a hat, two blankets, a canvas tent half, two sets of Union blue pants and shirts, two pairs of socks, personal gear (razor, comb, and soap), two small tins of matches, some dried bread, two bruised apples, some beef jerky, and dried pork belly. They then emptied the box from the boat and found a compass, more matches, two small jugs of water, and four small haversack canvas bags. There was a bag of coffee beans, a hardtack bag (dried biscuits), a bag with dried beans, and a salted pork bag. Willy commented, "I don't have anything.... I don't have a single thing except for what I'm wearing."

"Yes, you do! said Jimmy. "Half of all of this crap is now yours."

Finally, there they sat, amidst their provisions and Jimmy's personal bags. Jimmy spoke up. "I can't believe this is happening. I really thought we would catch a transport or a train to St. Louis and then go on to New Madrid. This flood emergency has fouled everything up. Nobody really knows what's going on and I'm sure that all of the transports are either shut down or getting ready to shut down. What should we do?"

"I don't know," said Willy. "Why don't we just relax, have a little food and water, and figure out our options. All I know is that I'm free, thanks to you."

"Right. Well, you can thank Colonel Kahn, commander of the Alton Federal Prison, for that."

"Well, thanks to him *and* you then."

"You're welcome, Will. But I don't think Colonel Kahn knew about this flood emergency, or he probably would have held us back a few days."

"No way. I'm glad we're out of there," said Willy. "Another day later and who knows what might have happened. I could have drowned or even caught real smallpox. We might have even got stuck in Alton for two or three weeks."

"Look, Will," said Jimmy, "I've also been thinking about our departure from Smallpox Island. I know that I showed your orders to the sergeant back there, but that was really hectic. A real emergency. It was so busy amidst all of that chaos, no one was sure of what the hell was going on. Once the smoke clears, I wouldn't be at all surprised if they thought that you were still there."

"Agreed, I wouldn't be surprised either, but we have our official orders. So, we're good to go, right?"

"Oh yeah, and Colonel Kahn also knows our mission. So, we're good to go."

"Hey, Jimmy," said Will.

"What?"

"That sergeant was really swamped…get it. He was swamped."

"Very funny, asshole." Jimmy smiled. "Make jokes in the midst of a disaster."

"Yep, how do you think I made it through two and a half years in prison? Well, it wasn't by sulking around and complaining. A lot of the time, I joked around with the guards and the other inmates. Just like you and I did back at the farm."

"That's good, Willy. I'm glad that you make stupid jokes."

"Thanks for that approval, Jim."

"You're welcome, Billy…oops, I mean Willy."

"Whatever."

They both looked over their supplies and reflected quietly for a few moments. There were a lot of unknown factors that could affect them and their path toward home. Finally, after about five minutes of rest, Jimmy spoke. "Well, Corporal Logan," he said in an official tone. "We have to consider our options. I'm working under military orders to escort you to your home in New Madrid, Missouri. I have a mission and I have to figure out how to do it. I have to figure out our plan of travel.

"Should we: a) continue on downriver to St. Louis and then try to get a military transport boat to New Madrid, b) continue downriver to St. Louis and then attempt to take our skiff all the ways home, or c) cross the river right here and work our way back to Alton on foot. From there, we could wait until the river opens. Then, after some unknown amount of time, we could take a transport to St. Louis and then on toward home in whatever manner."

"Understood," said Willy. "But for right now, Willy," said Jimmy, "I was hoping that you could change your clothing. I brought a blue shirt and blue pants for you with a brown leather hat. We need you to look a little less like a Rebel Prisoner and a little more like a traveler."

Jimmy picked up his bag and moved his guitar over to the side. He then shuffled through the clothing and handed the pants, shirt, and hat over to Will.

"Can I keep my gray pants for now? I kind of like these old pants?"

"I guess so, but be careful, Will. They look like faded Rebel pants."

"Okay."

As Will changed, Jimmy noticed how thin he was. He also noticed the zoster shingles blisters around his back, side, and neck.

"How's the zoster?"

"Hurts like hell. It sure ain't showing no signs of lightening up yet."

Jimmy then gathered some jerky, water, and other provisions for them to eat.

Since Will was skinny and most likely running on adrenaline, Jimmy gave him an extra piece of bread and had him drink some extra water. "You need this more than I do."

"Thanks, Jim. I want you to know that I always spoke to my guards and told them that you were my brother. Sometimes that got me a little bit more food and water. So, you were helping me even when you didn't realize it."

"Good, I'm glad. Colonel Kahn says it's a miracle that you're still alive."

After eating, Will took his old shirt and hat to the side. He then dug a small hole with his boot and buried them. The brothers then finished surveying all of their supplies. They determined that they had enough food for three to four days and enough water for about two to three days.

It was still not raining and the sun was starting to pop out. Jimmy spoke, "Will, as far as the flooding on the river goes, the damage has already been done. We know how this goes from our days on the farm. It's rained so much upstream and locally that the river will probably go up for at least another week. Then it will go down very slowly."

"Yep. We've seen it all before." After a few minutes of looking at the river through the trees, Jimmy spoke up. "How's this sound? Let's work our way down to the Great Confluence. It's downstream, not far from here. We can find some high ground there, make a camp, and try to dry out and rest a bit. I have that canvas tent half in my bag. We'll decide what to do later. Right now, we're safe, you're pardoned, and I have orders. I think we need to try to dry out and rest."

"I'm good with that," said Willy, "I want to take my boots off for a while once we settle in."

"Good, let's go."

"I have one question," said Willy. "What's the Great Confluence?"

"Ha! You'll see, brother! It's awesome! Let's load this crap up and get the hell out of here."

They loaded the boat and headed downstream. There was some agreeable high ground just before the Great Confluence, so Jimmy pulled the boat up onto the shore. Then, the brothers dragged the skiff out of sight and surveyed the area, looking for a place to camp. To Jimmy's surprise, he found a site that appeared to have already been cleared. There were even remnants of an old campfire and some unused firewood. After they brought over their supplies, they both gathered some wood for the fire. Then, Jimmy set up his canvas tent half and Will took off his boots, leaving them in the sun to dry out.

After a brief reconnaissance walk around the area, Jimmy also took off his boots. He then laid out his pistol and ammo in the sun, which was rapidly going lower in the sky. They both pitched in, built a fire, and noticed that the previous travelers had done an excellent job at concealment. The camp was in a perfect area that couldn't be seen from the river through the dense foliage and trees. Then Will asked Jimmy if he could use his revolver. "I guess so," Jimmy said. "You also have a knife, right?" said Willy.

"Yep, right on my belt...and I also have ammo for my Colt."

"Good."

Will walked off in his bare feet with the gun. About twenty minutes later, Jimmy heard a shot from his pistol. Five minutes after that, Will came walking up with a big grin on his face. He had a good-sized rabbit in tow. "Earlier, I saw two rabbits running around over there. Let's cook up a little grub, brother."

"Outstanding," Jimmy said. They cleaned the rabbit, cooked it over the fire, and ate it just like they had done back at the farm, many times before.

The sun slowly went lower into the sky. They had finished the rabbit and there wasn't a lot to do, so Jimmy started picking lightly at his small guitar. He worked his way up to playing the same tune that he had made up while traveling north on the paddlewheel from home. "I wish I had my harmonica," said Willy. Jimmy grinned and reached into his canvas bag. He then threw a harmonica over to Will. "Bought this for twenty-five cents about a week ago. I took it up to your room the other day, but you were gone when I got there."

"I was at the island?"

"Yup." Jimmy pulled out his pocket watch and looked at it for a while as he thought about their situation. "Hey, Jimmy, I didn't know you had a pocket watch."

"I'm a sergeant. I have to know what time it is."

"Nice. What kind is it?"

"It's a William Ellery model. Paid twelve bucks for it about a year ago."

"That's awesome. Is it tough?"

"Oh, hell yeah. I fell into the water today and it's still working fine. You can bang nails with this thing."

"Really?"

"No, not really. It's not *that* tough."

"Oh, I didn't think so."

"Anyway, we have a couple more hours of daylight. We can keep this fire going and dry out as best we can. Then, after a decent night's rest, we can load up, row down to St. Louis, and go to Benton Barracks. I'd rather show up there in the morning rather than later in the day anyway. I know a lot of people there. So hopefully, we can settle in at Benton long enough to firm up our plans."

"Sounds good to me, Jim. As long as we steer clear of the Gratiot Street Prison."

"Will do, Willy. Understood."

Jimmy picked his guitar back up and kept playing it as darkness closed in. Willy played the harmonica but only for a short while before he lay down near the fire and fell fast asleep. As Willy slept,

Jimmy added some wood to the fire and covered Will with a blanket. He then checked the area, sat down, and dozed off with his pistol in his hand. Jimmy tried to wake up every few hours through the night to recheck the area's security.

Chapter Eight

April 1, 1865

The following day, the brothers woke up just before sunrise. Jimmy found a small stream that was perfect for shaving and washing up. He said to Willy, "I have to look presentable today. I'll be reporting in at my old Headquarters."

They both ate some pork belly and hardtack for breakfast. No time for coffee today, so they only drank water. After cleaning the area, they loaded the boat with their supplies. When it looked like it was about time to go, Jimmy asked Will to follow him for a moment. "Where are we going?"

"You'll see."

They walked to the south through some woods until they came to an opening. Once there, they both stood and gazed in awe upon an enormous expanse of water. "Holy crap! What the hell is this? Where are we?" said Willy.

"It's the Great Confluence! The joining of the Missouri River and the Great Mississippi River. It's known as the finest confluence in the world. The Missouri River is here on the right. It's fast and really tough for boats to navigate. The ol' Mississippi on our left is usually slow, but not today of course. St. Louis is just down the Mississippi on the right. Just up the Missouri River also on the right is a town called St. Charles."

They both stood there quietly for a moment, gazing at the vastness. "It's beautiful... It's massive," said Willy.

"I know. I wanted you to see it from land before we floated through it. Remember the Great Confluence!"

"I will," said Willy. "Thanks, Jimmy. Hey... I wonder why there aren't any buildings and a grand town here."

"Good question. I don't know. Maybe the land here is too low, or it might be too hard to get to. I don't really know. I do know it's a beautiful sight to see."

"Agreed.... Let's go."

They loaded into their small boat and pushed off. Within a few minutes, they were smack in the middle of the Great Confluence. "Oh, my gosh," Will said. "It looks like it's over a mile to shore in either direction!"

"I know. It's huge, isn't it? A beautiful and majestic piece of God's work."

Suddenly, they could feel the current from the Missouri River pushing them from the right side. For a moment, the skiff was nearly out of control. The strong current was pushing their skiff toward the center of the Mississippi. Jimmy rowed hard to regain control. Then, Willy said, "Man, let's get through this and try to get closer to shore. I don't think I can swim that far."

"Right! I really don't like being so far out in this little boat," said Jimmy. The soldier and the former prisoner pushed ahead.

Within a few moments, they had regained control and were once again close to the Missouri shoreline. "I think we're about ten miles from St. Louis," said Jimmy. "We'll stop at Benton Barracks, consider our options, and get some supplies. I may try to send a telegraph to Colonel Kahn requesting guidance on our next actions.

Smallpox Island

Don't forget, we're legitimate. We have official orders. We don't have to hide out here on the river. We're only here on this little boat because we had to escape a flood emergency at Smallpox Island. Once we get to Benton Barracks, we'll have options. I know a lot of soldiers there, including the post commander, Colonel Bonneville."

After about an hour and a half of fighting the current and the river debris, they were finally at the St. Louis shoreline. They rowed up to the riverbank near a dock operated by the Union Army. A large portion of the dock appeared to be submerged by the flooding and several armed soldiers were working nearby. A large paddlewheel transport was tied up at the Union dock. In total, they saw at least eight big paddlewheel steamboats sitting at the St. Louis riverfront. Willy grabbed the dock and held on as Jimmy went up to two of the Union soldiers. He asked for some help pulling their little boat up out of the water. "Yes, Sergeant," they both quickly replied.

Willy promptly jumped out of the boat as the soldiers ran over. They pulled the boat far out of the water and agreed to guard it while Sergeant Logan and Willy walked up toward Benton Barracks. The brothers grabbed some of their gear but left the box under the seat. Jimmy told them, "Please guard it well. I have valuable gear in there."

"Will do, Sergeant!" one of the guards replied.

They started walking through the streets of St. Louis and went toward Benton Barracks. "How far is it, Jimmy?"

"Oh, it's a good half-hour walk. That's if we don't get a ride."

"Well, I know one thing. The Gratiot Street Prison is real close. It's right over that way. I really don't want to go anywhere near there," said Willy.

"We won't and I don't blame you."

A moment later, Jimmy flagged down a military flatbed wagon that was heading to Benton. The brothers loaded onto the wagon and were at Benton Barracks in about ten minutes. They jumped off the wagon and Jimmy led them straight to the Headquarters building. "Wait here, Will," Jimmy said as he went inside.

Will looked around the post as he sat there with their gear. It had been nearly a year and a half since he was in the Gratiot Street Prison and almost two years since he was a patient in the Benton Barracks Hospital. He gazed over at the hospital building, which was about a hundred yards away. *I wonder if Belle, that great nurse that helped me, is still there?* he thought to himself. *She probably doesn't know that I still think about her nearly every single day.*

Then, a Union soldier, a private, walked by and looked closely at Will as he sat there next to the HQ building. Suddenly, he stopped and came back to Will. "Hey! Those look like Confederate pants, boy! Are you a Rebel?" Will knew that he looked like a typical prisoner. Not only was he very thin, but he also was wearing gray pants along with his blue shirt.

"Well, not exactly. I've been paroled and I'm waiting for my escort. He's inside."

"Sure, he is, boy. Stand up and put your hands up!" Willy smirked as he slowly stood up and put up his hands. The soldier grabbed Willy. He spun him around and shoved him up against the wall. Willy resisted but not very much. He knew that Jimmy was nearby.

"Easy, Private! I told you the truth! You're gonna get your ass kicked and it's not gonna be by me!"

The Union soldier said, "Shut up, Rebel!" as he jammed his elbow onto Will's neck and shoved him to the ground.

"Arrrgh!! Take it easy, asshole!" yelled Willy.

Just then, Jimmy came walking out of the Headquarters building. He saw what was happening and in about two steps, he flew over to the private, who now had his knee in Willy's back. Jimmy plowed into the soldier and knocked him about ten feet away from Willy. He then grabbed the Union private and literally threw him through the air. The private crashed up against the side of the building. Jimmy then landed directly on top of him.

"What are you doing attacking my brother, you piece of shit!"

"I...err... He said he was a Reb. I thought he had escaped."

"You thought nothing, Private Idiot! I'm his escort. He is paroled and he's with me!"

"I'm real sorry, Sergeant. I should have listened to him, I guess."

"I told ya that you were gonna get your ass kicked!" said Willy with a broad smile on his face. With that, Jimmy let the soldier up. Straightening his uniform, he told him, "Now move out smartly, Private."

"Yes, Sergeant!"

As the soldier departed, Jimmy asked Will, "Are you okay?"

"Yeah, I guess so. My back hurts a little from having his knee smashed into it."

"Sorry about that. I guess I should have taken you in with me."

"That's fine. I gotta slowly get out of the mode of being a model prisoner and get back into being a free man. I need to gain some weight...and I gotta change these pants."

"Good idea! Anyway, I just sent a telegraph to Colonel Kahn requesting direction on our next move. I also spoke to the Headquarters clerk, Corporal Moore, and showed him our orders. I know him. Colonel Bonneville is also in there and he was real glad to see me. He took good care of us. We now have quarters to stay in while we consider our next move. I worked here for a long time. For years...and I just left a month ago. I know a lot more people here than I ever knew at Alton, by a long shot."

They went to the Billeting Office, where they met the NCO in charge of all the soldiers' quarters at Benton Barracks. Luckily, Jimmy also knew him. He was a black soldier named Sergeant George Williams. Jimmy showed Williams their orders and asked that they not be housed in an open barracks because of Will's shingles condition. He also didn't want to cause trouble with other

Union troops because Will had been a Confederate soldier. He still looked like an emaciated prisoner.

Sergeant Williams was glad to see Jimmy, "Sure. You know I'll take care of ya, Sergeant Logan."

He assigned them to a temporary officers' quarters that was a standalone building on the east side of the post. The one-room building was used as an officers' quarters for soldiers who were just passing through. The building had two bunks, two desks, some chairs, and a small fireplace in it. It was somewhat run-down and was part of a group of about seven other small buildings. Jimmy knew the building well because he had been tasked to make repairs on it numerous times when he was a carpenter at Benton.

Once inside, they quickly stoked up the fireplace. "Now, first things first," said Jimmy. "Please switch your pants to anything that isn't gray. I'd rather you be buck naked than wearing those gray pants. We don't need to fight that battle every day."

Willy laughed. "Good idea! I think I'll go for the blue pants rather than being buck naked."

"Great, I'm sure that the entire post will be very thankful for that."

Jimmy then laughed and said, "I'll be back." He then departed for about twenty minutes and returned with a fresh loaf of bread, some ham, and a jug of water. By the time Jimmy returned, Willy had put on the light blue trousers Jimmy had packed for him. "There. You look a little better now, Willy. Try to blend in."

"Yes, Sergeant!" said Willy as he ate a piece of ham. "Blending in is what I do best. It's how I've survived for the last two and a half years."

"Okay, eat something, stay here, and rest up. In a minute, I'm going to go back down to the river, secure our boat, and check back with HQ. I'm still not sure how long we'll be here and I don't want the boat to float off with the flood."

Smallpox Island

"Right, I'll stay here for now. Please give me my orders, so I don't have to fight again."

Jimmy laughed. "Good idea.... Here you go." He pulled them out and handed them over. "Remember, we are registered here for this room. We're legal. We are not on the run, even though it sometimes feels like it." Jimmy threw some wood into the fireplace and moved about the room for a few minutes. Just as he was ready to go, he looked over at Willy. He had fallen asleep, with his orders still in his hand.

Jimmy secured a one-horse wagon headed down the riverfront. He loaded up their gear and, with the help of the dock guard, he secured the skiff boat about fifty feet away from the river's edge. They pulled it up right next to the Union guard's shack. Then, Jimmy borrowed a quill pen and some paper from the guards. He wrote, "Property of Sergeant Logan, U.S. Army" on the paper and secured it on the seat with two rocks.

On the way back to quarters, he dropped by the Headquarters building. There was still no return message from Colonel Kahn. However, the post commander, Colonel Boonville, was still there and he talked to Jimmy. "Don't worry, Sergeant, I've contacted Colonel Kahn at Alton. He is well aware of your status. We'll be giving you more information soon."

Jimmy answered, "Yes, sir!" As he walked out, he thought to himself, *The Colonels are contacting each other? I wonder what the heck is going on with that. Something smells a bit funny.*

April 2, 1865

The next day was a Sunday. Jimmy's plan to get to the post earlier on the previous day had worked out well. They ate at the mess hall and Jimmy acquainted Willy with the Benton Barracks layout. Even though the war was in high gear in other places, there was currently no action near Benton. The only exception was the steady stream of wounded soldiers arriving for care at the Benton Barracks Post Hospital. Willy spent most of the day resting. His body was still very thin and weak from being incarcerated for two and a half years. He was also exhausted from the last two days of rowing.

April 3, 1865

It was Monday morning, the sun was out, and it still was not raining. Today, Benton Barracks was a bustling military post with a lot of activity. The general mood of the post was very upbeat because rumors were beginning to circulate. The word was now going around that the war could soon be over. The brothers were just hanging out as they waited on instructions from their superiors. They ate meals at the mess hall, walked around the post, chatted with Jimmy's friends, and rested a lot. While eating at the mess hall, they gathered some non-perishable food and supplies in anticipation of their upcoming travel back home. While Willy was starting to look and feel a little bit stronger, he was still very weak. His shingles were still hurting quite a bit and he was in some real pain. Several of the more painful shingles blisters had been oozing on his back and neck. Jimmy saw the weeping blisters and told Willy to try the post's infirmary to see what they could do for him. "Yeah, I'll go there soon if this pain doesn't let up. This crap is a real pain in the ass."

At about 1100 hours, Jimmy walked through the door to the room. "Well, Colonel Kahn finally answered my telegraph! Seems he was working a deal with the Benton Barracks commander, Colonel Bonneville. I knew that something was up. They issued temporary orders that supersede our other orders for the next nine days. I'm to go back to work as a carpenter here at Benton Barracks for those nine days."

"What?!"

"Yep. So, after nine days and a wake-up, we're gone. We will depart on April 13th. Apparently, they are really hurting for some emergent carpentry work here and the commander knows that I can knock it out without too much of a problem. Seems they really like me around here."

"They like you everywhere," said Will.

"Whatever. Well, anyway, their maintenance team here has been bungling since I left. Shoddy workmanship with slow results. I already know the ins and outs around here, so I agreed. We can kick some real ass here with nine days of work."

"We?"

"Yes, that's if you agree. I told them that maybe you could help me. Hell, Willy, you're as good of a carpenter as I am."

"Yeah, maybe, but I haven't swung a hammer in three years."

"I know. It's just like riding a bike. You'll be fine. You can continue getting stronger in the meantime. If you agree, you'll work with me as my assistant." There was an awkward pause. Finally, Jimmy spoke, "Willy, I have to do this. I'm on orders. I have no choice. You, on the other hand, don't have to do this. You're free to decide. If you decline, you'll just have to hang out and wait for me to escort you home."

"Are you kidding? I'm in! I'd love to do some carpentry with my brother," said Willy.

"Great!" Jimmy continued. "On the morning of April 13th, we are out of here. Until then, you and I can work. We can get some decent food and lodging before we leave."

"Okay, Jimmy. Wait a cotton-pickin' minute!"

"What?"

"I've eaten at that Mess Hall. Let's not get carried away. 'Decent' is being very generous. It's barely mediocre." They both laughed. "That's true, little brother, that's very true..."

April 4, 1865

The next day, Jimmy went to the Headquarters for a list of the most emergent carpentry work and Will went off in search of the Benton Barracks Infirmary. The infirmary was primarily a medical station for the troops serving at Benton Barracks. He soon found that it was not in the same building as the hospital and that it was better known to the soldiers as "Sick Call." Finally, he found the building and walked through the front door. It was a medium-sized barracks-style building. There appeared to be two doctors and two nurses working inside. Willy signed in and sat down, waiting for someone to see him.

After about five minutes, a doctor called him back and asked him to sit on a bed. After a discussion and a brief examination, the doctor said, "Well, son, that's a mighty strong case of the shingles. Have you had this before?"

"Yes, sir. About three years ago."

"Well, it's rare in young people, but it does happen. This may last for up to four or five weeks. I will have the nurse wrap up these weeping vesicles with some clean bandages. I'll also have her give you a bottle of laudanum. It's liquid opium for the pain, but don't use it unless you have to. It's powerful stuff."

"Understood. Thank you, sir."

The doctor departed and about five minutes later, a nurse walked up with a tray full of bandages. Willy couldn't believe his eyes. It was Belle! The very same nurse who had cared for him nearly two years before in the Benton Barracks Hospital. Will instantly recognized her. He stood up and said, "Hi, Belle!" The nurse stood back for a few seconds with a blank look on her face. Then her facial look turned to a bright smile. "I remember you. Your name is..."

"Will!" he said. "You were my nurse over at the hospital a couple of years ago."

"I do remember you! Ms. Parsons found your brother working here on the post."

"Yep!" said Willy with a broad smile.

"You're a farm boy from lower Missouri and you thanked me for being your nurse."

"That's right! I'm not a prisoner anymore. I've been paroled and I'm here with that very same brother." The nurse moved toward Will and sat her supplies down on a table. "I have shingles blisters. They hurt a lot and leak some fluid."

"Yes, I know. The doctor spoke to me about it. He sent me to wrap them up and to give you a bottle of opium for the pain."

Belle helped Willy remove his shirt. As she surveyed his wounds, Will was surprised that she didn't react to the severity of them. His blisters were not nice to look at. They covered about half of his back and wrapped around his torso. The blisters also came up the right side of his neck. Thankfully, the blisters that were on his neck had stopped right at his jawline just before his face. Will looked closely at her eyes as she cared for him. He remembered how beautiful she was when he last saw her. He thought to himself, *She still looks exactly the same as before.* Belle wrapped the gauze around him with such kindness and care.

As he gazed at her, she suddenly paused and looked at Will. "Are you okay?"

"Yes. I was just noticing what a kind and beautiful person you are, on the inside and the outside. I wanted to tell you that when you were my nurse before, but I was afraid to because I was a prisoner. I'm not a prisoner now, so there. I finally told you. Please excuse me if I seem forward. I'm just telling you the truth."

"Thank you, Willy. You are very nice to say that," said Belle as she wrapped Will's torso. "I've been approached by a few men since I've been here, but none of them have spoken to me quite like that. To be honest with you, I remember you very well from when I was your nurse. I remember how kind and courteous that *you* were. Actually, to tell the truth, I've thought about you quite often. I've wondered what had become of you. I wondered if you were still alive…and to be honest with you…I really didn't think that you were."

Belle finished wrapping Will's wounds and handed him the bottle of liquid opium. "Listen, Will. This medication is called Laudanum and it's very strong. Please try not to take it unless the pain is unbearable. It can knock you out, it can make your head dizzy, and it can lock up your bowels."

"Sounds really great. I can't wait to try some," said Willy with a grin.

"I know it sounds bad," said Belle giggling, "but it's actually okay as long as you don't use too much of it."

"Thanks, Belle, really. You know, I was wondering, would you like to eat dinner with me at the mess hall later? Maybe, if you'd like, we can take a walk afterwards. Just for something different to do."

Belle just sat there smiling at him. He continued, "I'm not crazy and I promise not to harm you. I've been sitting around my room every evening listening to my brother play guitar and I'd love to do something different. Like maybe walk through the countryside area just off post. I heard there are some nice prairies, creeks, and streams nearby. It would be kind of odd for me to walk around out there alone." Just then, Will realized that he was the only person talking. He wondered if he had been talking too much. He felt so nervous to ask her to meet with him.

Belle sat there for about ten seconds, smiling at him. Then she spoke. "I should be off work at about 6 p.m. Meet me at the mess hall. If we have a good visit during dinner, maybe we can extend our visit to the surrounding countryside. It gets dark around 7:30, so we won't have a lot of time."

"Great!!" said Willy with a huge smile on his face. He jumped up out of this chair and quickly put his shirt back on, smiling the entire time.

"I thought you were in pain!" said Belle.

"I am!" said Willy as he bumped into the chair. "I'm just in pain and happy at the same time. I never thought that I'd see you again, so I'm happy."

Their special moment was quickly ended as a doctor called out, "Ms. Palmer, I could use your help over here!"

"Yes, Doctor! On my way!"

Belle watched Willy awkwardly depart with a smile on her face, then she hurriedly went back to work.

Will briskly returned to the cabin and walked through the front door. He immediately told Jimmy that Belle, his hospital nurse from two years before, was still there and was working at the Medical Infirmary. "Wow, that's great. I know you had mentioned that you liked her. Are you going to try to meet with her before we leave?"

"Yes, we're meeting for dinner tonight at the mess hall."

"The mess hall...that's very nice. How romantic."

"Shut up, stupid."

At 6 p.m. that evening, Will and Belle met at the mess hall right on time. After some small talk and an uneventful dinner, he asked Belle if she would like to take that walk through the countryside just off of the post. She agreed and they left the mess hall together. They walked through the main gate of the post (both waving at the guards) and took a walk toward the river. The area that they strolled through was a bit off the beaten path. Spring was approaching and there were lots of wildflowers beginning to bloom. At times they could even see the Mississippi River off in the distance. They talked and talked about anything that came into their minds. As the walk continued, they became more comfortable with each other by the moment.

While walking in an area of prairies and trees, they noticed that darkness was quickly approaching. The sky became a beautiful rusty orange as the sun started to set into the horizon. "This area is beautiful and that may be the most stunning sunset I've ever seen," said Belle.

"I agree, Belle. I've seen a lot of sunsets, but I don't remember any quite as beautiful as this one," said Will as he was looking at Belle.

Belle added, "I just didn't know how nice it was out here."

"To be honest, I didn't either. I just wanted to take a walk with you, and I also love nature."

"So do I."

As dusk enveloped the area, they realized that they had to make it back to the main gate before dark. As they hurried back, Will reached out to Belle as they stepped across a creek. Belle took his hand for the first time and she kept it for the rest of their walk. After about ten minutes, they emerged from the countryside area. Will walked Belle back onto the post (once again, they waved at the guards), and he took her back to her quarters.

While standing at her door, they made plans to meet each other for dinner on the following day, if possible. After chatting for several more moments, Will said "Good night" as he leaned in to attempt a kiss. Belle also leaned in but turned her head ever so slightly, so they actually kissed each other's cheeks. They stood there looking into each other's eyes, then Will quickly moved forward and gave Belle a quick little kiss on the lips. They had kissed each other for the first time. Belle smiled and said "Good night!" as she hurriedly turned to enter her quarters and closed her door. Will smiled and walked away with a brisk hop in his step.

Smallpox Island

April 5, 1865

For the next several days, the brothers worked on some of the many carpentry and maintenance repairs all around Benton Barracks. Although it was raining sporadically, it seemed that the torrential rains had stopped. Jimmy checked with the Headquarters for flooding reports from upriver. It appeared that the Mississippi River was no longer rising. That was not only good news, that was great news!

That afternoon, the two brothers were walking across the post to fix the main entrance doorway to the hospital. Will was carrying a ladder, while Jimmy was carrying a saw and a couple of boards. As they were walking, an entire company of over one hundred black soldiers went marching by them. Will nearly dropped the ladder. His mouth fell open and he stood still in amazement. The sergeant who was on the side leading the march looked over and saw Jimmy. He nodded and yelled over, "Good morning, Sergeant Logan!"

Jimmy yelled back, raising his hand high in the air, "Morning, Sergeant Johnson! Good luck!"

"Jimmy," Willy whispered, "that's a full company of marching black soldiers. What the hell's going on? I've seen black soldiers here at Benton, but I have never seen a whole company like that."

"Well, I'm a little surprised that you haven't. You have heard of the Emancipation, haven't you?"

"The what?"

"President Lincoln issued the Emancipation Proclamation over two years ago. You haven't even heard of it?"

"Nope. As you may remember, Jim, I've been a little preoccupied in prison for the last few years."

"Right. Well anyway, he freed all of the slaves! The Emancipation also paved the way for black men to join the Union Army. Some of their units were organized and train right here at Benton Barracks.

That guy leading the march is my friend Sergeant Johnson. He's been a leader around here for a long time."

"Wow, what's the name of the unit?"

"Well, they used to be the Fourth Missouri Colored Infantry, but Sergeant Johnson told me that they've recently been changed to the 68th U.S. Colored Troops Regiment. He told me at dinner yesterday that they have orders to move out today. They're going down south to fight for the Union in Alabama."

"Ah, so that's why you said "Good luck" to him."

"Yep."

Willy just stood there in amazement, studying the large contingent of over one hundred soldiers as they marched by. It was an impressive sight to see. They didn't look like colored soldiers. They didn't look like white soldiers. They just looked like…soldiers.

"Well, I've seen colored soldiers here," said Willy, "but I didn't…I thought…I just didn't know there were whole companies of black soldiers."

"Don't be so shocked," Jimmy said. "They're all part of the USCT, the United States Colored Troops. They don't just march good. They're great fighting soldiers. They've been all over the country fighting for the Union, fighting for their freedom. They're awesome.

"The big fella marching the company is Sergeant Johnson. He's a buddy of mine. A great guy. He reminds me a little of our Amos."

"Well, I'll be," said Will.

"Come on, stupid," Jimmy said with a broad grin, "Let's go fix a door."

While they worked on the hospital's main entrance door, another large group of black soldiers went marching by. Willy looked over and told Jimmy, "Makes perfect sense, though, fighting for their own freedom. I can imagine a guy like our Amos fighting as a soldier. He'd be nearly invincible."

Smallpox Island

"Right! Now you're starting to get it," said Jimmy with a smile on his face.

Chapter Nine

April 7, 1865

After several days of sunny and warmer spring weather, it had begun to rain again. Jimmy and Will were continuing with their carpentry duties. Today they were working inside, fixing an area of flooring that had given way in the main hospital building. The floor had given way because of weak timber and heavy foot traffic. Then, a group of soldiers and civilian hospital workers came walking by with newspapers in their hands. They were all talking about some kind of big news in the St. Louis paper. Then, once again, they could hear another group excitedly chattering about something. Will looked over at Jimmy and said, "What's going on, Jim?"

"I don't know. Apparently, some kind of a buzz is starting to go around the post and we're out of the loop."

Jimmy tossed his hammer down and said, "I'll be right back." He rapidly secured a copy of the local paper and returned. After quickly reading the article, he spoke to Will. "Ah-ha! This is exactly as Colonel Kahn said. He knew this was going to happen."

"What do you mean, Jimmy?"

"Well, this paper confirms the same thing that Colonel Kahn had told me before we left the Alton Prison. It says here that General U.S. Grant and massive numbers of Union forces are moving against General Lee into Virginia. The article also mentions that the South is quickly running out of supplies, not only in Virginia but also everywhere else."

"Well, it would be good if this dreadful war ended before we left Benton Barracks to head home."

"Yes, it would, Willy, but I'll believe this if and when it actually happens."

"Me too," said Willy.

April 9, 1865
Lee Surrenders

The brothers continued to make repairs all around the post. Two days later, at about 1600 hours, a telegraph had apparently been received at the Benton Barracks Headquarters from Washington D.C. Shortly after that, a new rumor started rapidly spreading throughout the post. This time the rumor mill was churning out a great story. The end of the war was actually happening. The Benton Barracks commander, Colonel Bonneville, quickly confirmed the information and sent out couriers to all of the commanders on post. They delivered the following message to be shared with all of the troops:

"At Appomattox, Virginia at the Wilmer McLean home, Confederate Commanding General Robert E. Lee is currently in active discussions with Union General Ulysses S. Grant concerning the conditions of a Confederate surrender."

The buzz was everywhere, and the anticipation at Benton Barracks was so thick, you could cut it with a knife. Was it really going to happen? Could it really be over soon? Finally, at about 1800 hours, another message was sent out from the Headquarters. This one stated that an official Military Telegraph had been received from Washington. It was done. The war was over. At slightly before 1600 hours, Lee had surrendered to Grant at the Appomattox Court House. All of Benton Barracks company commanders were told by messengers to report to the Headquarters building. After a brief meeting, the company commanders quickly departed and assembled their troops into formations.

The following message was read to all of the troops:

"Lt. Gen. Ulysses S. Grant sent a telegraph on April 9, 1865, from Headquarters Army of the U.S. to Secretary of War Edwin M. Stanton in Washington that read: 'General Lee surrendered the Army of Northern Virginia this afternoon on terms proposed by myself. The accompanying additional correspondence will show the conditions fully.'"

> *Point of Historical Reference – Lee's surrender to Grant on April 9, 1865 marked the official ending of the Civil War. A total of over 620,000 men were killed from both the Union and the Confederacy.*

Huge roars and cheers came from troops all around the post at slightly different times while the messages were read. Sergeant Jimmy Logan and Corporal Will Logan worked directly for the post commander, so Colonel Boonville himself read the statement to their platoon. After the announcement, all of the troops cheered, hollered, and jumped up and down, grabbing each other in pure happiness. The long-enduring miserable war was over. After the statement, the commander added, "Listen up, boys. The war may be officially over, but the fighting probably is not done. The total surrender could take days or even weeks to be completed. So, I want all of my soldiers to stay vigilant until the total surrender has taken hold everywhere."

While everyone was whooping and hollering, Willy ran up and grabbed Jimmy by the shoulders. "April 13th is in four days!" he yelled at Jimmy amidst all of the noise and commotion. "We're still out of here, right?!"

"That's right, little brother! We're out of here, come hell or high water!"

"Ha!...I get it. High water! Like when we left Smallpox Island. Not funny!" Will said.

Will then ran over to the post infirmary to tell Belle that the war was over. She had already heard, so she gleefully met him about halfway there. He picked her up and spun her around and around as they both laughed and laughed.

Later, the brothers went back to their quarters and talked about their departure in four short days. Jimmy said, "I feel like we're getting ready to leave because of the end of the war announcement, but we're really getting ready because we are on official orders to take you home."

"I know. It's kinda strange. Have you decided how we are getting there? Horse, train, or boat?"

"Well, I'm glad you mentioned it," Jimmy answered quickly. "I want to talk to you about this. I went to Headquarters earlier tonight and asked about our travel home. They said many of the train tracks are out of commission. Blown up with dynamite by the Rebs. So, it could take weeks or even months to repair them all.

"They also said there are no Union horses available to give to us, and I sure don't have enough money to buy two horses. They also said that all available transport boats will now be tied up on priority missions taking Confederate prisoners back down toward their homes in the South. Everyone will be returning home after the war's end. Besides, I'd really rather not travel on a transport boat that's packed with sick and ill Confederate prisoners. I don't want to walk. It would take way too long.

"So…I was leaning toward taking our little skiff boat. It's our boat. It brought us here safely from Alton. The Mississippi River provides downstream travel all of the way, and now that the war's over, it might be the easiest way to get home."

Will didn't speak. He just looked at Jimmy while deep in thought. Jimmy continued, "To tell you the truth, Will, I was kinda leaning toward the boat anyway. We already know how to use it. Once we resupply it, it may be the easiest and best way. What do you think, Will?"

Willy just looked at Jimmy for about ten seconds. Then he finally answered, "Well, Jimmy. First of all, that was a lot of talkin'. Maybe you should run for office after this. But anyway, I think it's a pretty good plan. I was thinking basically the same thing. Even though I am a former Confederate, I don't think I want to be on a crowded transport with a bunch of sick Rebels. Besides, we live right on the river. We can take the skiff all of the way to our house. Hell yeah! I'm in! Let's do it!"

"Calm down, brother! We still have three more days and a wake-up."

"I'm good. I'm calm. I'm just glad this damn forsaken, son of a bitchen' war is going to finally be over."

Jimmy laughed. "Me too, Willy.... Me too!"

April 13, 1865

Three days later, after a good final day of carpentry work, the brothers turned in their tools to the quartermaster. That evening, Jimmy went to the Headquarters and sent a telegraph to Colonel Kahn notifying him that they were departing in the morning. Jimmy also acquired a flatbed wagon and they went back and forth preparing their little boat. After pulling the boat back down to the water, they checked it for seaworthiness and stocked it with some supplies to prepare it for travel. Jimmy then showed the dock guards his orders and asked them to keep a close eye on the skiff until their departure the next morning.

That evening, Willy spent a good amount of time visiting Belle since he wasn't sure when they would see each other again. They took another walk in the countryside, but Willy had to cut it short because he was getting ready to leave. "I don't want Jimmy to get too mad at me. He gets a little squirrely when it comes to military orders, and we have to get up early to get out of here. It's a long river trip to get home, so we don't have time to lollygag."

As they stood at Belle's door, Willy was in the middle of telling her goodbye when she said, "Wait!" and hurriedly ran into her quarters. She emerged with a quill pen and some paper so they could exchange addresses.

After they did so, Willy said, "Okay, Belle. We'll write to each other as soon as possible. Once you're released, I'll come up here to take you down to New Madrid, right?"

"Yes," Belle said. "I'll come to see you in New Madrid, but after that, I may have to move on. I have to help people. I'm a nurse, Willy. It's my calling."

"I know that, and I understand."

Belle continued, "There's a Union hospital in Nashville, Tennessee that needs help. I might go there, or I've also been asked to work right here in St. Louis. A group called the United States Christian Commission needs help. They assist Army soldiers as they transition from the military back into civilian life."

"That sounds like a great idea," said Willy. "Soldiers can use help switching from military mode to civilian mode. It's not as easy as people think it is. I have a good friend named Caleb who's been dealing with his transition from military to civilian life for over ten years. It's probably even harder for soldiers who have been seriously injured."

"That's absolutely true," said Belle. "I'm glad you think that way."

"Belle, as far as our future," said Willy, "I'm a prisoner on parole right now, so I have orders to return home. I have no choice. I can't stay here with you even though I would like to."

"I understand, Will. I think our relationship is headed somewhere special, but we can't rush it right now. Let's just see what happens," said Belle.

"Yes," said Willy. "If things go right, I have a feeling that we are going to find a way to be close to each other."

"So do I, Will. I haven't told you before, but I do love you."

"I love you too, Belle."

They kissed and held each other close while standing at the door to Belle's quarters.

April 14, 1865, 0700 hours
Going Home

Early the next morning, Jim and Willy sat at breakfast. Everyone at the Chow Hall was still laughing and joking because the war was really going to be over. "Better eat and drink as much as you can. We have a way to go," Jimmy told Will. "Wait a minute, Will. Did you say goodbye to Belle? Because we don't have a lot of time this morning."

"I already did that last night. We even have each other's addresses."

Smallpox Island

"Good. She's a good person. You'd have to look a very long time to find a woman as special as she is," said Jimmy.

"Right, I know that. She's one of a kind. I can't believe that I've actually met her and know her."

"I agree…she's definitely too good for you."

"Shut up, asshole," said Willy as he threw a piece of biscuit at Jimmy.

"So, how long do you think it will take us to get home, brother?"

"Well, I got a couple of maps from Corporal Moore at HQ. I think New Madrid is about 170 miles or so. It's been more than a week since we've traveled during the flood, so the river has calmed down quite a bit. There'll be a lot fewer trees and debris, but we can't just coast. We have to row to make good time. If we travel at six miles an hour, that would mean about twenty-eight hours of pure travel. That doesn't include any stops to rest or sleep. I'd say three days or so if we travel about ten hours per day. That doesn't include any extra stops because of weather or any other potential problems. It could take a little more or a little less."

"Potential problems?" said Will.

"Yeah, like maybe some pissed off Confederates taking potshots at us, or we get a leak in the boat. Hell, I don't know…anything."

"I don't care," Will answered. "I'll walk to New Madrid if I have to. I'm ready to be home again. It's been two and a half years."

"Agreed. After we eat, I still have the flatbed wagon, so we can finish loading up our gear. Then, after we're totally ready, I have to go to HQ and the Billeting Office to sign out of our room and return our linens. Then, we can finally get out of here."

"Great. Let's get moving!"

They loaded up on food and coffee and went out to load the horse-drawn wagon. After throwing their bags onto the wagon, they rode across Benton Barracks one last time. Jimmy signed them out at HQ and with the Billeting NCO. Then, just as they were pulling away in the wagon, the Headquarters clerk, Corporal Moore, flung the door open and yelled, "Wait, Sergeant Logan!"

"Oh boy, what can it be now?" Jimmy said.

Will added, "I hope whatever it is, it doesn't stop us from leaving."

Jimmy stopped the wagon and ran back into the Headquarters building. "What is it, Moore?"

"You got a telegraph from Colonel Kahn, commander of the Alton Federal Prison!" He handed it to Jimmy.

It stated:

"From Colonel Kahn, Commander, Alton Federal Prison to Sergeant James Logan: Message received. Depart on your mission on 14 April 1886 as reported. Per the end of hostilities, you will be officially discharged on 30 April 1866. Orders and remuneration will follow to your home of record.

Signed, Colonel Kahn, Alton Federal Prison."

Jimmy read it and started laughing. "Thanks! Please send a one-word message back stating, 'Received!'"

"Will do, Sergeant."

Jimmy ran out of the building and jumped onto the wagon. They headed down to the river.

"Well, what was it?" Will asked.

Smiling from ear to ear, Jimmy said, "It was a telegraph from Colonel Kahn. I'm out of the Army after we get home! I don't even have to go back! Orders will follow."

"Holy crap. Are you the luckiest son of a bitch or what!!" Will yelled.

"*What* did you say?"

"Oops, I meant son of a gun."

Jimmy took his elbow and jabbed it hard into Willy's shoulder. He kept laughing nearly all of the way to the river. It was about a

Smallpox Island

ten-minute ride, and near the end, Will looked over toward the Gratiot Street Prison for one last time. Once at the dock, they loaded and prepped the boat for travel.

It had rained, so they had to pull the skiff back out of the water, unload it, and tip it over to get all of the water out of it. Then, they pulled the boat back down into the water at the dock and reloaded their supplies. Jimmy told the guards, "I'm Sergeant Logan. This wagon and horse team belong to Headquarters Benton Barracks. Can you please take it back to HQ?"

"Yes, Sergeant," said the dock guard with a smile on his face. "We know who you are. We'll take care of it. We work for them as well so it won't be a problem. Be careful on your way down to New Madrid."

They both looked over at the guard, wondering how he apparently knew all about their mission.

"Thank you, Private," Jimmy told him.

They started to shove off and the other guard, a big fellow whom they had not spoken to, yelled, "Stop!!" He hurriedly started walking over to their little boat with an apparent frown on his face. The guard looked to be about six-foot-four and at least three hundred pounds. His rifle was pointed in their general direction. Willy said, "What the hell is going on?"

"I don't know," Jimmy said. The soldier walked up and put one foot down into their boat, essentially stopping them from leaving. Both brothers looked up at the soldier, a bit shocked as they wondered what had gone wrong. Finally, the soldier spoke to them.

"I wanted to tell you both...congratulations! I'm glad this hellish war is over. I have a brother that was fighting for the Rebels...he didn't make it.... He actually died at Alton Prison."

The guard then looked directly at Will as the boat bounced up and down in the river. "Did you know anyone named George Newsome over at the Alton Prison?" After a short pause, Willy shook his head. "No. I don't think so. No, I didn't."

"Well, I'm glad you made it out of there alive. Godspeed, boys." Then, the guard shook both of their hands. "Won't be long, and I'll be right behind ya. I live down in Cape Girardeau!"

"That's great. Thanks, Newsome!" said Willy with a nervous smile on his face.

The soldier nodded and grinned at them both, removed his foot, and helped them shove off. Willy's hands were shaking and he had broken into a sweat. He thought something bad was about to happen, but instead, something good happened. Apparently, a lot of people knew not only about their mission but also about their entire situation.

They shoved off and started heading down the river. Willy took the oars first and started rowing. The brothers took in the sights of the river and spoke very little for thirty minutes or so. Since they were floating and rowing along with the river's southbound current, it immediately felt like they were making good time. The two men quickly transitioned back into the groove of maneuvering their little boat. They kept to the west side of the river, not too far from the shoreline. The brothers automatically stayed alert for debris, although there seemed to be a lot less of it. The river had calmed down a lot in the two weeks since the flood emergency.

Even though it had rained recently, the weather was on their side today. They had mostly sunny skies and relatively warm temperatures. Jimmy finally spoke up as a huge transport came pushing loudly up the river right near them, "Hug the side, Willy. These big-ass boats could plow us over and barely notice it."

"Yup, I'm watching. I was just thinkin' the same thing," said Willy. "They seem to come up on us quickly because the current tries to drag us toward the middle, taking us right toward them."

"Right. Hey, look, Willy!"

"What?"

Smallpox Island

"See that building way up on that bluff to the right?"

"Yes."

"That's the Jefferson Barracks Headquarters building. I joined the Army there."

"You signed up right there?"

"Well, not that exact building, but right near there. Grant and Sherman served there too. It's a great Army post."

"Okay, good. Do we need to stop there?"

"Nope. No way! Just keep on rowing, brother."

They waved at a couple of Union guards who were standing on the bank down by the river. Willy then spoke, "You know, that big dock guard back at St. Louis scared the crap out of me."

"Ha! Yeah, that was kind of funny," answered Jimmy. "I wonder how these people know so much about us."

"Don't know," said Willy, "but people sure like to scuttlebutt about what's goin' on. They like to share interesting stories involving other people.

"Yep, the scuttlebutt really seems to get around, I guess."

"Well, everybody's got a story," said Willy, "and Jimmy, I don't think ours is quite over yet."

"Me neither."

After about an hour, they switched and Jimmy had started rowing. Suddenly, the brothers noticed that another strong current was dragging them toward the middle of the channel. It was similar to the current at the Great Confluence, but they could not see a cause for it. Jimmy fought the current and had some difficulty getting back to the side of the river. "Sheesh, I hope that doesn't happen when there is a paddlewheel boat coming," said Willy.

"Right," Jimmy added. "That was crazy. Let's just keep rowing and watch out for it."

About two hours later, the strong current started pulling them toward the center of the river again. It was happening again and

Jimmy was at the oars. The channel was not as wide at this point, and a large steamboat was coming right down the center of the river!

"Son of a bitch!!" Jimmy yelled. "I knew this would happen!" He rowed feverishly as the current kept dragging them toward the middle of the channel. The steamship captain saw them and hit his loud steam horn. "Waaaaaaaaaah!!"

"Row harder!!" yelled Willy. "I am! I am!" The steamboat approached closer as the brothers struggled to stop their little skiff from heading directly in front of the massive transport. Willy reached down into the water and was frantically rowing with his arm.

They finally seemed to get the skiff under control, but by that time, they were directly in front of the steamboat. "What do we do? Jump?" Will yelled.

"No, not yet. Hold on!" About thirty feet before the ship was going to hit them, the giant paddlewheel stopped. It just stopped. Right on a dime. The captain walked up to the front of the boat and cursed the brothers. He was a sharp-dressed riverboat captain with a large handlebar mustache. "What in the hell is wrong with you?!" The captain yelled.

Jimmy answered, "We were caught up in the current. We couldn't get out of the way!"

"Yep! I figured that. Not the first time that's happened. But it *is* the first time it's happened with two Union soldiers in a skiff."

The two boats peacefully floated down the center of the river together. The skiff had its oars up, and the steamship was on idle. The captain continued, "You're really lucky I'm going upstream. I can stop this boat on a dime when I'm headed upstream. Going downstream, I would have plowed you over. I wouldn't have been able to stop. Right now, we're floating downstream together with the current. Row over here, boys!" It was a very strange change of feelings. The mood had gone from a panicked feeling of immediate doom to a nearly calm feeling of relative safety and peace.

The captain guided the brothers and their little boat to the side of the large transport. "Crew, tie up with this little boat! We're going to take it over toward the shore." The crew members quickly threw the brothers a rope. They pulled the skiff over and tied it to the side of the larger boat. The captain then fired up the giant paddlewheel and slowly directed it over to the western side of the river.

After they arrived at the side of the river, the captain came over and talked to them. "Okay, there you go! Good luck, boys. Now listen, there are more currents just like that up ahead. Where are you going?"

"New Madrid."

"Okay, let's see... There's big currents just before and just after Cape Girardeau, then the next big one is right in the middle of the huge zigzag right before New Madrid. So, try to stay above water, boys."

"Will do, sir! Thanks!!" said Willy, yelling very loudly. He yelled so loudly that Jimmy immediately looked over at him. He noticed that Willy was visibly shaking. Willy quickly threw the rope back to the crew and Jimmy rowed their boat over toward the side of the river.

As they moved on and started to make progress down the river, it became apparent that the steamboat ordeal had shaken Willy up. He became very quiet and started looking all around them as Jimmy rowed. Finally, he looked over at Jimmy and said, "Listen, I'm sorry, brother, but I need a small break. I need to get out of this boat. I need to calm down."

Jimmy answered, "Okay, will do. What's up, brother? Are you okay? What's wrong?"

"I'm getting really shaky and a little jumpy. It feels like I'm super alert...too alert. I was really jumpy like this right after the Battle of Iuka, and I don't want to feel like that again. Don't really know why. I saw a lot of serious things. Explosions...people killed right in front of me...blood everywhere. Dead soldiers missing arms...legs...heads...whatever. I don't want to feel like that. Not now. This is not what that is. This is way too important for me to mess up."

"Understood, Willy. You're safe and I'm with you. Let's pull over right here. We'll get outta this boat, take a break, and get something to eat. You're gonna be okay."

"Good. Thanks, Jim."

They pulled up on a small sandbar that was in front of a large grove of trees. Jimmy jumped out and nearly pulled the entire boat out of the water. "Take it easy, Jimmy. Don't pull the dang boat apart."

Jimmy smiled and answered, "I had a good breakfast."

They grabbed some provisions and then covered up the boat with a couple of fallen tree limbs. Then, they walked into the wood line to find a good place to sit down, relax, and eat. After about twenty feet, they found a clearing. Just like before, it appeared that others had been there before them. The grass was matted down, parts of the area were cleared, and there were again remnants of a previous fire. The brothers sat down to a meal of biscuits, jerky, and water. Jimmy started eating and mentioned, "Looks like a lot of people frequent this river. I wonder who they all are. What they're like. Are they families, convicts, soldiers like us, or just travelers?"

"I don't know and I don't really care," said Willy. "As long as they are friendly and don't point a gun at us, I'm okay with 'em."

The boys had literally grown up on the edge of the river, and they had nearly always had good experiences with the people traveling on it. Will started chuckling. "The only bad thing I can remember from the river is when that one river rat fella snuck up on our chicken coup and tried to run off with one of our chickens."

Smallpox Island

Jimmy answered, laughing, "Yeah, that was great. Amos lit him up on his backside with a load of salt shot."

"I never saw a person run so fast!" said Willy.

The boys broke into uncontrolled laughter for nearly a whole minute. Partially because of the Amos story and partially because of the tension from the happenings of the day.

"Woooo!" Will said. "I feel better." Let's get back on the boat. New Madrid ain't gonna come to us."

"That's so true. Let's load up and cut through some water."

With that, the brothers loaded back into the skiff and were off again, moving down the river. They both seemed to be a bit more relaxed while still keenly aware of their surroundings. They made good time for the next several hours as they began to master the river again. After a few more close calls with the Mississippi current, they finally made it to St. Genevieve. They pulled over to the side of the river and Jimmy looked at a military map that he had been using since they departed. The sun was starting to get lower in the sky. He told Will, "Let's go downstream for a while and set up camp somewhere. We should try to go for at least another hour so that we can be about one-third of the way home."

"Okay. Aye aye, Captain Sergeant Logan!" yelled Willy (obviously feeling a lot better). "Shut up, Reb boy!"

"That's Corporal Reb Boy to you, Captain Sergeant!"

They both now moved down the river with small grins on their faces.

They went downstream about seven miles and found a large wooded island off to the left of the main channel. "Wadda you think, Will?" said Jimmy as he looked at the map. "Map says this is called "Liberty Island."

"Sounds good to me. I really like the name."

They pulled up to shore in a seemingly inconspicuous area and pulled the boat up through the sand. They both immediately noticed footprints in the sand. "We're not alone," said Will, "What do you want to do? I'm exhausted."

"Well, we have nothing to hide. We're legitimate. I have a gun and a guitar. If they're not friendly, I can shoot 'em, and if they are friendly, I can play guitar for them."

"Great idea. We're staying," said Will with a cautious smile on his face.

Chapter Ten

April 14, 1865, 8 p.m. Island Alliance

They pulled the boat up into the wood line and threw a couple of tree limbs on it. Then they grabbed a few supplies and walked toward the center of the island, looking for a good place to bivouac. Quickly, they realized that they were walking on a path. Then, they heard talking and laughing coming from the interior of the island. Willy looked at Jimmy. "What do you wanna do?"

"Just keep walking. Let's see what's up with all of this."

Then to their surprise, a tall, slim man came walking down the path right toward them with a shotgun slung over his shoulder. "Stand fast," Jimmy said to Will. The man was in decent, non-tattered clothing. He didn't look like a ne'er-do-well or a down-and-out drifter. He looked like any regular guy walking through the streets of New Madrid, St. Louis, or Alton. The man looked right at them. He nodded and smiled, saying, "Hi, how are ya?" He then kept walking right by them. Right after that, they heard uproarious laughter coming from up ahead.

"What the hell is going on here?" Will said. They went farther and suddenly they were at the edge of a large clearing that appeared to be right in the middle of the island.

In the direct center of the clearing was a massive fire with about ten people sitting near it. Jimmy assessed the situation. He counted five black people and five white people. Two of the white people appeared to be uniformed Confederate soldiers. "Come on," said Jimmy. They walked into the clearing. As they approached, the entire group immediately stopped talking and looked over at them. Jimmy was wearing his blue Union soldier uniform, and Will was wearing a similar blue outfit without any military markings.

One of the men in the group stood up, smiled, and spoke first. "Well, hello and welcome, soldiers. I'm Thaddeus Walker and I'm a musician. The war is over, so come on in and join the party. At last tally, we're drinking apple cider, beer, whiskey, tea, water, and coffee. You're welcome to sit and join us in a drink to peace." Thaddeus Walker was dressed in classy attire and he wore a vest and a railroad cap. He was clean shaven and looked to be in his forties or early fifties.

"Well, okay," said Jimmy.

Walker continued, "We don't have a lot of food flowing yet, but it's on the way. My friend, Mr. Benton, went to get a whole mess of rabbits he killed today on the mainland."

Jimmy answered, "I'm Sergeant Logan and this is my brother, Will."

"Good to meet cha! Have a seat. Relax and tell us more about yourself if you wish. There are no enemies here," said Walker as he looked over at the Confederate soldiers. "Our guards are down and our cups are up." With that, the group raised their cups and took a drink of whatever they were drinking.

"Okay, great, but what are all of you doing here in the middle of this river island?" asked Jimmy.

"Glad you asked," said Walker. "We are all travelers and we were all strangers to each other before our chance meeting here on Liberty Island. I've unofficially named our group the 'Island Alliance.' We are a few soldiers, some former slaves, a couple of farmers, a musician, and a merchant cook. We are mostly heading north for our own reasons that you could probably guess. We've all found this island at slightly different times and we've generally found it to be a safe and decent refuge while the perennial smoke of war clears and the high emotions of the times calm down a bit." Thaddeus Walker was a smooth talker, but he appeared to be sincere.

Walker then paused and looked seriously at the brothers. "We are all friends here. Even if it's only for a short while. If you don't want to be friends with our alliance, I will respectfully ask you to move on. We may have plenty of room here, but we have no room for petty quarrels, revenge, bad attitudes, retribution, or vindictive ways. Today, Liberty Island is an island of peace."

"Sounds good to me," Jimmy answered.

Willy added, "We're not interested in fighting and war. We're just trying to get home."

"Great! Where's home?"

"New Madrid, Missouri."

"Ah yes, that's about two days downstream. A nice easy trip. As I mentioned, most of us are heading north. It takes much longer to get anywhere heading upstream. There's also been a lot of rain up north."

"We know," said Will.

Jimmy added, "Listen, we have to get our gear and set up a place to sleep tonight."

"Great. You can bivouac and bed down in this area if you like. We will hopefully have a good fire burning through the night. Our fire can't be seen from the mainland or the river."

"Sounds good. Okay, we'll be back." The brothers headed back to their boat to get their gear.

On the way back to the skiff, they passed the same tall fellow that they had passed earlier. This time, the tall, slim man was carrying several rabbits and squirrels. They were hanging on a long stick and had already been cleaned and gutted. Again, he spoke in a friendly tone to them, "Hey, fellas, are you coming back?"

"Yep," said Willy. "We'll see you in a few."

"Great! That's outstanding," said the man. "We'll have some vittles cooked up soon and you can join us."

"Sounds good," said Jimmy.

The brothers returned to their boat and pulled it up a little further into the woods. As they were grabbing their gear, Jimmy said, "I don't know about all of this. I think it's almost too good to be true."

"I don't," said Will as he sat down on the side of the boat. "I think people are tired of war and most folks don't have a lot of money for a train or a steamboat trip. I also think some people are trying to get to a place where they can be safe and happy. Everybody's had enough of death, and sickness, and sadness. I know I've had enough."

"I know, brother. How's the shingles?" said Jimmy as he grabbed his personal bag with the neck of his guitar sticking out of the top.

"Hurts like hell."

"Hang in there, brother. Hey, do you still have your harmonica?" Jimmy asked.

"In my back pocket." Will grabbed his little personal bag and they both grabbed one side of the supply box from the boat.

As they walked back with their supplies, Will asked, "What do we have to drink with us? Those people are having a party."

"Well, let me think. We have some water and dried tea and coffee."

"Well, we might have to break it out."

"Sounds good to me, Willy. Sounds real good. You know, it feels like we haven't really had much time to celebrate the end of the war."

Willy answered, "Well, Jimmy, it looks like we may be fixin' to celebrate right now."

When the brothers arrived back at the large clearing, Thaddeus Walker was hard at work clearing a spot for them and the tall, slim man was prepping his rabbits and squirrels to cook on the fire. "Hey, boys, how about this area?" Walker said. "I don't see any bugs and there are some tree limbs above to keep some of the rain or dew from hitting you too awful hard. If you don't like it, you can sure pick another area. A soldier is better at this stuff than I am anyway."

"This will do just fine," said Jimmy. The brothers sat down their supply box and went to work. They finished clearing the area and started setting up their bivouac. Both had learned a lot about setting up a bivouac in their military duties, so they were quite adept at preparing their area.

They quickly and strategically moved some brush around, so they could see or hear anyone approaching. They also made sure that any approaching person could not see them. Then, they put up their leaning tent half and gathered large grasses for bedding. They even used their boots to dig a small ditch for drainage in the case of rain. The others sitting around the fire watched in awed amazement as the brothers moved like a finely tuned machine. "Wow...these guys really know what they're doing," one of them said. "Yeah, I think I need to improve my area."

"Me too!" another one said. Then several other members of the group jumped up and started fixing up their areas. They all kept looking over at the brother's area as a guide, even digging little trenches to drain any water away.

After about fifteen minutes, the brothers had finished setting up their area. "What do you say we go find some firewood?" said Jimmy.

"Sounds good."

"Listen, folks," Jimmy told the group. "We're going to go get some wood for the big fire. Also, we might make a little side fire over there by our bivouac."

"Okay then, super soldiers," Thaddeus Walker said, smiling. "You guys need to try to pull your load around here. Maybe dig a mote and build a watchtower before dinner if you can."

The whole group laughed as the brothers walked off into the woods. Willy grinned and waved his arm at them while they walked away. After about a half-hour, there was a giant pile of wood next to the big fire. The slim man, Mr. Benton, was cooking several rabbits and squirrels. He had them turning on sticks over the fire.

Finally, the brothers sat down by the fire as the others drifted in and out of its circle of heat. "Well, I guess introductions are in order," said Walker. "So, I'll go first. I'm Thaddeus Walker and I come from Mississippi. I do some acting, but primarily I'm a musician. I played in the Southern Community Band for two years. We played at battles and other events all around the South. We were paid salaries and everything, just like a soldier. But things got really slim and they stopped paying us about six months ago. Since then, I've been working my way north to find work. I play all kinds of instruments, but I only have a fiddle and a banjo with me. I'm headed up to Davenport, Iowa. My uncle has nearly a hundred acres up there about twenty miles west of Davenport. He's getting older and he says that he needs help with his farm."

Thaddeus Walker then looked over at the black man sitting by the fire with his wife and daughter. After a quiet period, the black man spoke up.

"Well, I'm Charles Douglass. This is my wife, Tanna. I got two boys back there sleeping. Robert and James. One girl right here name a Georgia. We from Memphis, Tennessee. Broke off from the master after he was shot dead by robbers. Didn't see no reason to stay. So, we been working our way up north by walkin' and raft… or any way we could muster."

Charles was a well-built black man. He stood about six feet tall and he wore brown pants and shirt with a small straw hat. His wife Tanna wore a pale-yellow dress and a matching headscarf. He continued, "Got here by foot and crossed over to the island by raft about three days ago. Mr. Walker came yesterday and told us about the end of the war. Now, we plannin' on leaving in a few days with Mr. Walker. He's gonna help us out."

"Your damn right I am," said Thaddeus Walker. "You got a real nice family. Here's what we got. As I mentioned, my uncle has near a hundred acres about twenty miles west of Davenport, Iowa and he needs help with his farm. He's wrote me about it several times now. Says he's gonna sell me half of his acres for five dollars if I help him out. At least that's what he said. He also wants me to bring more workers if I can. So, I need help giving him help. I recently spoke with Charles and his boys about helpin' me to help him. They already have extensive skills from farming down in Memphis. We need the work and he needs workers. It's a perfect matchup."

Walker continued, "So, if it all works out as planned, we're going to go to work in Iowa. If I do get some acreage, I plan to sell a nice hunk of it to Mr. Charles Douglass for one dollar. That's called 'passing it on,' you know." Walker looked over with a smile and saluted Charles Douglass sitting with his wife, daughter, and two teen boys that had come up to the fire. "I've talked enough. Okay, who's next?"

Then, the slim man spoke up as he was adjusting the meats on their sticks, "Well, I'm Thomas Benton. I'm from Lacrosse, Wisconsin. I'm a merchant and a civilian cook. I was working in Arkansas and lower Missouri supplying food to the troops. Primarily Confederate troops, but also some Union troops. Like Thaddeus said, things have been getting tough and cash pay has been getting down to either thin or none. So, right now, I'm heading home…and I'm mighty glad this good for nothing war is over." Benton was about six-foot-four. He was well dressed with a flat brimmed hat, a white shirt, and a gray vest. The slim man sported long sideburns and wore no beard.

Benton scanned the group for the next person. Then, the farmer spoke up. "Well, I'm Charles Mason and this is my son, Thomas. My wife died of typhoid, I lost my farm, and we're heading north to restart. We've been here about four days. That's all I feel like saying. I ain't really much for talkin'." Charles Mason looked to be around fifty years old and his son, Thomas, looked to be about sixteen years old. They wore non-tattered clothes that were dingy from days of rough traveling.

"That's fine," said Thaddeus Walker. "You don't have to even talk. As long as you agree to be peaceful here, and you have already done that."

Lastly, Walker looked over and nodded at the two remaining young men. They were Confederate soldiers in uniform and appeared to be less than twenty years old. "Yes, sir. Well, as you can see, we're Confederate soldiers. I'm Beau and this is Hector. We're done with it all and we lost. So, now we're going home to Festus, Missouri. We're damn near broke. Don't really wanna say much of nothin' else. We ain't here for no trouble and we sure ain't fixin' to hurt nobody."

Beau then looked directly toward the black family. He nodded at them with a faint smile. Then he looked at Jimmy and Willy. Then at Mr. Walker. "The soldiers have agreed to our island rules," Thaddeus Walker said, smiling, "and they are a welcomed part of our temporary little community. Is it time to eat something, Mr. Benton?"

"Indeed it is, Mr. Walker," Benton replied.

Mr. Benton started passing out pieces of rabbit and Walker started sharing drink from a large jug. Willy waved the rabbit off and went back to their bivouac for a moment. He quickly returned with several pieces of jerky, some hardtack, and a small jug of water to share. The group sat around sharing food, drink, and some stories for the next hour or so. "Mr. Walker," said Jimmy, "your jug of fine homemade moonshine tastes very, very good."

"Thank you, please enjoy!" Jimmy then passed the jug over to Willy and it continued around the group. Tanna Douglass and the children were all drinking tea, and nearly everyone else had a cup of something in their hand. At one point, Thaddeus Walker spoke up to the group. "Attention! I'd like to make a special toast. "To the war's end and to safe travels." They all raised their containers and repeated, "To the war's end and to safe travels for all!"

The next thing they knew, it was dark, but they hardly noticed because of the large fire. Just as it appeared that the group was starting to wrap things up, Thaddeus Walker pulled out his banjo and started playing a quiet little tune that sounded similar to "Dixie Land." Not long after that, Will pulled out his harmonica and slowly started joining in. Mr. Benton, the tall, slim man, was next as he grabbed Walker's fiddle. They all started playing along, with each one following the other's lead.

"Jimmy, go get your guitar," said Willy.

"Naa."

"You better!"

"What?!"

"Are you too good to play with us?"

"No."

"Good. Then go and get it. You're probably the best player here. Come on, let's have some fun. We deserve it."

"Okay, I'll be right back."

Jimmy grabbed his guitar and after some tuning, he was playing right along with the others. Then, suddenly, he took off with some improvised lead playing that made him stand out from the others. They all stopped playing and looked at Jimmy in astonishment. "Wow, your good, boy. Do you have a song that you'd like to play for us or with us?" said Mr. Walker.

"Well, sure. I have a couple. They aren't the best, but I like them."

"Okay, let's work on 'em and play them out." Jimmy went to his bivouac and pulled a book out of his bag. He opened it to a specific page. "I try to write down my lyrics and chords so I don't forget them."

"Smart. I have a music book too," said Walker. After about fifteen minutes of practicing Jimmy's song, the group was ready. Jimmy started playing the tune and they all joined in.

Jimmy announced the song. "Okay, here we go. This is called "Standing on the Rock." Jimmy strummed his guitar rhythmically and sang the song. It was an upbeat, good ol' timey country type song. It had a positive message with a cheerful mood and tempo. At one point, Hector, the rebel soldier, jumped up and shouted, "Yahoo!!" Then the soldiers, the farmers, Charles Douglass, and his sons all got up and started dancing and jumping around. By the tune's end, nearly everyone was smiling and dancing around with each other. It was a magical moment that reminded the brothers of the good ol' days of making music with their father. At the song's ending, the whole group was happy and laughing. It was as if the Island Alliance had finally loosened up enough to enjoy the end of the war. Even if it was with their new but temporary friends.

Since the entire group seemed to enjoy the first song, Mr. Walker said, "Hey, let's play some more. We got a whole band here with considerable skills. Does anybody else have a song? We can try to work it out and play it." One of the Confederate soldiers, Beau, asked, "Is it okay to play, 'I Wish I Was in Dixie'?"

"Well, hell yes," said Walker.

"It's more than okay with me," said Jimmy. "I heard that President Lincoln likes the song and plays it around the White House."

"Really?" said Beau.

"Yep. Let's work it out and then we'll play it. If we play it, can one of you guys sing it?"

"Sure. I can't sing, but Hector here sure can."
"Hector quickly looked at him with a smirk. "What, me?"
"Yes. I know you know the words."
"Well... Okay."

The band moved off to the side of the group and spent about five minutes getting ready for the song. The tall, slim man, Mr. Benton, and Thaddeus Walker were ready to play the song right away as they had obviously played it hundreds of times. Mr. Walker then pulled a book out of his bag and opened it to a certain page. Handing it to Hector, he said, "Here are the lyrics and chords to 'Dixie,' Hector."

"Thanks, but I don't think I'll need them."

Jimmy announced the song. "Okay, this is called, 'I Wish I Was in Dixie.' The fiddler, Mr. Benton, started it out and Hector joined right in.

"I Wish I Was in Dixie" – 1859 – Daniel Decatur Emmett

Oh, I wish I was in the land of cotton,
Old times there are not forgotten
Look away! Look away!
Look away! Dixie Land
In Dixie Land where I was born in,
Early on one frosty mornin'
Look away! Look away! Look away! Dixie Land

Chorus
Oh, I wish I was in Dixie,
Hooray! Hooray!
In Dixie Land I'll take my stand,
To live and die in Dixie
Away, away, away down south in Dixie,
Away, away, away down south in Dixie

Old Missus marry Will, the weaver
William was a gay deceiver
Look away! Look away! Look away! Dixie Land

But when he put his arm around her
He smiled as fierce as a forty-pounder
Look away! Look away! Look away! Dixie Land
Chorus
(SONG CONTINUES UNTIL ITS ENDING)

The island band played as Hector sang the song (with Walker's book in hand). Everybody was either nodding their head or slapping on their leg or both. Mr. Douglass's family seemed to particularly enjoy the song as much or even more than anyone else. Jimmy noticed this and thought to himself, *Perhaps that's because they were no longer going to be living as slaves in Dixie Land.* However, he didn't ask because he didn't want to spoil the moment.

The unlikely Island Alliance sat around eating food and drinking apple cider, beer, whiskey, tea, water, or coffee for the next couple of hours. They restocked the fire and continued to play music off and on. The island band played their favorite tunes and sometimes even made up the songs as they went along.

As the evening waned, a few folks started branching off to their personal areas to get things ready for bed. Then, Jimmy waved over to Charles Douglass and motioned for him to come over.

"Hi, Charles. Do you know how to read?"

"Yes, sir," answered Charles. "The old master had me learn to read years ago. I helped him with supply orders and such for the house. Really for the whole plantation. Even though he told me not to, I've been a learnin' my boys. Gonna take a lot more than muscle to make it in the new future. Gonna take brains."

"That's really good, Charles. Teach your boys and your daughter how to read. Then try to get 'em to school too! You can do that up north where you're headed."

"Yes, sir. That's my plan."

"Good. Listen, do you like to sing?"

"Yes, sir."

"Okay then, would you like to look through my songbook to find a song to sing...or do you have a song that you already know?"

"Well, I do have a song, sir. Been singin' it for years. Learned it from my uncle...my daddy's brother. It's called, 'Nobody Knows the Trouble I've Seen.'"

"I know that song. You can sing that song, Charles?"

"Yes, I can."

"That's a great song!" Jimmy gathered the island band back together. They worked on Charles Douglass's song for about five minutes and they were ready to go.

"Okay, listen up, everyone," said Jimmy. "Charles is going to sing 'Nobody Knows the Trouble I've Seen.' Quickly, there was a chatter in the group as Charles started getting ready to sing. His whole family moved up, anticipating the song that they had undoubtedly heard before.

"Nobody Knows the Trouble I've Seen" - 1867 - Traditional - Harry Thacker Burleigh

Nobody knows the trouble I've been through
Nobody knows my sorrow
Nobody knows the trouble I've seen
Glory hallelujah!
Sometimes I'm up, sometimes I'm down
Oh, yes, Lord
Sometimes I'm almost to the ground
Oh, yes, Lord

Although you see me going 'long so
Oh, yes, Lord
I have my trials here below
Oh, yes, Lord
If you get there before I do
Oh, yes, Lord
Tell all-a my friends I'm coming to Heaven!
Oh, yes, Lord
(SONG'S ENDING)

During the song, there was a lot of swaying and head nodding. At the end of the tune, nearly everyone jumped up and clapped. Charles' wife, Tanna, jumped up and yelled, "That was my husband singin' that song!"

"Thank you, darlin'!" The Island Alliance restocked the fire and chatted with each other as the musicians played more of their favorite tunes. The musicians even made up some music that seemed to fit with the evening.

At about 11 p.m., the group was starting to get tired. Mr. Walker mentioned, "Hey folks. You know after tomorrow morning, our unlikely 'Island Alliance' may not see each other again."

"Well, what should we do about that?" said Mr. Benton.

Then Willy spoke up. "Jimmy, why don't we write down everyone's name in your book and also in Walker's book?"

"Sure. That sounds like a great idea," said Walker. "Also, write down the town that you're planning to settle in."

Jimmy paused a moment and looked around at everyone in the group with a broad smile on his face. "Maybe we can even get this alliance back together someday and play some more music."

"That would be mighty good, Sergeant Logan," said Charles Douglass, "I really liked all the playin' and singin' tonight. Reminds me of when I was a boy singin' with my daddy."

"Good, but call me Jimmy."

"It's agreed then," Mr. Walker said. "We'll all make entries in Jimmy's book and in my book. We'll promise to write and maybe even get our island band back together someday." He looked at the Logan brothers. "I know the Logans' names and their town of New Madrid already, so I'll write them down first." They passed the book around and everyone entered their names and destinations. Several added little comments such as "Remember the Island Alliance" or "The war is finally over."

Soon after making their entries into the books, everyone started going back to their sleeping areas. Jimmy and Will started up a small bivouac fire near their area and they also added more wood to the big fire in the middle of the group. Exhausted, the entire group went to sleep in less than half an hour. The stars shined brightly in the sky and a chorus of grasshoppers, crickets, and frogs chirped away as if singing a continuous lullaby to the sleepy members of the Island Alliance.

Chapter Eleven

April 15, 1865

The following day was a Thursday. There was a lot of dew on the ground, but thankfully, it had not rained. Several people in the group started stirring just before dawn. At about 7 a.m., the brothers went off to gather wood. Then, they stoked up the big center fire that had burnt down to a bunch of hot embers. At about 7:30, they suddenly heard church bells ringing far in the distance. Oddly, the bells did not stop ringing.

"What the heck is going on?" said Will.

"I don't know," said Jimmy. He went over to Mr. Walker and Mr. Benton. "Have you guys heard that ringing? Typically, if a church won't stop ringing its bells, that means either really good news or really bad news."

"Agreed," said Mr. Walker. "The war's already over, so I don't know what it could be. Maybe it's some kind of local crisis or death."

A few moments later, a steamboat went by, blasting its steam horn continuously for over thirty seconds. Mr. Benton, Jimmy, and Mr. Walker all stood there looking puzzled at each other. Then Benton asked Walker, "What the hell's going on, Thaddeus?"

Smallpox Island

"Don't know, but something's up. I haven't heard horns and bells go off like this since the war ended," Benton responded. "There's a little town named Chester nearby. I can row over to the mainland and try to get some information."

"No," said Jimmy. "I'll try to holler over to a passing steamboat. It'll be faster. So, I'll be back in just a bit."

He walked across the island toward the main channel, where the skiff was hidden. After about ten minutes, a medium-sized riverboat approached, once again blowing its horn. Jimmy took off running across the sandbar in the direction of the boat. As the transport passed, it kept blowing its horn in long and short blasts. Trying to get the captain's attention, Jimmy jumped up and down in his Union uniform. He waved his arms and then grabbed his hat, waving it in the air. But the boat's captain kept looking straight ahead and didn't see him. With that, Jimmy stood there and waited, looking up and down the river for the next boat.

Five minutes later, another boat came by, but it was not blowing its horn. Again, Jimmy waved at the ship and this time, it slowed a bit.

The ship's captain stepped out of the pilothouse and waved back. "What do you need, soldier?!"

"Hello! I was wondering why all of the boats are blowing their horns and the churches are ringing their bells?!"

"Haven't you heard yet?!"

"Heard what?!"

With that, the captain looked down and went back into the pilothouse. He slowed the boat and slowly directed it over toward Jimmy. Once he had trimmed the boat off about a hundred feet from shore, he came out of the pilothouse, straightened his jacket, and spoke loudly toward Jimmy. "Soldier, I'm sorry to inform you that your commander in chief, Abraham Lincoln, was shot last night by an assassin while attending a play in Washington, D.C. He died this morning."

Jimmy stood there. He was too stunned to say anything. He just stood there looking at the riverboat captain.

Just then, Will walked out of the wood line and stood next to Jimmy in the sand. "I heard him. I was just walking up."

Jimmy and Will stood there staring off into space while looking toward the boat. The captain finally said, "I'm real sorry about this, boys.... I gotta go."

Jimmy finally spoke. "Oh.... Okay, thanks very much. Really!"

"You're welcome. Maybe you should check in with your unit. Take care, soldiers." The ship's captain waved, stepped back into the pilothouse, and continued his journey.

The brothers stood there for a few minutes, saying nothing. Then, finally, Jimmy shook his head and started to turn. Again, he had tears in his eyes, but this time they could not be hidden by the rain. Will put his hand on Jimmy's shoulder, "I'm sorry about this, Jim. I can hardly believe it."

"Neither can I.... Let's go back and try to tell the group."

They went back and gathered the "Island Alliance" to break the news to them. Jimmy spoke. "Okay, listen up, everyone. The bells and horns have been going off because..." He paused for a few seconds to gain his composure. "Because apparently, President Lincoln has been shot and killed in Washington."

There was an immediate gasp by nearly everyone in the group. Tanna Douglass spontaneously let off a brief and awkward shriek. Jimmy immediately continued, "I don't know any other details. The riverboat captain said the president was shot at a play last night and that he died this morning. At least that's what he just told me."

A low hush came over the group as they reacted with somber and somewhat mixed reactions. Charles Douglass immediately turned away and walked off into the tree line, as his wife Tanna started sobbing tears. Thaddeus Walker, Thomas Benton, and the

Confederate soldiers muted their response and kept looking around at the group as if to read the reactions.

Finally, Thaddeus Walker stood up and seemed to speak for the group. "I'm sorry about this news, folks. I know he was a good man. Unfortunately, this had to happen just when the country is trying to get back together. We could have used a strong president like Abe to help stitch this ripped quilt back together. I'm not that awful surprised though. I know a lot of Confederates are probably highly angered by the Southern loss and they are not going to want to give in easily."

Surprisingly, the Confederate soldiers, Beau and Hector, both commented almost immediately after Walker. Hector stood up and said, "Hey, folks, listen. I'm sorry for you all because I know you really liked him. As for me, I don't feel happy about it. I think some Southerners might be celebrating, but I ain't. If it is really true, it's just gonna put more hurt on top a hurt. I'm really done with all the fightin', death, and misery. They can kill whoever they want and the South ain't coming back to fight. At least I ain't."

Beau added, "Me neither. The South's dream of victory is over. And I'm tellin' you from the inside. They told us it was gonna be a glorious, quick, and easy victory for the South. Well, it turned out to be a long, miserable, and bloody loss. We were damn near starving at the end. I can't believe some idiot shot the president. It's only gonna make things worse."

The farmers Charles Mason and his son Frank just sat there quietly, shaking their heads in disbelief.

After the announcement, most of the people of the Island Alliance went back to their separate areas and sat around. Some others seemed to just be moping around the area as they stared off into space. It looked as if they all had nothing to do and nowhere to go. This, of course, was not the case at all. Thaddeus Walker walked over to the brother's area and sat with them on a tree limb. "How are you boys doing?"

Jimmy answered, "Okay, but why are we all sitting around? Why is everyone just sitting around? I thought we had to get outta here. I thought everyone had to get out of here."

"Not sure," answered Willy. "Maybe they are like us and are not exactly sure if they want to leave right now."

"What do you mean, Will?"

"I mean, maybe it would be smart for us to wait until the high emotions of this news have settled down. Who knows what crackpots from either side could do now that this has all been stirred up again?"

Thaddeus Walker then chimed in, "Good point, Willy. One more night here won't hurt anyone, and it might be a smart thing to do. It's safe here. We're among friends here. I think I'm with you, boys."

"Okay," Jimmy answered. "But tomorrow morning, we're leaving come hell or high water."

"Agreed," said Will.

"I'll go talk to the rest of the alliance and see what they want to do," said Walker.

After a short period, Walker returned and told the brothers that everyone had agreed to stay. "Maybe we can have some more music like we had last night."

"I'm counting on it," said Jimmy, "and I know the perfect song to start it off."

Later that morning, the thin man Mr. Benton addressed the entire group. He told them that, since they apparently were staying a bit longer, he would row west over to the Missouri side of the river. He explained that rowing west through the main channel was the shortest trip to the mainland from Liberty Island. Nearly everyone on the island had concealed a boat or a raft somewhere on the island's eastern side, away from the main channel. Benton then told the group that he planned to do three things:

1) Hunt for some more rabbits

2) Get a few jugs of clean water

3) Take a small ferry over to the nearby town of Chester, Illinois, in hopes of getting a copy of the local newspaper

After Benton departed, the Island Alliance generally returned into their little groups. Willy was tending to the fire so that it wouldn't go totally out. The Douglasses were chatting in their area while their boys were sleeping. The farmers were playing a card game. The \Confederate soldiers Beau and Hector were playing a made-up game involving the tossing of rocks and sticks. Thaddeus Walker was reading a news page (that had to be at least several days old) and talking to Jimmy, who was pecking and tuning his guitar. Generally, everyone's guard was down. Then suddenly, there was the sound of breaking sticks from someone walking through the woods. Walker mumbled to himself, "Benton is back already?"

April 15, 1865, 1 p.m.
Robbers Visit the Island

At that moment, two unknown men walked into the clearing. The men were armed but had not drawn their pistols. "Well, howdy folks!" announced one of the men. "My brother here and I were just passing by and we happened to see some tall fella rowing a boat from this island over to the Missouri side." The men were dusty from riding the trail. One was about three to four inches shorter than the other and they both wore leather coats and hats.

The shorter intruder continued, "Now it's not like us to let a possible monetary gain slip by, so we borrowed his little boat and came out here to this island. We thought he might just be on the run with maybe a stash of cash money out here."

While the intruders were talking, Mr. Walker whispered to

Jimmy, "Stay real calm, but I think I know that taller fella. Looks like one of Quantrill's boys.... They're pro-Confederate and they can be real butchers."

Walker then spoke up. "Hello, fine gentlemen. I am Thaddeus Walker. I'm a musician for the Southern forces until their untimely demise. These are travelers in my company. We are traveling via the river and we are about two dollars short of penniless."

The shorter of the two intruders again spoke. "Well, hello there, Mr. Walker! I believe you, but who was the tall fellow that we saw in the rowboat?"

"That was Mr. Benton. He's a former supplier of rations to the Confederate Army. He went to look for some water and some meager supplies for us."

"Well, we'll see about that," said the shorter intruder, as the two men slowly pulled out their pistols. The shorter man then said calmly, "Nobody move. I just need everyone to put all of your money on the ground in front of you."

The Island Alliance started fidgeting around and checking their pockets as if they were looking for money and the intruders scanned the entire group for the first time. They saw Willy tending to the center fire, Mr. Walker, the two Confederate soldiers, the two poor farmers, the five former slaves, and Jimmy in his full Union Army uniform.

The taller intruder spoke up. "Wait a minute," he said, speaking to the Confederates. "What are you boys doing here?"

Hector spoke up. "Trying to go home. Look here, sir. These people are travelers and they ain't got no damn money, and neither do we. If we did, we sure wouldn't be out here staying on this damn island."

Just then, Will took a log that he was prepping for the fire and hurled it at the men, hitting the taller man in the chest and knocking his pistol out of his hand. The other man's gun fired into the air as he ducked down, and Will instantly leaped forward and grabbed the man's pistol from the ground. At that exact second, Jimmy immediately pulled and fired his pistol two times over the shorter man's head. "I was trying to miss, but I won't next time!" yelled Jimmy.

Both parties stood there. Jimmy and Will had pistols aimed at the strangers and the shorter intruder had his pistol aimed at Jimmy. The taller intruder struggled to his feet and spoke to his partner. "Jesse, this ain't what we came out here for. These ain't the kinda people we're interested in. Hell, looks like most of 'em are poor ass Southerners anyway."

"I know it, Frank. I can see! But what are we supposed to do about these Yankee boys aiming pistols at us?"

Mr. Walker then spoke, attempting to defuse the standoff a bit. "You boys know about Quantrill's Raiders, don't ya? I was with him and Bill Anderson down near Sherman, Texas in the winter of '63."

"Okay, I know them, but I don't know you," said the intruder apparently named Frank. "But, I'd like to say something. Listen up here, Yankee boys. Let's go ahead and put down our pistols."

"Sounds good to me," said Jimmy as he nodded over to Will. Everyone slowly lowered their weapons.

The other intruder named Jesse then spoke slowly as he placed his pistol into its holster. "Look here, fellas. We didn't come out here to rob no poor people. Right now, we have other plans and we have better things to do. My brother Frank here has business in Kentucky and I'm heading up toward Lexington, Missouri."

Frank added, "Right. Like he said, we have more important things to do and bigger fish to fry."

Jimmy holstered his pistol and Frank held out his hand toward Will, asking for the return of his pistol. Will refused at first. "Come on, stranger!" said the intruder named Frank. You hit me with a damn log!"

Will looked over at Jimmy. Jimmy nodded again. "It's okay, Will, give it back. Willy slowly obliged.

Jesse then asked, "You fellers have anything to eat?"

"Well, hell yeah!" Mr. Walker said. "We got some hardtack, biscuits, and burnt-up rabbit." Suddenly, the tension seemed to dial down and everyone started to relax just a bit.

Frank and Jesse looked down toward the ground and then slowly walked up toward the fire. As they sat down, Jesse said, "We'll sure enough take a piece of the rabbit if you can spare it."

Then, Walker, Jimmy, and the Confederate soldiers walked up to the fire and sat down with the bandits. Willy stayed in the background. "Burnt rabbit's right there on that rock," said Walker. "There's a jug of water there too." Walker smiled as he pointed to the rabbit and the water. Jesse and Frank picked up a couple of pieces of meat and seemed to relax as they ate rabbit and drank the water.

The Confederate soldiers started talking to Jesse and Frank about military units and such. Jesse asked them, "Did you fellas hear about Dishonest Abe?"

"Yup, we heard he's dead," said Hector. "Too little too late. Won't change anything."

"Maybe not, but we're not changing any of our plans. We're gonna keep raising hell!" Walker then started chatting with the intruders, determining that they shared several mutual acquaintances. At one point, Frank slowly stood up. He turned and looked over at Will, still standing in the background. "Hey! That log hurt, you know!"

"Sorry about that. I thought you were gonna kill us."

Then Frank turned around even more, looking face to face at Willy. He paused for a second, grinned, and said, "That's okay, kid. I think I would have done the same thing." Will, took a deep breath and finally relaxed.

After drinking some water, Jesse started talking to Frank about working his way up toward northeastern Missouri. "Hey, Frank, on the way up there, maybe I can stay in that cave up by the Meramec River."

"You mean the one where we blew up that Union gunpowder factory a year or so ago?"

"Yep, that's the one," said Jesse as he smiled directly toward Jimmy, sitting there in his full Union Army uniform.

After about twenty minutes of food and talk, Jesse motioned to Frank and the two men stood up. They both walked to the side and spoke for about thirty seconds. Jesse then motioned to Mr. Walker, "Can I speak with you for just a minute?"

"Well, yes, sir," said Walker. The two men walked over to Walker's sleeping area and Jesse spoke. "Look here, I'm sorry about the trouble. We didn't know that all you people were out here. You see, my brother and me may have done some things that we ain't real proud of, but there are certain things that we don't ever do. Robbin' poor people is one of 'em."

Jesse then reached into his pocket and pulled out a large wad of Union Greenback paper bills. They were all Missouri one-dollar notes. Jesse counted off several of the bills and handed them to Walker. "Listen, I want to thank you folks for the food and drink. I know it's not a lot, but take this money for the food. Keep it or share it with the others if you like."

"Much obliged, stranger."

"Jesse... my name's Jesse James. That's my brother, Frank."

Jesse turned and walked back toward the center of the camp. Then, Frank stood up and the brothers looked at the whole group. "Listen, island people," said Jesse, "We gotta go now, but thanks for the food and water."

"We're real sorry for the interruption," said Frank.

Walker spoke up quickly. "Island Alliance!"

"What?"

"We call our group the Island Alliance!"

Frank and Jesse both chuckled. Then, Jesse answered while grinning from ear to ear, "Island Alliance! Well, that sounds like the perfect name for this odd little group! Listen, we'll put the tall fella's boat right back where we found it." He tipped his hat and said, "Have a good day, Island Alliance!"

The intruders turned and departed. About half of the group said goodbye to Frank and Jesse James, while the others just looked at them in silence. The James Brothers ferried themselves back to the mainland in Mr. Benton's boat and returned it to the same general area where they had found it.

About an hour and a half later, Mr. Benton returned to the island and found the group to be a bit dumbfounded. "Hey, folks! I got five more rabbits, a jug of water, and even a paper from Chester, Illinois." The group all just stared at him with blank looks on their faces. "Hey, everybody! What is wrong with you folks?!"

Mr. Walker answered, "You won't believe it, Mr. Benton. Two men held us up while you were gone. They saw that we didn't have any money, ate some of your rabbit, gave us ten dollars, and left."

"What?!"

"Yep, they saw you when you left the island earlier, so they used your boat to get over here."

Benton answered, "I just saw them on horseback when I was walking back. They both tipped their hats to me with big grins on their faces. One of them said, 'Thanks for the rabbit, Mister.' Now, I know what they meant."

"Yep. That was them. They told us that they would put your boat back."

"They did, sort of. I noticed that the boat was in a different place from where I had left it. I thought I was crackin' up."

The Island Alliance settled back in after the attempted robbery, turned courtesy visit. As they prepped the rabbits and started cooking them, Mr. Walker made an announcement: "Listen, folks, you know we are all in this together, at least for one more night. So, I'm going to share with you these ten Missouri dollars. That fella named Jesse gave these to me before he departed. Said he was, 'Sorry for the trouble.' So, I have a dollar for each person in the group. Everyone gets one, including the whole Douglass family. I'm excluding myself and Mr. Benton since we already have a little money." Mr. Benton shook his head yes in agreement.

"What? You got to be joking!" said Jimmy.

"No, sir. He gave me ten Missouri dollars to share with the group and that's exactly what I'm gonna do. Every single person is gonna get one dollar. It's not much, but it's money."

Mr. Walker walked about as pleased as he could be. He handed a Missouri dollar to Beau, Hector, Jimmy, Will, Charles Mason, and Frank Mason. He also gave one dollar to Charles Douglass, one to his wife, and one to each of his three children. "I did have to add a dollar so everyone in the group could get one," he said smiling.

The group was stunned. Nearly everyone sat or stood there grinning, some literally with their mouths hanging open. The group laughed and joked while Walker went around the camp handing out the money. Walker then exclaimed, "I just knew our alliance would pay off in one way or another! This must be the other!" Everyone looked around at each other and chuckled and laughed, with some waving their one-dollar bills in the air.

After a while, everyone had eaten and they all started to settle down for the evening. Jimmy and the other musicians began to pull out their instruments, preparing for another evening with music. Mr. Benton even pulled out a small mandolin from his bag that he had not mentioned before. He started pecking and strumming at it. Willy told him, "You've been holding out on us, Mr. Benton."

"No, I just didn't think anyone wanted to play it. I'm stuck playing the fiddle most of the time."

Hector immediately spoke up and said, "Hey, I play a little banjo. I might be able to play that mandolin in the background so you fellas can play something else."

"That's perfect," said Jimmy, "Every so often, you can strum the basic tune and I can play something else." Willy spoke up quickly, "Oh, you mean so you can show off!"

"Yeah, asshole, I guess so. Keep it up and I'm gonna poke your shingles with a stick."

"Go ahead, brother. Then I'll break it off in your nose!" Jimmy shoved Willy over. Then, Willy quickly jumped up and shoved Jimmy in the face with an open hand, walking away. Everyone broke into laughter while the brothers settled their playful fight.

April 15, 1985, 7:38 p.m. (sunset)

After about an hour of talking and playing small pieces of music, the musicians were almost ready to start. Mr. Walker and Jimmy both had their music books out and had practiced several new tunes for the group to play. Just as they were about to begin, Charles Douglass walked over to Jimmy.

"I think I might have a song, Mr. Jim."

Jimmy was playing a little tune on his guitar as he looked up at Charles. "Okay. Let's work it out, Charles. You did a great job yesterday and you have a great voice."

"Well, sir, I've been mostly workin' on the song in my mind since we finished last night. I can write some of it down."

"Great. We can take it from there. Here you go," said Jimmy, handing Charles his book and writing pencil. They both stepped over to the side and practiced the new song that Charles had conceived. After about ten minutes, they were ready. "Well, Charles, do you want to do your song now or a little later?"

"How about a little later so I can get up my nerve?"

"Ha! That sounds good, buddy. It will be a great tune. I guarantee it!"

"Mr. Walker, do you want to kick it off for us?" asked Jimmy.

"I certainly do, sir. This is 'My Old Kentucky Home, Good-Night,' written by Stephen Foster. Jimmy brought this song to my attention since our late President Lincoln was born of humble beginnings in the great state of Kentucky."

Mr. Walker then launched into an incredible lead banjo as he sang the song with Jimmy also playing guitar. Walker played and sang the song to perfection. It was obvious that he had performed 'My Old Kentucky Home' many hundreds of times before.

My Old Kentucky Home – 1853 – Stephen Foster – John Prine Style

Oh, the sun shines bright on my old Kentucky home
'Tis summer, the old folks are gay
Where the corn top's ripe and the meadow's in the bloom
While the birds make music all the day
Weep no more, my lady
Oh, weep no more today
We'll sing one song
For my old Kentucky home
For my old Kentucky home, far away
(SONG CONTINUES UNTIL ITS ENDING)

At the song's ending, everyone applauded and the farmer Charles Mason stood up and spoke. "That's a truly great song, Mr. Walker," Mason continued. "It almost made me cry." He wiped a tear from his eye. "My wife and I were born near London, Kentucky. We moved out west to Paducah, Kentucky and started a farm after we married. That's where we had my son, Thomas here."

Charles' son Thomas then spoke. "Yes, sir! Thanks for playing that, Mr. Walker. My dad here sings that song all day long when we are working."

"You're welcome, son," said Walker. "Charles, you know I never asked, and you don't have to say, but what happened with your farm?"

"Well, first my horses were stolen and then my house was burned to the ground. We think by Southern soldiers, but we're not totally sure. Tom here and me barely made it out alive. My wife, Dorothy, had died just before the war started. So, after we lost the house, we didn't really see no reason to stay. So, I sold my land and my barn to my neighbor. Decided to head up to northern Missouri. Got a brother up there with a big farm way up near Kirksville, Missouri. He's been writing and asking us to move up there for years."

"That's really good, Charles," said Mr. Walker. "I think you'll like it up there. Well, good luck to you on your journey, Mr. Mason."

"Thanks, Mr. Walker."

Then Jimmy readied his next tune by practicing with their island band for about ten minutes. "This is a song that I learned at Benton Barracks in St. Louis. Learned it from a fella named John Dillon from out of the Ozark Hills of Missouri. The song is called 'Walkin' Down the Road.' I added a little guitar intro called 'Tullamore Dew.' That's a type of Irish whisky."

Jimmy then played "Walkin' Down the Road." Everyone who had an instrument played as loudly as they could. It was an upbeat up-tempo song about a fellow leaving his home. At Jimmy's prompting, there were several parts of the song where everyone sang, "Choo-choo, choo-choo!" It made the song even more fun for the group. Everyone was jumping around and making funny dance moves during the song. Willy played harmonica with one hand and kept the beat by beating on a tree stump with a short, strong stick in his other hand. At the end, everyone clapped and hollered, "Choo-choo, choo-choo!" Mr. Benton yelled, "Now that's a real good down-home kinda song, Jimmy!!"

"Thank you, sir."

After the song, everyone took a break and had a drink of either apple cider, beer, whiskey, tea, water, or coffee. They chatted about the previous song and all of the roads that they might find in their future travels. Then, Jimmy called Charles Douglass over. "Charles, get ready to go right after the next song."

"I'll be ready, Mr. Jimmy," said Charles.

A few minutes later, the musicians noticed that Jimmy was getting ready to play a song. Quickly, Mr. Walker and the others came over to him and asked about practicing for the next song. "Well, fellas. I only know how to do this one by myself. Willy, you can join in on harmonica if you like, but I'll have the largest portion covered. This is one that I wrote myself."

"Okay," said Walker. "The rest of us will all have a little break and enjoy the music."

"That's fine. Whatever you like."

A couple of minutes later, Jimmy was ready to play his song and Charles Douglass was standing by, waiting to do the next song. Then, Jimmy announced to the group, "Okay, the name of this song is 'Georgia Train.' I wrote it a few years ago after talking to a fella at the train station in my hometown of New Madrid. He said he was planning to go down to Georgia to get his girl. Apparently, he had let her go and he knew it was a mistake. Now, I don't know for sure if he ever actually left to go find her, but I sure didn't see him after that. So, I'm guessing he went down to make up with her."

G. S. Spooner

Georgia Train – 2015 – G. S. Spooner

Well I'm gone down to Georgia,
Going to bring my little girl home.
Well I'm gone down to Georgia,
Going to bring my little girl home.
And if I don't get to Georgia,
My little girl will be long gone.

Gonna tell the train conductor, to put some more coal on.
Gonna tell the train conductor, to put some more coal on.
We gotta get this train a movin', gotta bring my little girl home.

Guitar Interlude

Now the ticket man he tells me, I gotta get off the next stop.
Now the ticket man he tells me, I gotta get off the next stop.
I only made down to Memphis, oh Lord please help this stop.

Now I gotta get some money, gonna back on that train.
Now I gotta get some money, gonna back on that train.
Man I gotta get to Georgia, oh Lord please help this pain.

Guitar Interlude – Repeat First
(SONG CONTINUES UNTIL ITS ENDING)

After the song was over, everybody seemed to be in a good mood. They all talked about the character trying to get down to Georgia on a train. Hector said it was kind of funny that he wanted the train to go faster by putting "some more coal on." Hector

Smallpox Island

continued, "I don't really think that I would chase down a girl that left me." Thaddeus Walker answered, "Well, Hector. That might depend on the girl," spurring a chuckle from nearly everyone.

Next up was Charles Douglass and the song that he had worked out with Jimmy. Before they could start, Jimmy asked everyone with an instrument to come over for a few minutes to work on the musical part of the song. "Okay, Hector and Mr. Walker. I want you fellas to strum quickly and follow my lead. It will go like this." He strummed his guitar, saying, "1 2 3, 1 2, 1 2 3, 1 2, 1 2 3, 1 2." He added, "Willy, I want you to cover the drumbeat by beating on that stump just like you did earlier. Look here, everyone, we're gonna have a dramatic pause at a couple of points. You'll see, we'll just stop playing for a few seconds. I'll hold up my hand, so just watch me for it and follow me." Jimmy started practicing the song and the musicians quickly caught on. They were ready. Jimmy said, "This is gonna be the best song of the night. Maybe even the theme song for the Island Alliance."

"Here here!" said Mr. Walker. "Hoorah!" added Will and several of the others.

"Okay, are we ready?" Everyone nodded. "Charles, are you ready?"

"Yes, sir," said Charles Douglass. "I'm gonna sing this one for Mr. Lincoln. May he rest in peace." Everyone paused at his comment. They all stared kind of stunned at Charles. A chill came over everyone. Everyone…including the Confederate soldiers and the farmers. The group had almost forgotten that President Lincoln was no longer alive. Charles Douglass looked down and wiped a small tear from his right eye. Then, he announced his song. "Okay. Name of this song is "Freedom, Motherless Child."

G. S. Spooner

Freedom (Motherless Child) – 1899 – Traditional – Richie Havens Style

Freedom, Freedom, Freedom, Freedom,
Sometimes I feel like a motherless child (Repeat x3)
A long way from home, a long way from home.

Sometimes I feel like I'm almost done (Repeat x3)
And a long, long way from home, a long way.. from home.

True believer, true believer
I got a telegraph in my bosom, and I can call him up from my heart (Repeat x2)
When I need my brother…brother, When I need my mother…mother.
A long, long way from home, a long, long way.. from home.
(SONG'S ENDING)

The song built to a crescendo as Jimmy kept the beat by quickly strumming his guitar while looking at Charles and the others. They all were playing their instruments as perfectly and as hard as they could without breaking them. Will was beating on the giant log with two thick sticks as if it were a sanctioned instrument known around the world and he was a quantified master at playing it. Charles sang the song with great bravado and deep vocalization as he stood still at first and then started walking around. His strong vocals and poignant lyrics pulled the group deeper and deeper into the song.

The dramatic pause came off perfectly as Charles sang, *"…a long way…a long way (pause)… from home!"* At one point, he walked around clapping and added, *"Clap your hands! Clap your hands. Clap your hands!"* Everyone without an instrument started clapping their hands instantly. Near the end, Charles was singing, *"When I need my brother...brother. When I need my mother...mother."* He was moving around the group, looking around at everyone, bouncing his head and upper body up and down. The entire Island Alliance was either playing an instrument, clapping, or trying to sing along. They had all effectively become one perfect instrument, belting out the song "Freedom, Motherless Child!"

When the song was finally finished, they all cheered and looked around at each other in amazement. "What just happened, Beau?!" said Hector. "I don't know, but I feel like I just ran around the island five times."

"Me too!" said Charles Douglass.

"I'm beat," said Mr. Walker. They were all excited and exhausted because of the beautiful and almost tribal noise that they had just made. Even though it was only April, Charles Douglass was sweating like it was July. He walked around to everyone in the group and said, "Thank you," as he shook their hand.

When he got around to Hector and Beau, Charles Douglass said, "Thank you," and held out his hand. Hector stood there and looked intensely at Charles. Suddenly, he pushed his hand away, grabbed him, and hugged him.

"Thanks, Charles," said Hector. "I've never been a part of anything like that before."

Charles looked at him and flashed a broad smile, saying, "I never been a part of anything like that before either. And I don't think I ever will again. Not unless all you people are there with me." He then firmly shook Beau's hand and moved over to his family. They all grabbed onto him and he started hugging them all at the same time. Then, the entire alliance walked around from person to person, smiling, shaking each other's hands, and patting each other on the back. The Island Alliance had now become their tribe. Their tribe was now the Island Alliance.

After about twenty minutes, Jimmy announced, "My friends, I don't think we can follow up with anything that comes even close to the level of the song that we just did. So, if it's okay, I'd like that to be the final song of the night."

"Great. That was a perfect ending," said Mr. Benton.

"You're not gonna beat that last song anyway," said Mr. Walker.

"A real good ending," said Charles.

Willy added, "I suppose it's a good time to stop and cool off so we can go to sleep. But man, we were just getting to sound really good!"

"Agreed!" several of the others said at the same time.

April 15, 1865, 10 p.m.

The Island Alliance started winding down as they prepared their sleeping areas for another night on Liberty Island. Several people in the group began walking back and forth into the wood line to gather timber for the big fire. The brothers saw this and joined them. A short while later, everyone bedded down for the night and started to go to sleep. "How many more days until we get home, Jimmy?" Will asked.

"Two days, little brother. I think. I hope...two days." During the night, Jimmy arose to walk the perimeter of the clearing. He thought it was important to check the area's security from time to time. While he was walking past the Douglasses's area, Charles spoke quietly to him. "Hey, Mr. Jim, just so you know, I tend to sleep with one eye open." Jimmy smiled, nodded, and went back to his sleeping area.

Chapter Twelve

April 16, 1865, 6:22 a.m.

The morning came quickly and the sun began to rise upon Liberty Island. It was a cool awakening, but thankfully it was another dry one. With light breaking, nearly everyone had started to stir with the exception of Charles Douglass's two sons and Hector. The woken travelers began chatting with each other as they began to rekindle the big fire. It had dwindled through the night, but it was still smoldering. Within a half-hour, everyone was up and coffee was brewing. They all generally functioned in their own little groups, eating something for breakfast and completing their individual morning routines. It only took the Logan brothers about fifteen minutes to break down their bivouac. By 7:30 a.m., they were packed up and ready to go.

Others in the group seemed to be preparing to depart but at a much slower pace. Jimmy and Will walked up to Thaddeus Walker and Mr. Benton. "Gentlemen, it's been a pleasure, but we have many miles to lay down today and we have to make haste," said Jimmy.

"I'm sure you do. The pleasure has been ours," said Walker. "I think the last two evenings will be engraved in our minds forever. Listen, we have each other's addresses, so we'll be in touch. It's good to have friends in different areas. You never know when destiny might bring us back together again."

"Yes, sir," said Jimmy. "Don't forget that we live right on the river, so we're easy to find."

Then, Mr. Walker handed Jimmy a small leather flask. "It's for you both. It's Tennessee whiskey and it's really good for medicinal purposes."

"Thanks!" the brothers said simultaneously.

Benton added, "We may have lost a president, but we've gained two friends. Be careful and get home safe."

"We will," answered Willy. The brothers went around to everyone in the group and said goodbye. Hector and Beau looked sad at their departure, and Charles Douglass brought his entire family around them.

"You fine gentlemen have brought a piece of happiness on us that we haven't felt for a long time," Charles said with a sad yet smiling face. "I feel that I'm gonna be singin' a might bit more than I used to, thanks to you."

"I certainly hope so, Charles. You made the night."

"Thank you, sir."

The three men shook hands and then hugged each other. As they finished their embrace, the entire Douglass family surrounded them and pushed into them, hugging all of them together. Willy looked around at the joined group of seven people as they all started laughing (with some sobbing) seemingly at the same time.

After the big hug, the brothers waved and said goodbye to the group as they walked into the woods toward their skiff. As they started to walk away, Jimmy whispered something to Will. Suddenly, they both turned and simultaneously yelled, "Long live the Island Alliance!!" as loud as they could. The entire group quickly returned the call, "Long live the Island Alliance!!" with equal passion and volume.

> *Point of Historical Reference – During the Civil War, the islands of the Mississippi River served as a refuge for soldiers, deserters, fugitives, outlaws and regular travelers. The Mississippi River was a main conduit for the Underground Railroad, ushering many former slaves toward their freedom.*

By 8 a.m., the brothers were off in their little skiff and were heading down the river. Once again, they moved to the right bank on the Missouri side as they rapidly regained their skills concerning the navigation of the river. At one point, they were rowing as fast as they could to keep pace ahead of a Union transport that appeared to be filled with prisoners returning to the South. In about five minutes, the transport steamship caught up with them, seemingly going at the same speed for a brief moment. The brothers waved at the boat that appeared to be overloaded with former Confederate prisoners heading back to their homes. Many of the former prisoners waved back and one yelled over to them, "We're going home faster than you are, Yankees!"

Will said, "I wonder if any of those guys are from Alton."

"I don't know, Willy. But I sure hope so," said Jimmy.

After hours of hard rowing, the brothers decided to pull the skiff over to take a break. They found a sandbar that looked pretty good and rowed up to it. Once ashore, they pulled the boat up into the wood line and hid it with some brush. Then after a brief scouting mission, they went inland to relax, drink water, and eat some food. They found a few fallen trees to sit on and they took their break. As Jimmy ate, he was busy looking at the map and at local landmarks.

"How far are we from home?" asked Will. "I'm not exactly sure, but it looks like we're on pace to make camp about ten miles south of Cape Girardeau."

"Then after that," said Willy, "how far until we get home?"

"Well, I think we'll be home tomorrow. Maybe late tomorrow, but no guarantees."

"Tomorrow sounds damn good to me," said Will. "Momma's gonna pass out. Does she know we're coming?"

"Probably not. I wrote her a brief letter telling her that I was bringing you home, but I don't think it will get there before we do. I hear the mail is really slow these days."

"No doubt!"

Within ten minutes, the Logans were back on the water. As usual, they traded off with rowing duty. "Looking at the map," said Jimmy, "we're gonna have to beat feet if we want to make it to ten miles south of Cape Girardeau."

"All right then," said Will.

"Pull harder, bro!" yelled Jimmy. "Let's row!! Let's go!!"

Down the mighty Mississippi they went, as fast as they could go and as fast as they could row. About four hours later, Jimmy said, "Look, I think that's Cape."

"Yep, me too. Dad and I rode horses up there to get some supplies when I was younger. Took all day. We got back home in the dark. Looks right, but I didn't see the town from the river."

"It's Cape Girardeau. Gotta be. Let's pull over briefly to see what's going on."

They pulled up to a muddy shoreline that had a few steamboats docked at it. Jimmy saw a dock worker. "Sir, is this Cape Girardeau?"

"It sure is, soldier. You need a place to stay?"

"No, not really. We need to get downstream a bit more before we camp."

"Suit yourself."

"Any good places downstream to camp?"

"Well, Price's Landing is downstream about fifteen miles. There were two small buildings he put there as a Headquarters, but it's all abandoned now. They're about a quarter mile from the shore on the right side, the west side. I think the buildings are still there, but I'm not sure. You have to look close, or you'll miss them."

"Okay, thanks." They hastily departed. "Let's go!" said Jimmy as he earnestly rowed. "We gotta get there before dark and figure out what the hell we're gonna do. We don't have much time. Let's pound ground!"

"Ground?" said Willy.

"Let's splash water!" said Jimmy, laughing as he rowed.

About an hour and a half later, Jimmy said, "Eyes right, Willy. Those old buildings should be somewhere around here. We have to look close or we'll miss them."

All of a sudden, Willy spoke up. "Right there. I see them."

"Are you sure?"

"Well, I think so. I fought for Price, but I can't really tell you whether or not those are his buildings."

"That's them," Jimmy said. "Let's pull over and check 'em out before it gets too dark."

"Okay."

The brothers pulled the boat over and walked through the lightly wooded area to check out the two small buildings. As they walked through the structures, Jimmy said, "These are kinda okay, I guess. That one looks like animals sleep in it."

Willy added, "This one looks like people use it every so often. There are old coals here from a fire."

"How's the roof look?"

"Fair. There's one small hole in the corner, and there ain't no door." Then, Jimmy said while grinning, "Man, this is perfect. Hey, those Rebel boys build a pretty good little building, don't they?"

"Screw you, asshole!" Willy snapped back, shoving his older brother.

Within a half-hour, they had checked the area, hidden their skiff, and brought over some supplies. Then, they started a fire on the outside of the small building, on the side away from the river. The light wood line had several thickets. It offered limited cover and concealment, but they decided it was better than nothing.

"Not every place can be as perfect as Liberty Island," said Jimmy.

"So true."

They then grabbed some loose trees and brush and stacked them up about eight feet high, to partially hide their fire from passersby on the land side. The shack hid the fire from the riverside. Jimmy took out his tent half. He attached two corners to the building and held up the other two corners with several stout tree limbs. "We can sleep under this, Willy. We'll just keep the canvas about three or four feet away from the fire."

"Perfect."

As darkness set in, they had a fire going and had set up their bedding areas. They finally had time to eat and relax. After playing a little harmonica, Willy was asleep, the harmonica still in his hand. Jimmy stayed up for a while and did a walkthrough of the area for security. It seemed to be a peaceful night. He then took a small drink of whiskey from the leather flask that Mr. Walker had given them that morning. He made a face after he drank it.

The old Price Landing buildings seemed to be in a quiet area with little or no traffic. "Blessed again," Jimmy whispered to himself, "Thank you, God and Jesus."

After about five minutes of sitting by the fire, Jimmy started to bed down and go to sleep. He leaned back and slowly closed his eyes while looking at the light of the fire. A bit later, Jimmy awoke. The fire had seemed to smoke up and his eyes were glazed over by the sleep and the smoke. As the smoke cleared, Jimmy saw what appeared to be an American Indian, standing on the other side of the fire, holding a long staff. At first, Jimmy shook his head and blinked his eyes. He had been on night guard duty before and he had seen things that weren't really there. He blinked again. *Am I seeing things, or is this vision real?* he thought to himself.

Jimmy focused. It was real. The Indian was holding his right hand slightly raised up as if in a wave or a sign of peace. Jimmy gradually stood up and slowly approached the Indian with his pistol still holstered. Then, as quick as he could, Jimmy lunged at the intruder. The intruder ducked down and quickly swept Jimmy's feet out from under him. In one fluid motion, the Indian spun around. He landed on top of Jimmy with his knee on his chest and his pole across Jimmy's throat. Willy had woken up with the commotion and was standing nearby holding a large stick. The Indian then quietly spoke to Jimmy in English, "Do not shoot me, soldier. I am no threat to you." With this, Jimmy took a deep breath and made a deep guttural sound as he started to lift the Indian (who was on top of him) into the air. Jimmy extended his arms until the Indian's entire body was now about two feet in the air over Jimmy.

Now extended above Jimmy, the Indian said loudly, "I only seek to cross the big river from this place!"

"Okay, why are you by my fire in the middle of the night?" said Jimmy as he quickly sat the Indian down to his side, grabbing his holstered pistol. "I want nothing but to pass by this area and cross the big river. I've grown tired of hiding from you. I was here before you and I've been hiding in the thicket," the Indian said, motioning toward a nearby brush line. "I had my right hand up as a sign of peace."

"I saw it, I think. But it was dark."

"I did not want to startle you, but as I said, I am tired of hiding in the bushes," the Indian said. "How come I didn't see you earlier?"

"You have walked past me many times since you came."

"Really?"

"Yes."

Jimmy lowered his pistol and holstered it. Then, the two men moved further apart and continued to look at each other. Will was still standing nearby, holding the large stick. The Indian continued, "My people have crossed the river here for many years. Long before the white man came. Tomorrow, I am going to make a good raft to get across the river."

"Okay, how do you know that you people crossed here?"

"I came here with my father when I was young and he took me to our ancient home to the north."

Jimmy seemed to relax. Then, Willy tossed some wood on the fire and sat down. "How do you speak English so well?"

"I was taught by white teachers on the reservation in Oklahoma. Good teachers."

"Well, I'm Jimmy Logan. That's my brother Will over there."

"Hello," said Willy. "What's your name?"

"I am Makwa. I am from the Cahokia tribe. I am grandson of the great Keetinsa. I am the son of Kanto."

"Okay, Makwa. Why do you want to cross the river? It's not exactly an easy thing to do," said Willy.

"I cross because my father crossed here with me. This is the ancient path of my people. I will go over the big river tomorrow, into Illinois, and then I go north. Up to the lands of my ancestors, near the great mounds east of your big white town of St. Louis."

With this, Will stood up. He walked right in front of both men and placed some more wood on the fire. "Looks like we might be up a while," he said. He then tried to calm the situation a bit, saying,

"Yeah, when I was at Gratiot Street in St. Louis, the Graybeards told me about the Indian mounds at a place called Cahokia, about eight miles to the east. They said there was a massive mound there like a hundred feet high. Did your people build that mound?"

"No. The mounds were already there when the Cahokia moved there. My people do not know who the builders were."

Willy gestured to the ground and they all awkwardly sat down around the fire. As a peace gesture, Will walked over and handed a wedge of jerky to Makwa and then to Jimmy. Then, the three men began to talk about their recent journeys. At one point, Will asked Makwa, "What happened to your Cahokia tribe and why are you going back there?"

"I make my journey because my father took me there when I was young. We went over the river here. This is an ancient crossing. We go there to remember our ancestors. My son is no longer of this world, so I go with his spirit to the same place... to remember."

Makwa looked at a small necklace that he was holding in his hand. "I made this for him while he was alive," said Makwa.

"I'm sorry that you lost your son," said Willy.

"Yes. But isn't that a long way to travel, Mister?" said Jimmy.

"Makwa. My name is Makwa. It is important to go there to keep the ancient memories alive. My ancestors are remembered and they live on in the spirit world. They will never die there. It is also like this for my son. His spirit now goes with me to the land of the big mounds."

"That's good," said Willy.

Makwa continued, "You asked what happened to the Cahokia Tribe. Have you not heard of the Cahokia people?"

"No, Makwa," said Jimmy, "I haven't."

"I think that most of your kind do not know what has happened to my people. Most white men don't know about the plight of Indians from the place that you now call Illinois."

"No, not really. Other than what we learned from school or read in the paper."

"The story of my tribe should be known by more people," said Makwa. "What has happened to my people and many other tribes is not good."

Jimmy answered, "I heard of the Trail of Tears. I know that was a bad deal. Tell us the real story of your people."

Makwa answered, "I have learned the 'real story' from my father and from tribal elders. I have even learned some of it from the history lessons from the white teachers in school."

"I will tell you our story, soldier."

"Jimmy. My name is Jimmy and this is my brother, Will."

"Okay, Jimmy and Will. For many years, my Cahokia tribe was part of the great Illini Nation. We lived in the place that you call Illinois. Our numbers lessened with time as the white man moved into our land. In 1803, my people and others were the last of the Illini Nation. We did not have enough warriors to stand up to the white man's army. So, we had to give in and sign away nearly half of the lands now called Illinois. We were forced to sell almost nine million acres to the white man. We received $12,000 and two small tracts of land in Illinois.

"Then, in 1832, those two small tracts were taken away and we were sent to other land tracts in the eastern Kansas Territory. Then, that land was also taken away and we were sent to other lands in Oklahoma."

Jimmy and Will just looked at Makwa, nearly unable to speak. "I never knew about any of this," Will said. "I really had no idea."

Makwa continued, "Later, even that Oklahoma land was taken as more white settlers moved to the west. Our numbers are very few now. For the last eighteen years, my people have joined with other tribes in northwest Oklahoma." Makwa paused. His face became very tight and his eyes welled up with tears. "There are not many real Cahokia Indians left. I fear my people will all be gone by the time that I die."

The three men sat around the fire speechless for some time. Then, Makwa took a deep breath and sat up straight. He finished his story with one more statement. "Just as you travel with your brother, I travel with the spirit of my son. My people have lost our land, our streams, and our rivers. We have lost our deer, our rabbits, and even our birds. But our spirits can never be taken away.

"I have told you the story of the great Cahokia tribe...of my people. Many other proud Indian nations have stories much like mine. Many tribes have had it much worse! We still live on. We are strong and I tell my people's story, so it will not be forgotten."

"Don't worry, Makwa, we'll tell your story to many other people," said Willy. The men sat and spoke about the evening's weather for a while. Then, after a short period, Jimmy announced, "Listen, Makwa, we really need to sleep. We have a big day tomorrow. You can sleep here by our fire if you wish. We will keep it going until the morning."

"I will sleep here," answered Makwa. The Indian turned and went behind the thicket, returning quickly with a pouch of provisions and another long pole staff. He found an area, moved some dirt around, placed a small blanket, and lay down. Within a short period, all three men were asleep and the sounds of the night surrendered to crickets, grasshoppers, frogs, and the other creatures of the darkness.

April 17, 1865

At 6:21 a.m., the sun's morning light peaked over the horizon from the east. Its light began to blanket Prices Landing with warmth as it reflected off the river. It shined through the trees like a beautiful painting.

The brothers arose and quickly started moving about. Today was an important day. Will found a small stream nearby and the men took extra time getting ready. They washed up and even shaved by the creek's side as they talked about returning to their home later in the day. "I can't wait to see the look on Momma's face," said Willy.

"Me neither."

Within an hour, everyone had eaten and finished their morning activities. Jimmy was taking supplies back to the boat and Will was busy putting out the fire. When the three men were together, Makwa spoke to them. "Thank you, soldiers. May you find your home safely on this day." He turned and started to walk off.

"Wait a minute!" Will said. "Where are you going?"

"I have a hatchet and I have rope. I am going to make a raft to go across the big river."

"Well, we have a boat! We can take you to the other side. Right, Jimmy?"

"Damn straight, Willy. We sure can. Makwa, you can go with us to the other side. We have room for you."

"No!" said Makwa. "I do not need help in my journey. I will make it alone."

"That's bullshit, Mak," said Willy. "You told us yourself that you were not alone! You're not alone now and neither are we! We are all here together, even if it's just for this short little time. Even if it's never again!"

Jimmy joined in. "We know you and we know your people's story! Now, we can tell other people of the Cahokia and we will! Makwa, you are now a part of our story and we are a part of yours. We will help you cross because you are our friend!"

"Right," said Willy. "Friends help each other and they become a part of each other's story!"

Smallpox Island

After a long pause, Makwa agreed, saying, "I will go across the big river with you in your boat."

"Great!" With that, they all loaded into the little skiff. After about ten minutes, they had reached the other side. Makwa disembarked to the shore. He took a knee quietly and looked at the ground and then the sky. He then stood up straight and told them, "Will and Jimmy, you have helped me and I will remember you. Remember me and remember the Cahokia."

"We will. Be careful!"

At 7:30 a.m., they all waved at each other and the brothers started paddling down the mighty Mississippi River. When they were about fifty feet away, Makwa yelled to them while smiling, "Hey! You know, I will still have to make a raft when I return!"

"Yes, Makwa," said Willy. "But not today!"

The three friends laughed and continued their journeys. The brothers quickly worked their way back over to the western side of the river since they were more accustomed to navigating from the Missouri side.

For the first hour of rowing, not a single word was said. No words were needed unless something came up. Jimmy and Will simply navigated the river. They had become accustomed to the actions of the river and were moving like a finely tuned machine. Then, all of a sudden, Will spoke. "I can't believe that Abraham Lincoln is dead."

There was a long pause. Then Jimmy said, "But you fought against him. On the other side."

"I know, but I didn't want him to die. Did you want Jefferson Davis to die?"

"No, not really," said Jimmy.

"Besides, the war is over," Will said. "Both sides can use a strong president right now. To fix things up. I'm sure the South is torn up and Lincoln could have done a lot to help fix it."

"Well, I hope the new president will do a good job."

"Oh yeah, who is the new president?"

"Some guy named Johnson," said Jimmy. "Never heard of him."

"Me neither."

They both broke into laughter, which slowly waned into a nervous chuckle.

After another hour of rowing, they were passing the Ohio River. Holding his map, Jimmy told Will, "Eyes left, Will. That's the confluence of the Ohio and the Mississippi Rivers. See that Fort right there?"

"Yep."

"That's Fort Defiance. I heard General Grant built it to watch over the military river traffic."

"Yeah?" Will said. "I think I might have seen it as a prisoner when I was heading upriver on a transport ship. That was way back after I was captured at the Battle of Iuka. But that was a very long time ago and I'm really glad to be going the other way now."

"Me too, Willy. I'm glad we both are."

Three hours later, the brothers were exhausted. They had been trading off with fast rowing at every ten minutes. Finally, they slowed their rowing down and let the current take them for a while. "Looks like a town up here on the left," said Will. "Do you know what it is?"

"Well, it should be Columbus, Kentucky. It's about twenty miles north of New Madrid on the eastern side of the river."

"Okay. I remember that town. Dad had to go there to get some farm supplies way back in the day." After a few moments, they were on the opposite side of the river from the town. "Let's row past Columbus and pull over," said Willy. "We need to take a break to eat and rest."

"Agreed."

Smallpox Island

They rowed past the town (that actually was Columbus, Kentucky) and stopped their boat on the Missouri side of the river just about one-half mile after the town. They pulled the skiff up onto a sandy area and ventured inland to find a place to recharge. After about twenty minutes, they both were rested, fed, hydrated, and back on the river. Jimmy yelled out to the empty river, "Hey! In about three hours, we will be in New Madrid, Missouri!"

"Hee-haaw!!" Willy chimed in.

After their out-loud declarations, the brothers paddled their way down the river with newfound enthusiasm. The time was passing quickly as they paddled closer and closer to their home. As they traveled down the river, Will and Jimmy both started to look toward the sky. The clouds were becoming darker and darker. In the distance off to the west, they could see rain and some lightning flashes.

Within ten minutes, it had started to rain. For the next twenty minutes, they just kept paddling right through what was becoming a rather strong rainstorm. Even with the heavy rain, the brothers were not ready to stop since they were so close to home. Then suddenly, lightning crashed and flashed nearby. The brothers nearly jumped out of the boat.

"What do you want to do, Will?" yelled Jimmy through the loud storm.

"I wanna keep on going!" said Willy. "I've survived a lot of things, and I don't think my time to go is going to be on this river in this little boat."

"Okay. But normally, I would pull over and seek some kind of cover. Let's be careful anyway."

"Okay, Jimmy, got it!" yelled Willy through the rainstorm. "We'll make a point to try to steer around any lightning bolts!"

"Noted. That's a good safety tip!" They both laughed heartily as they rowed their boat through the rain and the lightning.

After about fifteen minutes, the storm had relinquished into a drizzle and the brothers rowed with enhanced vigor. Will took a cup and removed rainwater from the bottom of the boat. A couple of hours later, Jimmy slowed down his rowing. He gazed at a vast worn-down stretch of riverbank on the west side of the river. He knew this area all too well. It was his old unit's landing area just before New Madrid. General Pope and thousands of soldiers had disembarked on this now-abandoned spot.

Jimmy told Willy, "This is the area at the top right part of the 'N' of the Mississippi River. We're just east of New Madrid. My unit brought in thousands of soldiers here." He pointed to the massive area of land that had been nearly worn bare. "This was the Army of the Mississippi's landing area. We shelled New Madrid, dug a twelve-mile canal, and defeated Island #10."

"Wait a minute. You shelled New Madrid?" said Will.

"Yeah, but luckily it was abandoned."

"What do you mean you dug a twelve-mile canal?"

"Well, we dug a twelve-mile canal across the top of the 'N' all of the way to New Madrid," said Jimmy. "We hand-dug and blasted through trees, valleys, and hills. All of the way to Wilson's Bayou, and we did it in just nineteen days!"

"Bullshit," said Willy.

"I know. It sounds crazy, but we really did it. We did use dynamite. It's not like we dug out the entire thing by hand. Just most of it. We also had thousands of soldiers working on it." Jimmy continued as they floated along, "Then, we ferried hundreds of soldiers right around the Rebs and surprised them from the rear. We barely fired a shot. Island #10 was defeated and the river was opened again."

"Wait a minute," said Willy. "You're telling me that you built this magical canal and ferried hundreds of soldiers behind the Rebs and surprised them?"

"Yes, sir. And the transports went right past our farm, I might add."

Smallpox Island

"That sounds like one of the greatest military maneuvers of all time. Why haven't I ever heard of it?"

"I don't know, but there's the canal right there." They sat there in their little boat and gazed at the now impassable canal. It appeared to have been partially destroyed on purpose and had been largely overgrown with vegetation in the three years since it was completed.

"I can't believe it," said Will as he stood up in the boat, gazing deep into the canal. "Well, one thing's for sure. I don't think we can use your canal to get to New Madrid today."

"Nope. Looks like we wouldn't get too far."

"Come on, let's get going," said Jimmy. "We probably have another hour to New Madrid and another half hour after that to get to the farm."

"Great, let's go!"

About half an hour later, they made the river's hard-right U-turn as it turned back to the north. They looked to the left and Jimmy pointed at Island #10. "Look, Willy! There's #10." The small island was utterly pulverized, with trees splintered apart and bomb craters everywhere. "Holy crap!" said Jimmy. "I know we bombed #10 for days, but I never saw it until now."

"Glad I wasn't stationed there," said Will.

"I'm glad you weren't too. My unit never faced yours and I thank God for that." After another half hour, they were cruising up to their town of New Madrid. "You know, the last time I came through here, I took off my uniform. The place was mostly Rebels back then. But this time, I think I'm gonna leave it on. The war is over and my side won. So, I'm keeping it on this time."

"Good idea. I don't feel like stopping to change anyway. I just want to get home." They paddled past New Madrid with little fanfare. Will saw one fellow that he knew and waved at him. That was about it. "Well, I guess there's not going to be a big parade for us," said Willy.

"Guess not, little brother."

"Too bad. I was preparing my speech." They both laughed.

"That's funny. Let's keep rowing." They followed the current as the river made another hard left U-turn to the south.

Jimmy and Willy traded off at rowing as they picked up the pace toward their home. About a half-hour later (at about 5:30 p.m.), they were finally coasting up to their family farm.

They pulled over nearly one-quarter mile from the house, right alongside the main farm field that they had both tilled for years. "Let's pull the boat up here," said Jimmy. "I want to straighten myself up a little bit before Momma sees me."

"Me too. Do you think she knows we're coming?"

"Well, like I said before, I sent her a letter from St. Louis before we left, but I doubt she has it yet."

Willy snickered and said, "I'm sure."

The boys combed their hair and straightened up a little bit. They looked at each other and with a brief nod, they started walking down the field to the house.

"Look!" said Willy. "That stupid plow is broken down again, and it's right in the middle of the field."

"So what else is new?"

Chapter Thirteen

April 17, 1865, 5:40 p.m.
Home

At exactly 5:40 p.m. on April 17, 1865, Martha Logan's two sons walked through the front door of their family home. At first, they just stood there quietly. Jimmy held his finger up and went, "Shhh." No one noticed them. Grandma Logan was sound asleep in the front room. They caught a brief glimpse of their mother walking around in the kitchen, but still they were not noticed. Then, after about one minute, they heard steps coming up behind them from outside. They moved over to the side and Phyllis came walking through the front door carrying a stack of firewood in her arms. As soon as she saw them, she dropped the wood on the floor and screamed out loud. "Oh, my great God!! Ms. Logan!! Ms. Logan!! Your boys!! Your boys!!"

Martha came running to the front room. "What? Do you have a letter?"

"No, Ma'am!" As Martha entered the room, she saw Phyllis with her arm stretched out, pointing at her two sons.

Jimmy and Willy stood there with giant grins on their faces.

Martha Logan saw her two sons, blinked her eyes, and fell to her knees as the boys went to her side. She broke into tears and kept saying, "My boys... My boys ..."

Grandma Logan woke up, stood up, waved her arms, and did a little jump with a yip! Everyone in the room started crying, including Ms. Logan's boys. After about five minutes of small talk with their mother, they walked her into the front room and she sat down in a chair.

"Why didn't you tell me you were coming?"

"We did. I sent you a letter," said Jimmy. "You should get it any day now." They all laughed and slowly started calming down from the moment.

Jimmy and Will gave their mother a brief update of the happenings since their last letter. It was more than a small task to fill her in on everything. "To put it in a nutshell," said Jimmy, "as you know, I started working at the Alton Prison. Then, they sent Willy to a place called Smallpox Island because they thought that his shingles were really smallpox. Then, I asked the prison commander to allow him off the island. So, he paroled Willy and ordered me to bring him home because he knew that the war was nearly over. It's all in my last letter that you haven't received. Then, lots of other interesting stuff happened to us as we headed home on the river, but I'll tell you more about all of that later."

Their mother then updated them about some recent events on the farm. She told them that many Confederate soldiers had walked through the property and passed by on the river.

"Oh, I went by on the river, Momma," Will said.

"So did I, Momma," Jimmy added.

"Well, why didn't you stop and see me?!" said Martha.

"I couldn't, Momma," said Willy, chuckling. "I was a prisoner!"

"I couldn't either, said Jimmy. "My unit was doing a night attack."

"Well, okay then," Martha said. "I guess I'll forgive you this time."

They all laughed again and finally started to relax.

As darkness approached, the brothers went out to retrieve their little boat. They floated down to the area right in front of the house. After pulling it up onto shore, they brought all of its contents either back to the house or the main barn. They were surprised to see that they still had a decent amount of supplies left, including some matches, some beef jerky, a jug of water, and a bag with dried beans.

"Hey look, Jimmy!" Will said. "We could have gone a lot further."

"Great! Let's load this thing back up and get down the river!"

"No way, Jim. I've had enough of the muddy ol' Mississippi for a while."

"Agreed. Me too."

Martha prepared a special homecoming chicken dinner for the evening. After that, the boys went upstairs to their shared room and started organizing it for the first time in a very long time.

"Wonder how long we'll be livin' here, Jimmy?"

"Not too awful long, Will. If things go right, I'll be building a house soon for Patsy and me."

"Right. I'll help you. If things go right for Belle and me, I just might need your carpentry help as well."

"That sounds like a good deal," said Jimmy.

April 18-21, 1865

The next day Martha, Jimmy, and Will went out and found George Cribbon and Tom Machins while they were out working in the fields. They thanked the men for working the farm while they were gone.

"Great to see you both, boys," Tom said. "Take your time coming back out to these fields. They sure ain't going anywhere."

George Cribbon added, "Well, you can start out working on

that old plow of your daddy's. That piece of crap hasn't worked right since you left. I've been using mine. That rusty ol' thing's right out in the middle of the field waiting for you!"

They all laughed. Tom grabbed and hugged them both with a big bear hug. George added, "We're really glad you boys are back. We missed ya!"

Later, Martha told the boys that she was going to plan a homecoming party for them in four days, on Saturday, April 22. But first, she wanted everyone to settle in a little and try to catch up with normal life.

That afternoon, the boys started walking toward the house of their old girlfriends, Patsy and Bonnie Caldwell. As they walked there, Willy said, "I know Bonnie has married and moved away, but I think it's right for me to drop by with you."

"Sure, Patsy likes you, too."

They made it to the house and knocked on the door. Patsy's mom opened the door and then opened her mouth with surprise. "Shh, I'll send her out," she whispered.

Jimmy's girl Patsy walked through the door, looked at Jimmy, and instantly started crying. She rushed into his arms. She kissed him and then she stood back and punched him in the chest. "Why did you stop writing to me?" she said.

"I didn't stop! I've just been busy. I've been workin' for the Army and it wasn't easy getting this guy outta prison! It's been a real whirlwind. I haven't even hardly had time to write my own momma! I also couldn't write about every single thing that I was doing because I didn't know if it would all work out. I also didn't want you to worry about me."

"Well, it didn't work!" she said, grabbing him with a firm hug.

She quickly turned to look directly at Will. She frowned and gave him a brief hug. "Willy, I guess you've heard that Bonnie has married and moved west."

Smallpox Island

"I know."

"She heard that you were a prisoner. They told us that your chances of making it back were not very good."

"Yeah, I knew all about it," said Will. "Momma told me in one of her letters that she had married and moved away about a year ago. It's okay. I didn't expect her to wait that long. I'm glad for her. Heck, I didn't think I was gonna make it back either."

Bonnie continued, "She married a good man named Thomas Jamison and they moved way out to Colorado. I'll let her know that you're okay." She paused and then looked Willy straight in the eyes, "Will, in every single letter she writes to me, she asks about you. She is going to have her prayers answered when she finds out that you've made it home alive."

Jimmy then told Patsy about the homecoming party on Saturday and told her to also ask her family to come.

"We'll be there!" she said. "I'm sure everyone will be there. The whole town loves you guys." Jimmy and Patsy shared an uncomfortable kiss since Will and her mom were standing there watching. "I'll try to come visit you later in the day tomorrow."

"You better," Jimmy said.

The brothers headed home. Jimmy said, "Well, that went much better than I expected."

"Yes, it did," said Will, "and it's good to know that Bonnie still cares about me."

"Don't get too excited, lover boy. You already gotta real fine girl named Belle."

"I know, but it's nice to know that Bonnie still cares."

For the next two days, Jimmy and Will tried to get back into the groove of the farm.

Will's zoster shingles condition was quickly diminishing and was much less noticeable. It was also hurting much less. On the day before the party, Martha had the boys clear a large area near the river that the family used for large gatherings. The boys spoke back and forth to each other while they worked. "What time's the party tomorrow?"

"She told me it's from 5 p.m. to 9 p.m., or whenever. After we clear this area, we're going to get the horse and wagon. We have to bring a whole bunch of wood down here for a big bonfire."

"Phyllis is killing about fifteen chickens tomorrow to cook up for people to eat."

"Wow! Good thing we have forty chickens."

"Tom Machin's wife is also bringing over a big tub of beans. George Cribbon told me yesterday he's bringing over a whole keg of beer that he had delivered all the way from St. Louis. Lemp Beer. That's the good stuff. He said that he ordered it right after Lee surrendered and he finally got it yesterday."

Point of Historical Reference – The production of Lemp Beer was started in St. Louis by German immigrant John Lemp around 1840. The lager style beer became immensely popular throughout in the entire Midwest region. Lemp's son William, later took the helm and built a large new brewery in St. Louis in 1864, right in the middle of the Civil War.

"It's starting to sound like a dang good party to me."

"Yes, sir."

"Are we going to play some music?"

"Don't know, but I hope so."

The following evening, Jimmy and Patsy met in the same gathering area in front of the Logans' house. It was chilly, so Jimmy brought a blanket. They sat together on a hay bale that had been brought down for the next day's party. They chatted with each other

Smallpox Island

as they watched the river roll by, much as they had done many times before. "So, let me get this straight," Patsy said. "You're still in the Union Army, but you don't have to go back and you still are getting paid. How does somebody get a deal like that?"

"Well, my commander sent me here to take Willy home. I'm on orders and I will officially be discharged on 30 April 1865. So, I'm on duty and I'm actually on the clock and getting paid."

"So, you are a public servant and you work for me then!"

"Well, I guess so. What do you have in mind?" Patsy stood up, grabbed his hand, and pulled him up. Then, she grabbed the blanket and led him away into the nearby wood line as the moonlight reflected off the river. The frogs and crickets serenaded them as they walked off into the darkness.

April 22, 1865
The Day of the Welcome Home Gathering

The next day was Saturday. It had rained early in the morning, but by noon, the sun had appeared. Martha Logan and Jimmy took the wagon into town to pick up a few things before the homecoming party. It was turning out to be a good day after all. As they entered town, one New Madrid resident noticed Jimmy and yelled, "Welcome home, Jimmy!"

"Thanks, Henry! Good to see you!"

Another man yelled, "Hey Logan, did you kill any of my friends while you were fighting for the damn Yankees!"

Jimmy yelled back, "Don't think so! I hope not!" He then spoke quietly to his mother. "Hey, Momma, who the heck was that?"

"I've seen him before, Jimmy, but I don't remember his name. Wait, I remember. I think that's Emil Hastings," she said. "Your father knew him. He was around years ago and he's not a very nice person. I haven't seen him around here for a long time."

Several other locals waved and smiled at Martha and her son. The sting of the war was diminishing, but it was certainly still present.

As they pulled up to the general store, the manager, Mr. Kimmel, was standing on the front porch. He saw Martha and Jimmy approaching and spryly walked out to the wagon with a big smile on his face. "Hey there, Logans! Hi, Jimmy, I'm sure glad that doggone war is over. It's a dang miracle my store wasn't hit by the shelling." Kimmel ran over to Jimmy and shook his hand as he exited the wagon.

"Good, I'm really glad it wasn't!" said Jimmy as he jumped off the wagon. Jimmy couldn't bear to tell Mr. Kimmel that he had actually taken part in the shelling of his own hometown.

He immediately thought about his unit and the bombardment of New Madrid. Jimmy had a brief flashback of kicking the mortar cannon just a bit to make it miss its target. Then, he remembered that he had actually vomited during the shelling. Just the thought of what had happened made his stomach a bit queasy at that very moment. While they were at the store, Jimmy was busy gathering his mother's order. He found Mr. Kimmel and whispered a few words into his ear. The manager came back a moment later with a big smile on his face, "Here you are, Jim. Four new sets of catgut guitar strings."

"Thank you, sir," Jimmy said cheerfully.

Jimmy and his mother made a few other quick stops and within an hour they were approaching the farm. As they pulled up in the wagon, she asked Jimmy for the time on his pocket watch. "It's two o'clock, Momma."

"Oh my," his mom proclaimed. "It's two o'clock! I have to get busy. I have a party to get ready for. My sons have come home from the war!" She jumped from the wagon and quickly entered the house as Jimmy brought in her purchases.

At 4 p.m., Martha asked the boys to start up the big fire. Tom Machins and his wife were there setting up some tables. George Cribbon then pulled up in his wagon with his keg of Lemp Beer that had come all the way from St. Louis. He also brought some blocks of ice that he had purchased in town. First, Tom dug a good-sized hole in a shaded area near some trees. Then, he put his big keg of beer right down into the hole. Finally, he broke up his ice blocks with a hammer, placed them all around the barrel, and covered it all with two large blankets. "That will sure help to keep that beer cool! I don't like hot beer," Cribbon proudly proclaimed.

At about 4:30, Martha and Phyllis were busy setting up decorations. Then, Martha told the boys to go back to the house. "Go get cleaned up and put on some real nice clothes, boys. Half the town is coming to see you tonight. We'll take care of everything else." As they walked up to the house, Willy said, "I wonder what I should wear tonight."

"Well, I'm sure you'll find a nice dress to wear."

"Screw you, asshole!" Will said as he shoved his big brother.

At 5:10 p.m., Jimmy and Will came walking down from the house to a group of about thirty people. Both of the brothers smiled, pointed, and waved as everyone started clapping, whooping, and hollering. Phyllis was proudly standing behind a big "Welcome Home" cake that she had baked. The whole area was set up with food, drink, and decorations.

As the evening developed, it was evident that the word had spread about the boys' big party. More and more people started showing up as the evening progressed. By the time that darkness had arrived, there were at least fifty to sixty people there. Everyone was talking, eating, drinking, and having a good time. The sounds of laughter and chatter filled the air. At one point, Jimmy stole away to have some time alone with Patsy. Two guests had started to play a fiddle and a banjo, so no one really noticed that Jimmy wasn't there for a while.

Suddenly, Emil Hastings, the same disheveled person they had seen in town earlier that day, came walking into the party. No one really noticed him at first. He zigzagged through the party and gradually started talking louder and louder. Most of the partygoers still ignored Hastings until he went into a loud rant about slavery, the Confederacy, Lincoln, and John Wilkes Booth. Finally, one person yelled, "Shut up, Emil!" while nearly everyone else still refused to pay attention to the intruder. Then, Hastings pulled out a pistol and fired it into the air. Then they all paid attention. Hastings quickly ran up to Martha Logan and grabbed her from behind. Martha fought him, but she did not scream. Hastings then started backing up the hill toward the house while holding the gun up to Martha's head.

The men at the party quickly started moving around, but there wasn't a lot that they could do, primarily because of the angle and the fact that Hastings had a pistol to Martha Logan's head. George Cribbon quickly came up and said, "Give me the gun, Emil!"

"Get away, George! All of you! Don't make me kill her! I told this bitch's husband John Logan ten years ago not to go about freein' any damn slave! He wouldn't listen. I told him that I wouldn't have it. He told me to 'get lost!' Called me an 'idiot!'" Hastings kept dragging Martha up the hill, away from the party, while facing toward the crowd. "You know what I did then? I'll tell you. I followed him one day! Came up behind him and hit him with a board. When he didn't die all the way, I shot him three times!! Then Martha here goes about to freeing the damn slave anyway!! I'm not about to have it. The Confederacy almost proved me right! I waited ten years! I'm gonna kill this nigra-loving mother of a Union soldier!"

At that second, Jimmy returned to the party after hearing

the gunshot and all the yelling. He found Willy and they saw their mother being dragged up the hill. Will and Jimmy looked at each other. Then Jimmy yelled, "Let's go!!" They rushed directly at Hastings as he backed up with their mother. Immediately, Hastings shot his pistol straight at Jimmy. The round hit Jimmy and he spun around, hitting the ground. Will stopped quickly as Hastings leveled his pistol directly at him. "You're next, boy. I got four more rounds in this chamber! You know I've been waiting for you and your brother to come back home! If you weren't a Rebel soldier, I'd shoot your ass right now! Aw, hell, I'm gonna kill your whole family anyway! Then, I'll take your slave and I'll sell her ass!"

Will looked at Jimmy and helped him to stand up. Jim had only been grazed in the shoulder. He whispered to Willy, "That looks like a seven-shot Remington revolver. I think he might have five rounds left, not four. Be careful."

Then, Tom Machins started walking up to Hastings with his hands up. By this time, Hastings had dragged Martha halfway up the hill to the house. Machins yelled, "Now Emil, I've known you since we were kids. You don't need to do this!"

"Shut up, Machins! You don't know me! Get away or I'll shoot you, too!" Hastings kept backing up with the crowd following him as he went up the hill. Just then, a shadowy figure started quietly walking toward Hastings and his captive from behind. Some in the crowd saw the figure, but nobody acknowledged it. The figure then disappeared. Hastings kept backing up while he ranted about his cause.

Will and Jimmy kept approaching closer and Hastings again leveled his pistol directly at the boys. Then like a flash, out of nowhere, the shadowy figure jumped up directly behind Hastings. Immediately there was a loud *Boom!* and a muzzle flash. The unknown man had shot Hastings point-blank in the side of his neck, with the pistol aimed away from Martha Logan. Hastings dropped immediately to the ground motionless. He didn't even know what had hit him. Martha temporarily fell to the ground, holding her ears, before jumping up and running over to her sons. The unknown man stood silently and directly over Hastings, still pointing his pistol directly at the intruder's dead body.

With the sun going down behind him, it was hard to see the face of the man who had just saved Martha. Martha, Jimmy, Will, and indeed the entire crowd moved forward to look closely at the man who was standing over the body of Emil Hastings. The man who had just saved Martha. It took a few seconds for their eyes to adjust and for their minds to realize exactly who the man was.

It was Caleb Bullman! Martha, the boys, and indeed the whole crowd were gobsmacked as they all looked aghast at him. "It's Bullman!"

"Who?"

"It's Caleb Bullman!"

Bullman leaned over and disarmed Hastings, making sure that the intruder was dead. Martha spoke up while crying, "Oh, my God! What has happened? I can't believe that man killed my John. My husband!" Still crying, she said, "Oh, thank you, Mr. Bullman. Thank you!"

Bullman spoke up. "You're welcome, ma'am. Are you okay?"

"Yes, I'm fine. My right ear is ringing a little bit."

"That'll go away soon. Jimmy, are you okay?"

"Yes, sir. He grazed my left shoulder, but it didn't go in."

Bullman continued, "Good. You're a very lucky man. Good thing this dirtbag is a bad shot!" He then looked toward Will. "Mr. Will, do you remember what I told you a long time ago at that dance in New Madrid?"

With that comment, Jimmy instantly remembered Bullman whispering into Will's ear when they were at the town dance. "Yes, sir," said Willy.

"What did I tell you, boy?"

"You told me that you would watch out for my momma while I was gone."

"And I did. The whole time you were gone, I tried hard to keep an eye on what was going on around your farm here. I told Confederate soldiers to steer clear of your house many times."

"Did you know about this man?" asked Jimmy.

"You better believe I did. A long time ago, this here scallywag, Emil Hastings, thought I was akin to violence. He told me that he wanted to go after anyone that was for the North and anybody that freed any slaves. He mentioned your family and several others. When I told him that there had been enough stirring of the waters, he made the mistake of pointing his rifle at me. Threatening me. So, I took his rifle from him and butted him in the face with it. I've been keepin' an eye on this bastard ever since."

"Thanks, Mr. Bullman," said Jimmy. "I guess...I guess I really had you figured all wrong. And I'm sorry."

"That's okay, son. I know you didn't really like me. A good amount of the time, I don't really like me much either."

Some people in the crowd started moving back down the hill. Caleb Bullman looked toward Hastings' dead body and started talking quieter to Jimmy, Will, and Martha. "I learned a long time ago to try to do what's right. It don't always turn out that way, though. But I do try."

Then, some of the partygoers began gathering around Caleb Bullman. They started thanking him and shaking his hand while looking at the body. Martha and some friends took Jimmy up to the house and attended to the small wound on his right forearm. About ten minutes later, they all came back down from the house. Martha then announced, "My friends! The Welcome Home gathering for my boys will be rescheduled until tomorrow night. Sunday night. Once again, from 5 p.m. to 9 p.m., or whenever. That's unless something else goes wrong."

"It won't!" yelled Jimmy, gesturing toward Caleb Bullman. "We've got a Guardian Angel here to make sure of that!"

With that, the entire crowd erupted into a roar of clapping, cheers, and "Hip Hip, Hoorays!"

As sunset advanced, the crowd started dispersing. George Cribbon, Tom Machins, Phyllis, and the Logans started cleaning up the party sight. George and Tom quickly covered the body. Then, they brought a horse-drawn wagon and loaded up the would-be murderer. "I know his sister and her husband," proclaimed Cribbon. "We'll take the body over to their house and help them to bury him. They live a couple miles west of town, so we're going to leave now to try to get there before dark." They quickly departed.

After a short while, it was apparent that Jimmy had not been seriously injured. He brought down a couple of shovels and a bucket. Together, he and Caleb Bullman started scooping up the bloody soil where the body had fallen. There was a lot of blood. With no one near them, Bullman spoke casually to Jimmy. "You know, Jimmy, I too fought for the Union at one time."

"I know. Willy told me."

"I'm kinda more of a fighter than a policymaker. Fought with General Zachary Taylor in the Mexican-American War from 1846 to '48."

"Wow! You knew the future president! Willy told me a little bit about that. What battles were you in?"

"Well, the biggest ones were the Battle of Resaca de la Palma and the Battle of Buena Vista."

"You got hurt?"

"Got hurt pretty bad. That's why I have trouble walking sometimes." Bullman reached over with his shovel and tapped his left leg. "This here leg is mostly wood.

"I've seen some rough things. It all messed me up in more ways than I'd like to admit. I really still feel like I was more comfortable as a soldier, even though it's many years later."

Smallpox Island

"I understand that," said Jimmy. "I've seen a couple of rough battles myself, like you have. I also feel like I'm more soldier than I am anything else."

Bullman answered, "Jim, once you've been a true soldier, it becomes part of you. It doesn't really go away. You can't seem to get rid of it, even if you want to."

As dusk approached, the two former rivals then took their shovels, their bucket of bloody dirt, and they walked. They headed down toward the river, turned to the south, and found a thicket next to a little creek. There, they started to dig a small hole to dump the bloody dirt in. Caleb Bullman spoke. "Jimmy, I know I drink too much sometimes and I know you didn't like me very much. But I do follow orders and I really try to do what's right."

"Yep, Will told me a lot about you being in the military," said Jimmy. "To tell you the truth, I found it all was kinda hard to believe. Now, I know that it was true. Now, I also know that you saved my momma's life. Aww hell, Caleb, you saved the whole damn party. You're a hero in the truest sense of the word."

"No, I ain't. I feel like I only did what I had to do. I did what I had promised. I kept an eye out for your momma. Even though you boys were home, I knew that dirtbag was on the prowl. I got lucky and I got him."

"Well, I'm grateful," said Jimmy.

Caleb Bullman then asked, "You know what I think would make someone a hero?"

"What?"

"Well, I heard about someone that got their brother out of a prison full of sick people. I heard he went to the prison commander and somehow got permission. I also heard that he went out onto some quarantined island full of people dying of smallpox, rescued him, and brought him hundreds of miles all the way home. Now, that's what I would call a hero."

"I just did what I had to do," said Jimmy.

"Exactly. Just like I did."

The men had finished covering up the hole. While they leaned on their shovels, Caleb said, "I've got something to show you."

"What's that?" said Jimmy, patting down the dirt on top of the hole. Caleb reached in his pocket and pulled out a large gold coin. "Wow! What the heck is that?"

"This is a Congressional Gold Medal. Zachary Taylor gave it to me before he was president. He ended up with three of them. He got this one for a battle we were in. The Battle of Resaca de la Palma. He said I'd saved his life in the battle. I really don't talk about this, but I'll tell you because you're a soldier.

"We were temporarily overrun and I laid in front of him while he returned fire. I took about three rounds to my left leg and one to the left arm. That's why my left leg is mostly made of wood."

"Holy crap, Caleb," said Jimmy. "You were like a human bunker for Zachary Taylor!"

"I guess so. Didn't feel like it at the time. It just happened. I just did what I had to do. I had to provide cover for General Taylor, because I was expendable and he wasn't."

"I always heard that Taylor was a remarkable soldier," said Jimmy. "He was. We were outnumbered and we ended up pushing the Mexican Army back out of Texas. It was a real big deal at the time. Ulysses S. Grant also served in our unit. We were a great outfit. Everyone knew each other and we were prepared to die for each other if necessary."

"Anyway, he gave this to me. It's a Congressional Gold Medal."

Bullman showed Jimmy both sides of the coin. He then placed the coin in his palm and reached out his hand for Jimmy to shake it. He put the large coin-like medal into Jimmy's hand, while shaking his hand at the same time.

Smallpox Island

"What's this, Caleb?" said Jimmy, holding out the medal back toward Caleb.

"Now, I'm giving it to you," said Caleb.

"What!"

"Yes, you earned it. Let me tell you. Your brother, Will, is one of the few people that I can call a real friend. He was gonna die and you saved him." There was a long pause.

"Just like you saved Zachary Taylor," said Jimmy.

"Sure, I guess you can say that. I know I couldn't have saved Willy," said Caleb. "Look, maybe someday you can give it to somebody else. Someone that does something beyond belief to save someone. Something like you did for your brother."

"Or something like you did for Zachary Taylor," said Jimmy.

"By the way, Jimmy. You may never find that person."

"Well, I think I may have already," said Jimmy. "You saved my momma's life tonight. It was beyond heroic."

"Hmm, good point, kid. Keep it anyway. I've carried that heavy ass coin around long enough." As they turned to leave, Jimmy stared at the medal and Caleb patted Jimmy on the back. "Son, you may have to keep that medal for a very long time."

Jimmy slipped the medal into his pocket. Caleb Bullman put his hand on Jimmy's shoulder and the two men started walking back toward the farm. Caleb was walking with an empty bucket, and Jimmy was carrying two shovels, with a smile on his face.

As they approached the farm, Caleb said, "You know, now that this Civil War is over, I'd fight for the Union again, if my body would let me. The South lost, but I'm over it."

"Right. People need to heal," said Jimmy.

"There is no Confederacy anymore," said Caleb. "Dixie's big dream turned out to be a nightmare, but now it's over. The South will survive, but it's gonna have to be part of the United States.

Jimmy answered, "Agreed. The war is finally over and the killing is done."

Later that evening, nearly everyone had departed and the activity of the canceled gathering had subsided. Jimmy was carrying a lantern while walking Patsy back home in the dark. "Jimmy, do you think we will ever be married?" said Patsy. Jimmy stopped and stood there, holding his lantern. After a few seconds, he then started walking again. "Well, I would certainly like to hope so. I don't think I would want to go through my whole life without you."

"Good. I feel the same way," said Patsy.

"You know, Jimmy, I'll be twenty-three years old soon. That's darn near an old maid around here." Jimmy looked at her as if a light had gone off in his head. "Wow. I understand now. I think I better get my head outta my butt and actually ask you soon. Especially, now that I know you might say 'Yes.'"

After about ten minutes, they were in front of Patsy's house. Jimmy reached in to kiss her and she turned her head and pranced away. "That's right, James. I *might* say 'Yes!' See you tomorrow!" She smiled and then started laughing. "Bye-bye!" she said as she tossed him a wave while entering the front door.

Chapter Fourteen

April 23, 1865
The New Day of the Welcome Home Gathering

The next day was Sunday. Martha made sure that everyone was up early and off to church. The church was a good half-hour wagon ride from the Logans' farm and a lot of people that were at the party were also there. After the service, many people came up to Will and Jimmy. They all shook their hands and said things such as "Good to see you, again" and "Glad you're back." To the boys' surprise, nearly everyone shook both of their hands, with seemingly no regard for who had fought for the North or the South. As they went back to the wagon, Willy mentioned this to his momma and to Jimmy. Martha said, "I noticed that, William. Maybe the healing has begun. I'm proud of you boys and I think a lot of these people are proud of you too, regardless of which side you fought on."

That evening, the welcome home party was back on. Everyone pretty much repeated the previous day's activities and got ready for the party again. The boys gathered some wood and prepared for the fire. Tom Machins set up the beer keg. He picked up ice from the ice house near New Madrid for the second day in a row. It was early in the season, so there was still plenty of river ice for sale.

At about 5 p.m., the party began. Everyone seemed to enjoy the food and the drink. As more guests arrived, some people seemed just a little nervous until someone saw Caleb Bullman. He was on guard, sitting on a tree stump about fifty yards over to the side, with his hand on his pistol. He waved at the guest and yelled over to them, "I'll be staying right over here. Have a good time, folks!" Every so often, Bullman would disappear for a while and then he would be sighted at another location.

Later in the evening, Jimmy and Martha brought some food and a beer over to Bullman. "Thank you much. I'm really just not that comfortable in crowds. Besides, I can keep a good eye on the area from over here."

"Thank you, sir. I think this may be the safest party in the world," said Jimmy.

"Haaa haa!" chuckled Caleb. "Now get back to your party and have some fun. Jimmy, if you like, you or Willy could bring me over a beer every so often."

"Will do, Caleb."

Jimmy couldn't believe it. A person (Caleb Bullman) who was a disliked enemy only two days ago was now a good friend. A good friend that had not only saved his mother's life, but had also given him a Congressional Gold Medal that was once owned by Zachary Taylor. It was a change of heart and of feelings that was almost beyond belief.

The party was turning out to be a success and later that night, it was time to play some music. For about half an hour, Jimmy and Will walked around with pencil and paper, writing down song titles that anyone wanted to hear or play. After noting that several people wanted to play and sing, Jimmy walked over to Caleb. "Mr. Bullman, sir. Would you be interested in playing an instrument or singing a song this evening?"

"Caleb. Call me Caleb, Jimmy. My gosh, I gave you my Congressional Gold Medal yesterday and rescued your momma. You can call me Caleb now."

"Okay. Caleb, would you be interested in playing an instrument or singing a song this evening?"

"I'm glad you asked. I have a song that I wrote with a friend of mine after the end of the Confederacy."

"Okay, what's it called?"

"All for Dixie."

"Great. I'm putting you down to play second, right after me. We're going to practice for the next half hour and kick the music off around 7:30. Do you need any backup musicians to assist you? Looks like we'll have a guitar, fiddle, banjo, harmonica, and a drum."

"I play a little bit of guitar," said Caleb. "I think I could use some drum."

"Great. Talk with Will. He's going to be beating on the big hollow tree stump for our drum."

"Ha! Okay," said Caleb. "I'll talk to him. Thanks."

Jimmy and Will then went over to Tom Machins and George Cribbon. Tom played the banjo and George played a mean fiddle. The Logan brothers had played music with them as far back as they could remember. Before long, Jimmy completed a list of eight songs on his paper. Then, all of the musicians gathered off to the side of the party to practice. Since darkness was falling upon the party, Martha and Phyllis walked around and started placing lanterns on tree stumps and on some hanging poles that they had put up earlier. As the night progressed, it became abundantly evident that much of the evening's light would be provided by the roaring fire in the center of the gathering.

The musicians worked together on the chosen songs until they felt ready to go. At about 7:30, ready they were. They found something to drink and took up an area about twenty feet from the fire.

Jimmy then spoke to everyone at the gathering. "On behalf of my momma, Will, and myself, I want to thank everyone for coming to our gathering tonight. Willy and I are glad you're all here. If you allow us, we're going to play a few songs for you tonight."

"Welcome home, boys!" several people yelled from the gathering. "Thank you," said Will. "We're mighty glad we made it back."

"Okay," said Jimmy. "Here we go. The first song was requested by several folks at our party. It's called 'Old Blue.'"

Jimmy played his guitar and walked around as he started singing. Will quickly started clapping to the snappy beat and the whole party quickly followed, clapping to the tune right after it started.

"Old Blue" – Late 1800s – Traditional

I had an old dog and his name was Blue,
Betcha five dollars he's a good dog too.
Every night just about good dark,
Blue goes out and begins to bark.
Here old Blue, you're a good dog you. (Repeat x2)

Blue chased a possum up a 'simmon tree,
Barked at the possum and grinned at me.
Chased that possum way out on a limb,
Blue sat down and he talked to him.
Here old Blue, you're a good dog you. (Repeat x2)
(SONG CONTINUES UNTIL ITS ENDING)

As Jimmy sang the last line, *"You're a good dog you,"* he held the word "dog" to imitate a howling dog. *"You're a good dooooooouug you!"* As Jimmy finished, nearly everyone jumped up, clapped, and cheered. One fella was so happy he jumped up and knocked his drink over. "Wow, that was fun. Go and get you another drink, Howard," said Jimmy.

"I think I will."

"Okay, the next song is from Mister Caleb Bullman, our party's guardian. We're all glad he's here and I personally want to thank him for saving my momma. And well, for saving the whole darn party. I want to also thank him for his service to the Union Army in years past. Some folks may not know it, but Mr. Bullman is a great and honored soldier. Years ago, he saved the life of our former president, Zachary Taylor, just like he saved my momma's life last night."

The crowd was quiet, awed, and a bit dumbfounded. Caleb Bullman walked up with his noticeably awkward gait. He seemed a bit embarrassed by Jimmy's introduction. "Folks, please keep my military journey under your hat. It's in the past, and believe me, I want to just leave it there. All right, this is called 'All for Dixie.' I wrote it with a friend after the Confederacy fell. Caleb then took Jimmy's guitar as Will stood by with two stout sticks in his hand while sitting on the big hollow tree stump.

"All for Dixie" - 2017 - G. S. Spooner

Oh, the South had the right
And the South had the might
We'd fight, and the Union would fall

Well, the South had the right
Good ol' Dixie had the might
We'd fight, and the Union would fall

All for Dixie. All for Dixie. The South is alive. All for Dixie
All for Dixie. All for Dixie. The South will survive. All for Dixie

G. S. Spooner

With brave valor to the man
As we stand for Southern land
We take the Union to our cause

But our soldiers they are hurt
Many buried are in the dirt
We fought, but the Union would not fall

All for Dixie. All for Dixie. The South is alive. All for Dixie
All for Dixie. All for Dixie. The South will survive. All for Dixie

The Mason-Dixon line is gone
And the slaves are not for long
We fought, but the Union would not fall

Now the time has come around
To finally lay our rifles down
And try to repair our broken land

All for Dixie. All for Dixie. The South is still alive. All for Dixie
All for Dixie. All for Dixie. The South will survive. All for Dixie
(SONG'S ENDING)

While Bullman was singing his song, he sat and looked around at the people. Willy beat his tree drum with one lone beat for each line of the song. Caleb looked everyone straight in the eye as he strummed the guitar, singing with a solemn look on his face. Many of the people at the gathering had been on the side of the Confederacy. His resonant, clear, and deep tone caught everyone

Smallpox Island

off guard. Who knew that Caleb Bullman could sing? Quickly, nearly everyone joined along in the catchy chorus singing, "*All for Dixie. All for Dixie. The South is alive. All for Dixie.*" Even Jimmy and the people who were for the Union joined in. While everyone might not have been for the idea of slavery, they all seemed to like the idea of "Dixie."

Bullman's song was so poignant that a few people quietly wept. When Bullman finished, most people clapped and nearly everyone stood up. A few of the older men stood and gave a slow and solemn salute. It was as if they were rendering one last gesture to the passing of the Confederacy. Then, Bullman quietly handed the guitar back to Jimmy and started walking back to his guard post. "Thanks, Caleb," said Jimmy. "That was a great song. All for Dixie!"

After a brief pause, Willy spoke up. "Listen, friends. I fought for the South. I'm all for Dixie. But I'll tell ya, I've seen the evils of that war and I'm real glad that it's over. Believe it or not, I'm glad that Dixie is finished with this war. I'm hopin' we can all heal and I pray for God to take away some of the hate that has come over our country in the last three years." After Willy's comment, most of the partygoers looked around and nodded in agreement.

There was a quiet pause and then Jimmy spoke. "Okay, the war is over, but this party is just getting started! Caleb moved us with that amazing song, but now I think it's time to pick things up just a bit. Willy was supposed to be next, but we need an upbeat song right now. So, give us just a minute and we'll do a little shuffling."

Jimmy went to the side with Will and the other musicians. After a moment, Jimmy returned. "Okay, folks, this next song will have me on guitar and Willy on the harmonica. It's called 'Country Girl.' I learned it in Alton, Illinois, from a gentleman named Randle Chowning.

The song began with Willy playing the harmonica. Then, Jimmy joined in playing guitar and singing the song. After the song finished, everyone jumped up and clapped. It was an upbeat tune and it did a lot to lift the mood of the gathering. Caleb Bullman had brought reality to the party by mentioning the war. While it may have been proper to mention it, it was even more fitting to leave the topic behind, so they could all enjoy themselves.

"Okay!" said Jimmy, now the apparent master of ceremonies. "Now we're going to pick up the pace a little more with a tune that includes all of the musicians. In particular, you'll notice Tom Machins on the banjo and George Cribbon on the fiddle. We worked on this one a good amount, so I hope it comes out right," Jimmy continued. "It's called 'I Will Wait.'"

"I really like this one because it reminds me of a soldier coming home. It also seems that a lot of us have spent a good amount of time waiting for each other…or for someone or something else. I learned it from a fellow named Corporal Mumford. I met him while working as a carpenter for the Army up in St. Louis. So, after this song, I think we'll take a short break."

The song "I Will Wait" seemed to start at a hundred miles an hour with a predominant banjo from Tom Machins. Jimmy sang it and Willy kept a steady beat with the stump drum. The sound of the banjo, the fiddle, and the guitar all started to meld together. The song had several pauses where the band quieted down and then built the music back up. It was uplifting and rambunctious with everyone getting involved. As it built up to a crescendo, the band and the audience started moving with the music. For a moment, it felt like the dirt under their feet and even the Mississippi River had joined in. Many folks started jumping up and down.

At the song's end, everyone roared with delight while clapping, jumping, and hollering. Caleb Bullman even yelled over loudly from his guard post, "Now that's a damn good song! Even had my bullets dancing in the chamber!"

"Wow!" said Jimmy. "That was even better than I hoped it would be!"

Smallpox Island

"That's because it's just a real good song!" said Will. "It sure was fun to play, but man, am I thirsty!"

"Yep," said Jimmy. "Time for a short break." The musicians all sat down their instruments and went to find food and drink. Everyone at the party seemed to be energized by the evening's music. During the break, many of the guests gravitated toward the musicians. Several people even walked over to chat with Caleb Bullman.

During the nearly thirty-minute break, Jimmy and Will walked around enjoying the food, drink, and friends while speaking to nearly everyone at the party. At one point, they both walked over to Caleb Bullman, who was still sitting about fifty yards over to the side of the party on a tree stump, a bottle of whiskey at his feet and a rifle in his hand. "Caleb, you know you can come over and join in," said Jimmy. "You're as much a part of our party as everyone else is. Besides, you're even a band member!"

"Thanks, Jimmy, but like I said, I don't take much to crowds anyway. So, I think I'll stay over here for the most part. But I might still come over there from time to time."

"Good, I'll take that. Thank you very much for being here tonight."

"Well, apparently, it's where I'm supposed to be. I'm liking it all quite a bit."

"Good. Let's go, Will. We've got a couple more tunes to go through."

The people at the party all seemed to be having a wonderful time. The gathering appeared to be a welcomed release from some of the angst and frustrations that had accumulated during nearly three years of war.

Then, the band members again assembled off to the side of the party to work on the next set of tunes. After a few minutes, they were ready. They approached the gathering over by the big fire. "Okay," said Jimmy, "this is a song that I actually wrote myself many years ago. It was a dark, cold winter right here on the farm. So, for this song, I'll be playing alone. It's called, 'Happy Day Blues.' Jimmy sat on a nearby tree stump with his guitar. He played and sang the slow, rolling, and melodic song by himself. The band and the gathering looked on quietly while Jimmy played his home-brewed song.

"Happy Day Blues" – 2015 – G. S. Spooner

Cold moon is rising, closing back the day
Bright sun is hiding, coming back to stay

And I feel...like she's dragging me along
Dark cold winter, leaves me pining...to go home

Winter is leaving, melting away
Bright sun is shining, hope it's back to stay

And I feel...like it's shining through my bones
Bringing light, into the memories...of my own

(Guitar interlude)

Moving life everywhere, warmth holds the day
Rolling through hill and dale, oh happy day

And I feel...peace that I have never known
Feeling light, upon the lifetime...of my home
(SONG'S ENDING)

At the end, Jimmy sat there looking down at his guitar. No one clapped. The group sat in stunned quietness after the thoughtful and somewhat moving song. Then one person slowly clapped. Then another...and another. Gradually, the applause went up to a loud pitch. It seemed as though the group was somewhat surprised by Jimmy's own personal song. Then, Jimmy interrupted the clapping.

"Okay, here's a song by another Missouri Ozark guy named John Dillon," said Jimmy. "I also met him in St. Louis several years ago while I was stationed there. It's called 'You Made It Right.' Those Ozark fellas seem to have a lot of real good music."

The song started with Jimmy pecking at his guitar and Will playing his tree stump drum. At the song's ending, everyone clapped and hooted. The song included the words "Thank you, Lord" in the chorus. One guest commented, "I really liked the part about 'Thank you, Lord!' Nobody sings about the Lord much in anything other than a church song."

"That's right, neighbor. But we do!" said Jimmy.

"Okay," said Jimmy. "We need to keep the line moving. Next, we have my neighbor, Tom Machins. He is going to sing and play a song that will use the whole band. It'll probably be the best song of the whole night. Again, Tom is featured on the banjo and George is on the fiddle. It's a song that he won't have to read from my songbook because he knows it by heart. This is one of my favorites and it's called 'The Glendy Burke.'"

Immediately there was a buzz in the crowd. Everyone in the band looked excited and got ready to play. The partygoers started smiling and shaking their heads in anticipation. Then, the musicians all moved forward and prepared themselves for the upbeat tune that was obviously a favorite of the band and of the crowd.

The Glendy Burke – 1860 – Stephen Foster

The Glendy Burke is a mighty fast boat
With a mighty fast captain, too

G. S. Spooner

He sits up there on the hurricane roof
And he keeps his eye on the crew.

I can't stay here for they work too hard
I'm bound to leave this town,
I'll take my duds and tote 'em on my back
When the Glendy Burke comes down.

Chorus:
Ho for Lousiana,
I'm bound to leave this town,
I'll take my duds and tote 'em on my back
When the Glendy Burke comes down.
(SONG CONTINUES UNTIL ITS ENDING)

By the end of "The Glendy Burke," everyone was swinging back and forth as they sang along with the chorus, "Ho for Lousiana, I'm bound to leave this town, I'll take my duds and tote 'em on my back, when the Glendy Burke comes down!" They all cheered loudly at the end, not only for the band but also for themselves.

"Wow, that was awesome!" said Jimmy. "Well, this next one will have to be the last song." Some folks booed and hollered, "No!"

"Yes. This is the last song because Will and I want to visit with you all for a bit before you go. We also don't want to take up all of the attention of the evening. This party is not only about Will and me coming home. It's also about the end of the war and all you good people coming together to enjoy the night."

"Okay, the last song is called '*I'll See You in My Dreams*,'" said Jimmy, "Will is going to sing it and I'm going to play the guitar with Tom playing the banjo. We hope you like it. Will and I have been working on it since we were floating down the Mississippi River on our way home. I heard a fella singing it at a saloon in St. Louis and I wrote it down. We're still trying to learn it, so I hope we get it right. Here we go."

Tom Machins strummed his banjo and Jimmy played his guitar while Willy sang the tune. He read many of the words from Jimmy's songbook while walking about the crowd. The guests instantly seemed to like the song as they nodded their heads and started swaying back and forth. The other musicians all started to gently join in as the tune progressed. Caleb Bullman stood up and appeared as though he was coming over to the gathering, but he then sat back down at his improvised guard post.

"I'll See You in My Dreams" – 1924 – Gus Kahn and Isham Jones – Public Domain in the U.S.

Lonely days are long,
Twilight sings a song
All the happiness that used to be

Soon my eyes will close,
Soon I'll find repose
And in dreams, you're always near to me

I'll see you in my dreams
Hold you in my dreams
Someone took you right out of my arms
Still I feel the thrill of your charms

Lips that once were mine
Tender eyes that shine
They will light my way tonight
I'll see you in my dreams
(SONG CONTINUES UNTIL ITS ENDING)

The slow-paced rhythmic song was perfect to wind down the musical portion of the evening. Will liked the song because it touched on losing a love while keeping a positive approach to the future. Everyone, including the musicians, stood up and cheered at the song's end, marking the end of the evening's music. Martha and Phyllis walked straight up and hugged both Jimmy and Will. Then, everyone started chatting and discussing the evening. The troubles from the previous night were seemingly forgotten. Caleb Bullman finally came over and joined the party, smiling and shaking hands. He cheerfully talked with several attendees, although it seemed to make him just a little bit uncomfortable. The party's ending was full of joy and happiness until it wrapped up a couple of hours later.

Chapter Fifteen

July 10, 1865

Two and a half months later, Jimmy and Will were sitting on the deck of a large paddlewheel boat heading up the Mississippi River toward St. Louis. Jimmy was wearing his Union military uniform and Will was wearing casual civilian clothing. They both had a personal leather bag and a canvas bag sitting next to them on the deck. The bag next to Jimmy had the top of a guitar neck sticking out of it. Today, the large ship only had about fifty travelers, which was only about one-fourth of its maximum passenger limit. Jimmy was holding and reading a telegraph message. The telegraph read:

From: Colonel Kahn, Commander, Alton Federal Prison 2 July 1865

To: Sergeant James Logan, New Madrid, Missouri

Greetings, Sergeant James Logan. Per previous communications, you were honorably discharged from the United States Army on 30 April 1865. Official discharge orders sent to home of record in New Madrid, Missouri. Remuneration of active duty pay cannot currently be sent securely to home of record. Please report to Headquarters Alton Prison NLT Friday, 14 July 1865 to receive all pay due. Alton Prison will be officially closed down on Friday, 7 July 1865, but my office will remain open through 14 July 1865 for administrative activities. Per our records, you are due approximately three months pay totaling fifty-four dollars, plus eight dollars for travel to complete this action. Total due sixty-two dollars.

Colonel Kahn, Commander, Alton Federal Prison

> *Point of Historical Reference – Union sergeants earned about seventeen dollars per month while privates pay was only about thirteen dollars. The monthly pay for Union lieutenants was about one hundred dollars per month. Their Confederate counterparts were paid approximately the same amounts.*

The cost for the ride from New Madrid to St. Louis was only two dollars per person.

The sound of the *chug chug chug* came from the paddlewheel in the background as it pounded against the water. "What's the plan, Jimmy?"

"Well, we go upriver for two days, stop over at Benton Barracks in St. Louis tomorrow night, and then report to Alton prison the next day."

"And then you get paid, right?"

"That's right, sixty-two dollars."

"That's great. Jimmy, do you think they will let us look around? Like at my old cell? Maybe even at Smallpox Island?"

"Don't know," said Jimmy. "I don't know why not. The prison will have been empty for almost a week."

"I'll tell you something else, Jimmy," said Will.

"What?"

"I can't wait to see Belle again."

"I understand, Willy. I know you've only traveled up to see her in St. Louis once in the last couple of months."

"Yep, and we've written each other a lot, but this just isn't working for me. It actually hurts to be away from her, but I can't afford to travel up to St. Louis every couple of weeks."

"I know it, Willy. I can tell that you miss her. If she wasn't so far away, you could see her a lot more. I get to see Patsy anytime that I want. We'll be married in a few months and I'll get to see Patsy all of the time."

"Well, Jimmy, I feel like I need something like that. I wonder if Belle likes me enough to see me all of the time?"

"I have a feeling that she does, Willy."

Then, both of the brothers went into silent contemplation as they browsed around the deck, taking in the peaceful beauty of the river. They experienced the water, the land, the passing birds, and the hypnotic sound of the paddlewheel. Finally, after about a half-hour, Will spoke up.

"You know, Belle doesn't even know we're coming. I wrote her, but I'm sure the letter hasn't reached her yet."

"Well, that will be a real nice surprise for her. I'm sorry about that, but I didn't realize that I had to head up to Alton until a few days ago."

"Jimmy, do you think that Benton Barracks is still fully operational?"

"I hope so, because we're planning on staying there tomorrow night."

That evening, the ship pulled over to the riverbank in Perryville, Missouri. The town was about halfway between New Madrid and St. Louis, making it the perfect place to pick up supplies and dock for the night. The ship's captain preferred not to travel at night because of the many difficulties of navigating the river. As the evening waned and darkness came upon the river, the mystical sights and sounds of the river changed. The birds became quieter and the insects became louder and louder. The brothers sat on the deck and worked through a couple of tunes, with Jimmy playing guitar and Will on the harmonica. Later, the brothers found a couple of bunks below deck and they bedded down for the night.

July 11, 1865 Back at Benton

The next morning, the brothers slept in and were woken by the movement of the ship and the pounding of the paddlewheel. The sun shined brightly as they walked out onto the deck, wiping the sleep out of their eyes. For ten cents per person, the brothers enjoyed a breakfast of hard-boiled eggs, bread, and coffee. The day seemed to go by quickly and before they knew it, the steamboat was pulling up to the muddy banks of St. Louis, Missouri. There were at least twenty other big paddlewheel boats docked up against the bank. Jimmy and Will spoke with the boat's captain as they disembarked. The captain confirmed that he was departing for Alton at 9 a.m. the following morning. He also mentioned that the cost would be only thirty cents each since Jimmy was in Union military uniform.

They walked over to the military dock and sure enough, Private Newsome, the big soldier who had shoved them off nearly three months earlier, was still on duty. "Hey, Newsome, do you remember us?" yelled Willy.

The soldier looked up from his work. He was now wearing the rank of sergeant. After a short pause, he said, "Logan brothers! Well, hell yes, I remember you fellas! What are you doing here?"

"Going back to Alton Prison to get my pay," said Jimmy. "We're planning on staying at Benton for the night."

"Oh, yeah," said Newsome. "I heard that the Alton Prison was having some soldiers show up after they were discharged to get their money. Sounds like a bunch of crap."

Will asked, "What are you still doing here? I thought that you'd be discharged by now."

"Well, Benton Barracks is closing down at some point in the next few months and they needed a dock sergeant," said Newsome. "It's easy duty, I know how to do it, and it's five more bucks a month. So, in about two months, I'll be discharged and headed back home."

"To Cape Girardeau," said Will.

"That's right! I'm surprised that you remembered that. As for me, I never wanna go to Alton Prison, that hellhole. My brother, George, died there. Heck, I wouldn't go there if you paid me."

Jimmy answered, "That's the whole idea, Newsome. They're going to pay me."

"Haa ha!! That's right! I understand. Well, be careful anyway. Who knows what kinda nasty germs are still lurking around there."

"Oh, we will," said Willy. "Brother Jimmy here wants me to go with him. I kinda won't mind seeing the place from the other side of the bars, as a free man."

"I see. Well, good luck to ya, boys. Holler at me tomorrow before you leave."

"Will do."

The brothers then found a wagon ride up to Benton Barracks. As they traveled in the back of a wagon, Will gazed over toward the Gratiot Street Prison. "I guess that rat hole is closing too," he said to Jimmy.

"I don't know, but I hope so."

When they arrived at Benton Barracks, they quickly saw an Army post in transition. Soldiers were working in the garrison, but they noticed only about half as many as before. They went to the Headquarters building to sign in and then over to see Sergeant

George Williams at the Billeting Office. With his assistance, they secured a place to bunk for the night. With the low census on post, Williams even assigned them to the same small cabin that they had stayed in three months earlier.

Later, they settled into their quarters and had already eaten dinner. They were just passing time in their cabin and Jimmy was laying on his bunk. "Hey, Will. The billeting NCO, Sergeant Williams, told me that Benton Barracks is going to start shutting down in about a month."

"What? Closing totally? I thought it was closing in two or three months."

"Yep, but Sergeant Williams said it'll be a long period of transition. They're going to be selling some of the land and buildings to locals for cheap. He said the other buildings will be either disassembled or burned down. After that, this place is going to be gone. The soldiers and the local mission are going to be transferred to Jefferson Barracks."

"Wow, that's crazy. I need to go and see if I can find Belle."

"How come? Are you going to ask her to look at your wounds?"

"Yeah right, I guess so. As a follow-up."

"Your wounds have healed, though," Jimmy laughed.

Will continued, "Shut up, stupid! I need to talk to her in person to find out her plans now that Benton is closing. We've been writing to each other, but she doesn't even know I'm coming. This trip came up so fast. I really want to find out if she's interested in spending time with me in New Madrid after all of this is over."

Will quickly left the quarters and went directly to the post infirmary. As he entered the clinic, the first person he saw was Belle. She was changing a dressing on a soldier who had lost his arm. She looked over at Will while she was working and immediately gave out a small gasp,

"Will! What are you doing here?"

Smallpox Island

"I'm here with my brother. He's going over to Alton to get his military pay, so I came along. I wrote to you about it, but I'm sure the letter hasn't arrived yet."

"Oh my," said Belle. "I can't believe you're here. Hold on, I'll be finished in just a few minutes."

Belle finished taking care of the injured soldier and kindly escorted him to the door, asking him to return the next day. Belle closed the door, turned around, and walked directly up to Will. She stood there and looked straight into Will's eyes, then she reached out and hugged him tightly. Will embraced her as she spoke. "I don't really know why, Will, but I've thought about you every single day. Even though you've written a lot and you came up to see me four weeks ago, I find myself wondering if I'll ever see you again."

Will looked at Belle. She had tears in her eyes. "I've thought about you too, Belle," said Will. "That's why I'm here. Even though I came up here once and we've been writing letters, the mail is so slow and I really needed to see you again, in person."

"Well," Will said, "When you're finished here, would you like to go to the mess hall and get something to eat?"

"Yes, I'm starved."

"You say that every time," said Willy with a big smile on his face. Later, as they sat facing each other at the mess hall, it became apparent that Will and Belle were extremely happy to see each other.

"Will, I'm so happy that you came up to visit me four weeks ago. And as I said, I also love getting letters from you. But honestly, all of that just makes me want to see you even more. Being away from you is not a good feeling. I'm so glad to see you. You have no idea."

"Oh, yes I do, Belle. I know that exact feeling," said Willy. "I can't stand it. It actually hurts to be away from you. Does that make any sense?"

"Yes, it does," said Belle. "I feel that too. I think it means that we love each other."

"I think that's what it means, too, Belle…. It means I love you."

"I love you too, Will."

They left the mess hall and without even thinking about it, they walked through the main gate and started taking another scenic walk in the country. As they walked through the gate, one of the guards yelled over to them, "Hey, you two lovebirds! I haven't seen you together for a while."

Will waved and smiled yelling, "We're back!"

This time, they walked for well over an hour. They talked and walked amidst the trees and across the same creeks just as they had before. While in the country, Will stopped and looked deeply into Belle's eyes. He held her hands and told her, "Listen, Belle, I'm just going to the Alton Prison for one day. After Jimmy gets paid, we'll be back the very next day. Then, we're supposed to leave the following day to take a steamboat home. Belle, I'm asking you if you'll marry me."

Belle gasped. "Marry you?"

"Yes, will you marry me?"

"Yes, Will! Yes, yes, yes, yes, yes!"

They grasped each other and held a long kiss.

They headed back toward the post with smiles on their faces that could not be erased.

"Belle, I want to be with you and I really can't see any future of mine that doesn't have you in it. I love being with you and I don't like being away from you."

"I feel the same way, Will. When and where do you want to get married?"

"Soon Belle, if that's okay. And in New Madrid, if that's agreeable to you."

"That's fine," said Belle. "I don't know if I can step away from my job early."

"Right. If you can, I'll take you back with me to get married in

New Madrid right after we come back. If you can't come to New Madrid then, I'll come up here to get you whenever you're ready. I just don't want to wait a long time."

"Okay, I'll talk to the doctor tomorrow," said Belle. "I'll know what I can do by the time you get back in two days. I'll either leave with you then or I'll go with you in about a month or whenever the infirmary closes. Either way, we'll go to New Madrid to get married. It's just a matter of when."

"Great! That's a good plan," said Will. "So, let me go over all of this. In two days, you'll either be waiting to go to New Madrid with me or you'll have me come back and get you in about a month, or whenever the Benton Barracks Infirmary closes. Right?"

"Right."

"Another thing, Belle," said Willy. "Once we're married, if you still want to work at that hospital down in Nashville or maybe up here in St. Louis, I'm with you, so I'll go with you. I want to be where you are. I can find work as a carpenter in either Nashville or St. Louis until the time is right to go back to New Madrid."

"Okay, Will. I guess we'll see what happens," said Belle.

"No, Belle. That's important. You're a good nurse and you do great work that helps people. I don't want to mess that up."

Suddenly, they both realized that they were standing at the door of her quarters. They had totally lost track of time and place. He held her close and they kissed a very long kiss. They kissed some more and after a while, Will departed, saying, "Good night, future Mrs. Logan! I'll see you early tomorrow for breakfast." He and Belle were both smiling immensely.

"Okay, good night, future husband!"

Will headed back to his quarters, whispering to himself, "This is gotta be the best feeling that anybody has ever felt!"

At 11 p.m., Will came walking into their quarters with the same broad smile on his face. Jimmy was practicing his guitar while writing in his music book. "Well! I guess you found her," said Jimmy.

"Yes, sir, I found her all right."

"I hope so. You've been gone for almost three hours!" said Jimmy with a grin on his face. "Well, how did it go?"

"It went great. She was glad to see me. We went to the mess hall and then took a long walk on the countryside. We talked and talked.

"Jimmy, I asked her to marry me and she said 'Yes!'"

"I knew it!" yelled Jimmy as he jumped up and happily grabbed his brother.

"She's coming down to New Madrid either in two days with us or whenever she gets released from here!"

"Ha!!" said Jimmy. "A three-hour walk! I just knew you two would be together! Just how big of a kiss did you give her?"

Will threw his bag at Jimmy and said, "Shut up, idiot!"

"Okay, lover boy! You're walking about two feet off the ground!" said Jimmy. "Anyway, we need to try to get some sleep. We have to be on the boat to Alton before 9 a.m. tomorrow."

With that, the brothers wrapped up the day on a positive note as they sacked down for the night. As they lay in bed, Jimmy thought about how happy Willy was and about getting paid the next day. Willy was only thinking about Belle.

July 12, 1865

The morning light came quickly. Jimmy squinted, blinked, and opened his eyes as the sun shined through the eastern window of the small military cabin. With a quick look at his pocket watch, he saw that it was 7 a.m. The next thing that he noticed was what he didn't notice. Will was not there. Jimmy sat up on the side of his bunk and pondered his brother's absence for about a minute. Then, suddenly, Will came walking cheerfully through the door.

"Mornin', Jimmy!"

"Mornin'. Did you have...?"

Will interrupted. "Morning chow with Belle? Yes, sir, I certainly did. I figured we didn't have time to lollygag, so I got that out of the way early. We've already said goodbye and we're good to go."

"Great."

The brothers washed up and shaved. Jimmy dressed in his Union military uniform. Then, they both went to the mess hall and Jimmy ate a quick breakfast while Willy drank coffee. They kept their sleeping quarters since they would be returning the very next day. Before they knew it, the time was 8:30 a.m. and they were down at the riverfront. As they walked past the military dock on the way to their transport ship, Willy saw their friend, Sergeant Newsome. "Hey, Sergeant Newsome! We'll probably see you tomorrow!"

"Okay, Logans. Don't catch nothin' in that crappy hellhole!"

"We won't! It's closed anyway!"

At 9:05, the riverboat departed and at 11:15, it was docking in Alton, Illinois. As they disembarked, Jimmy immediately stopped and looked down at his boot. He noticed dry ground underneath his feet and on the entire riverbank. In the past, the ground had been so muddy for so long that in his mind, it was always muddy there and never dry.

"Wow, it's actually dry here," Jimmy announced to Will.

"Sweet," said Will as he took a few more steps before also stopping. But Willy didn't look at the ground. Instead, he gazed straight across the river, at Smallpox Island.

It only took about ten minutes for the Logans to make their way to the massive Alton Prison. Once they made it to the site, Jimmy immediately noticed that the perimeter checkpoint was gone. Apparently, so were all of the prisoners. Soldiers were bustling back and forth hard at work, shutting down the prison. The sun was shining, it was a beautiful day, and the building was towering over them. The entire feel of the place had changed from dark, cold, and wet to light, warm, and free. It felt a lot more like an Army post and a lot less like a prison.

Will stood there looking up at the gigantic building. "What do we do now, Jim?" said Will.

"Well, I need to go up the hill to the Headquarters building. You can come with me or do something else until I get back. It's up to you."

"I think I'll just sit here on this rock wall and look at this old prison. It's kinda nice to be a free man on the outside of it. Especially after being a prisoner on the inside for nearly two years. So, I'll just stay here and watch our bags."

"Okay, I don't blame you. I should be back before too long. Be careful."

Jimmy started walking up the steep hill to the Unit Headquarters. It was a familiar journey that he had traveled many times before. He thought about his many treks up the hill to secure the release of his brother. While looking around at the buildings, the trees, and the bushes, it seemed so much nicer than he had remembered it. Jimmy thought to himself, *This might be the last time I ever walk up this hill. But, this time the war is over and the sun is finally shining. I won't miss the time that I spent here, but I'll try to remember this nice final walk up the hill to HQ.* Jimmy went directly to the Headquarters building and was met by an armed guard who stood at the door.

The guard spoke loudly to Jimmy. "Halt! State your business!"

"Sergeant James Logan, reporting to Colonel Kahn, as ordered," Jimmy answered.

"Stand fast!" said the guard as he opened up a ledger and looked for Jimmy's name. "Okay, Sergeant. You may enter. Once inside, the line forms on the right."

Smallpox Island

"Line?" said Jimmy. "Yes, Sergeant. There are about four other soldiers in there right now. We've had soldiers reporting for pay all week. Sometimes the line goes around the building." Jimmy went in and stood in the short line. It took about five minutes per soldier to verify the paperwork and receive their pay.

After about ten minutes, Jimmy was second in line and there were two more soldiers behind him. Then, all of a sudden, Colonel Kahn came out of his office. He stood there, scanning the soldiers in the line. He was smoking a cigar and seemed to be in a good mood. "Hey there, Sergeant Logan! Didn't I tell you I was going to be shutting this joint down in a couple of months?"

"Yes, sir!" answered Jimmy with a smile on his face.

"Well, I'm glad you got out of here ahead of the rush. How's your brother?"

"He's good, sir. Thank you. His zoster has mostly cleared up and he's sitting down at the bottom of the hill."

"Outstanding! Give him my best. I'm so damn happy that this war is over!"

"Yes, sir! So am I," answered Jimmy.

Colonel Kahn continued speaking to Jimmy and the four other soldiers that were in line. "Gentlemen, I didn't want to bring you in for your pay, but I had to. We had an infiltrator stealing outgoing pay while in transit. So, I've instructed my clerk, Private Brockman, to pay each soldier all pay due, plus travel, plus two 1861 silver dollars from myself. Thank you for your service to me, to the Alton Prison, and to the nation."

The men were all surprised by the kind gesture. Colonel Kahn then walked over to Jimmy and the four men. He shook each man's hand and took time to chat with them about their families and their well-being.

Just then, a commotion was heard from outside. A man charged through the door and started ranting about the Confederacy. It became obvious that the man was drunk. "What about the burning of Atlanta, boys?! Huh?! What about the Shenandoah Valley?! They burned down our mills, barns, and even our fields!" Then, the man looked directly at Jimmy. "The Yanks even killed all of our cattle and sheep!"

With that, the door guard rushed up and butted the man in the head with his rifle. Then, the guard and another soldier dragged the unconscious drunk out of the Headquarters and order was restored. "You know," Colonel Kahn said. "He's right. There's not a lot of good thoughts about the burning of Atlanta or the Shenandoah Valley. But all I know is this evil war is finished. Good riddance...and may God help us all."

Jimmy was finally paid and he started walking back down the hill. It was still a beautiful day. The birds were singing, the war was over, and he had sixty-two dollars in his pocket, not including the two silver dollars! Once down the hill, he went to the rock wall where Will had been sitting. Their bags were there, but Willy was nowhere to be found. Then, Jimmy looked around and saw a soldier with a shovel digging a hole nearby. "Soldier! Did you see the slim fella that was sitting here?"

"Yes, Sergeant. I think I saw him go in that door over there." The soldier pointed to a door leading into the prison. He asked me to watch these bags for a few minutes."

"Do you need some help, Sergeant?"

"No, Private. I think I know where he is."

Jimmy went into the unguarded building and walked up the stairs to the fourth floor.

As he entered the fourth floor, he saw that all of the cell doors were wide open and the rooms were totally empty. It was a sight that shocked him at first, but it was okay. The prison was closed. He walked seven cells down the hall, turned right, and entered cell 423W. Will was standing in the room silently, looking out of the opened window. Jimmy stood quietly in the doorway. Will broke the silence without even turning to see if Jimmy was there. Because he knew Jimmy was there. "I spent a year and a half here. Right in this room. Going in and out. Looking out of this window. Opening and closing it...wondering if I would ever be allowed to leave."

He turned around and looked at Jimmy. Although Will wasn't openly crying, his voice was clear and tears were running down his face. He turned back toward the window. "See that group of trees over there on the bluff?"

Jimmy looked over his shoulder at the stand of trees. "Yes."

"I watched them change color through the seasons. It helped me to feel normal. It helped me to keep my sanity. See that big evergreen over there on the right side?"

"Yes."

"I watched it drop its pine cones through the summer. Then it would drop some of its needles in the fall and in the winter. Then, the next spring, I watched it become full again. The pine cones would start out small and green. As it warmed up, they would get larger. The tree's needles would fill out and the cones would drop to the ground in the fall. Then, the next season came and it would all happen again. I watched it come to pass. It was like a story. The story of those trees. It helped me to focus on something good. I watched them nearly every day...from this window. I think I just might miss those trees...but I don't think I'll ever miss this place."

Then, Jimmy spoke. "You were finally allowed to leave, Will. You made it. I think you are the strongest man I've ever known. Some men are strong by pure muscle. Some men are strong by their willpower and their soul. You are strong by your willpower and your soul. I'm not only proud because you're my brother but because I actually know someone that is that strong. Someone that endured that. Endured this! A year and a half here and another year at Gratiot? You're a freak of nature, Will. You're almost like a superhuman."

Will answered, "Thanks, brother, but it's not like I had any other choice once I was captured. I had to make it."

"See, that's what I mean. I probably wouldn't have made it more than a month. I'm not strong enough, in the soul."

Will smiled and walked directly at Jimmy, shoving him out of the way as he walked through the cell door. "You're an idiot. Let's go."

They walked down the stairs, left the prison, and headed down toward the river with their personal bags in tow. All of a sudden, Jimmy yelled, "Hey, look! It's *The Wiggins!*"

It was the small steam-powered flatbed boat that had ferried soldiers out to Smallpox Island. The captain was working on the deck with the same two deckhands alongside. "Hey, Captain! How're ya doing?" yelled Jimmy. The captain looked up and stared at them blankly for a second. Then he said, "Well, son of a bitch! Hey there, Sergeant! Let me guess. You're here to get paid."

"You bet I am. Do you remember us? It was about three months ago."

"Oh, I remember, Sergeant. How can I forget? We all could have drowned. It was flooding with a lot of crap in the river. A house hit the boat, and we barely made it over to the island. Later, I gave you two fellas my side boat to head downstream. It was a real flood emergency."

"Hey, did you make it home?" said the captain. "How did my little skiff do?"

"It did great, Cap! We took it all the way to our farm in New Madrid, Missouri. We still have it."

"That's great! I was wondering what happened to you fellas."

"I don't remember if I ever had the chance to thank you," said Jimmy.

"Well, you're very welcome! Hey boys, we're fixin' to head over to Smallpox Island in about five minutes if you want to ride over. The weather's great, the waters down, and the pressure's off! We have

Smallpox Island

to go over and bring back some crap that the Army wants to keep. Hell, we could use a little help loading it up anyway."

"I don't know," said Jimmy. "Our paddlewheel back to St. Louis doesn't leave until tomorrow morning. So, we don't have anything else to do right now, except find a place to sleep tonight."

"Well, come on then," said the captain. "After we come back, we're done for the day."

Jimmy looked at Will. He was staring over toward Smallpox Island. "Well, what do you want to do, Will?"

After a short pause, Will answered, "You know something? I might as well put a bow on this trip and face another shadow of my internment. Why not? Hey, Captain, are there still any prisoners with smallpox over there?"

"No son, it's been emptied of all prisoners for over a week."

"Okay, let's do it," said Willy. "It's a beautiful day and maybe I can say a prayer for the soldiers that are in that burial pit over there."

"I think that's a dandy idea, son. Let's load up!"

The brothers loaded onto the ship with their personal bags and the captain started the trek across the river. It was a clear and beautiful day. The water was calm and about as clear as the Mississippi could get. Large white cranes and many other birds crowded the sky as they swooped back and forth, looking for fish to eat. Within ten minutes, they were docked at Smallpox Island. The deckhands secured the boat and everyone started loading the Army supplies onto it. The cargo included four big wood stoves and several boxes filled with pots, pans, nails, and brass doorknobs. With the brothers' help, they finished loading up the supplies in about fifteen minutes. Then, Will walked away to explore the island. He yelled over to the group, "Hey! I'm heading over this way!"

"Take your time, son!" said the captain. "Today is an easy day. We're done for the day after this. As a matter of fact, we're done period as of tomorrow. My men and I get paid and I'm taking *The*

Wiggins back up to Quincy, Illinois."

Will casually walked past his formerly assigned barracks, noticing that the doorknobs had been removed. He did not go in. Just as before, he always tried to stay out of that building. Then, he walked past the mess hall that he had tried equally hard to stay out of. Will stood there and looked around the island for a brief moment. Suddenly, he made a beeline toward the Lincoln Tree located on the back side of the island. He was there in less than a minute. Will stood there studying the tree and then slowly started laughing. He began to laugh louder and louder. Will laughed so hard that it was as though he was purging his soul of all of the pain of his captivity.

As Will laughed, Jimmy was nearby and he couldn't help but to hear him. He came walking up to Will and the big tree. He stood next to Will and said, "What?"

"Look!" yelled Willy while laughing. "Look, Jimmy!"

"What? I don't see anything."

Will then pointed at three initials on the tree that were nested next to several other carvings. The initials he pointed to were engraved with 'W.G.L. 1865.' "See? I misspelled my own initials!"

"What?"

"Yeah! I meant to carve "W.L.L."

Jimmy smiled. "Why do you think you did that?"

"Stress? I really don't know. My name is William Lawrence Logan. I do know that I signed in as Private William G. Logan when I came out here. Maybe that's why. All I know is that I meant to carve 'W.L.L.'"

"Wait a minute," Jimmy said. "You signed in as Private William G. Logan and not Corporal William L. Logan?"

"Yes," Will said, still chuckling. "I didn't want them to know my entire real name or rank."

"Why not?"

Smallpox Island

"Because I was thinking about maybe trying to sneak off and swim over to the Missouri side of the river."

"What?!" said Jimmy. "You were going to try to escape?!"

"Not really. Not unless I was sure that I could get away with it. But I wanted to keep my options open. So, I also signed in as being a private from the 8th Missouri Infantry."

"What?! I thought you were in the 1st Missouri."

"Right. I was. I didn't give them my real name or my real unit. Just something kinda close. Look, Jimmy, I would not have survived very long out here on this island. Eventually, I would have caught real smallpox and died. So, I had to make plans to try something."

"Wow," said Jimmy. "Maybe you subconsciously became William G. Logan instead of William L. Logan."

"I don't think so," said Will, still chuckling. "Did you see this one?" Will pointed at one large carving. It was in the center of all of the rest of the engravings. It said, "A.L. 1842."

"What is that?" said Jimmy.

"Well, like I probably mentioned back when I signed my non-battle pledge here, this is called the Lincoln Tree. The guards told me that Abe Lincoln came out here in 1842 to fight a duel with some guy."

"Are you kidding?"

"No!"

"What happened?"

"Well, they said the other guy chickened out and they all went to a saloon in Alton instead."

"Ha! That sounds like a classic Lincoln story," said Jimmy.

"Yeah, I don't know if it's true, but I do know that this carving says "A.L. 1842.""

"Come on, Jimmy, let's go over to the burial pit."

The brothers started walking over to the pit where over three hundred soldiers had been laid to rest. As they headed over, the captain and crew of *The Wiggins* walked over and joined them. The five men looked down at the ground at the vast area that was obviously disturbed by digging. It was easy to see the locations of the three burial trenches. "Jimmy, could you maybe please say a prayer?" said Will. "You're better at prayers than I am."

"Okay, little brother," said Jimmy. He bowed his head. "Heavenly Father, please bless all of the soldiers and other people buried in this place. Please allow them into your kingdom if it is your will and ease the pain of their family and friends. In the name of your son Jesus Christ, Amen."

"Amen!" said the four other men simultaneously.

As they all walked back toward the boat, Will remained somewhat cheerful. "You know, I was destined to be thrown in that trench back there." He then chuckled. "Ha, I can't believe I'm here. It's like a great weight has been removed. I'm still alive!" Willy almost started to cry while he was talking. He shook it off and continued, "I actually came out on the other side of all this!"

"You sure did," said the captain. "Listen, boys, I have one skiff left on my boat. I leave tomorrow and I don't want to drag it all the way back to Quincy. Do you want it?"

"Sure," said Jimmy. "What do you want for it?"

"Nothing! The war is over. The Army gave those skiffs to me for safety reasons, and Colonel Kahn told me that he doesn't want them back. So, I don't need it. If *The Wiggins* sinks, we just swim to the side. Hey, you could take it downstream to St. Louis if you like. You wouldn't have to wait until tomorrow for a ride. Hell, you can take it all the way to New Madrid again if you want to."

After a short pause Jimmy said, "Give us just a minute, Cap." He and Will then stepped off to the side to talk. After about sixty seconds, they walked back over to the captain. "We're in!" said Jimmy. "We'll take it! Heck, we have all of our stuff with us. We

Smallpox Island

can leave from here today for St. Louis and not have to wait until tomorrow. Besides, it's only three o'clock and it's all downstream rowing. So, if we leave now, we should make it to St. Louis before it gets really dark."

Will cut in, "Heck, we might even take it all the way home. We know the way!"

"Outstanding!" said the captain. "Crew! Grab their bags and prep the skiff."

With that, the two crew members darted off. They quickly prepped the small boat and put the brothers' personal bags into it.

Will and Jimmy were all grins as they climbed into the skiff, delighted with the way the day had went. "Consider this little boat as a token of my appreciation for your service," said the captain. "Listen, just like the other skiff, there's a compass, water, jerky, and dried bread in the box under the seat."

"Okay," said Jimmy. "Thank you, Captain, and thanks, guys." The brothers waved at the captain and the two crew members. The crew tipped their hats to the brothers as the captain himself pushed them off, saying, "God speed, boys. Be careful!"

Jimmy and Will thanked the captain again and started their navigation of the great Mississippi River. As Jimmy rowed, both he and Will gave Smallpox Island one final look. Will gazed at the Lincoln Tree that he had carved his initials into. The giant tree was easy to see from a distance as it was the tallest natural feature on the island. About five minutes into the journey, Will asked Jimmy if he could use his guitar. "Of course you can." Will pulled out Jimmy's guitar from his personal bag and kicked back into a relaxed posture. He was still feeling happy and light-hearted. As he pecked away at the guitar, he asked, "Jimmy, do you think we will be able to stay in our usual quarters in St. Louis?"

"Yep. That's a safe bet. Remember, it's still signed out to us. Sergeant Williams knows we're coming right back."

"That's good. I'll have to go see Belle while we're there."

"Well, I certainly hope you do. She'd clobber you if you didn't. I have a feeling that before too awful long, you and your future wife are going to be spending a lot more time together."

"I hope so, Jimmy. It seems like all of my thoughts of the future have her in them."

"That's good, little brother," said Jimmy. "I feel the exact same way. All of my thoughts of the future have Patsy in them. I think that's a good thing. We both need to just keep playing our cards right and we'll see how it all goes."

"Right!" said Will, chuckling again. He kicked back and started strumming a familiar tune on the guitar. Then he started singing "I'll See You in My Dreams."

"I'll See You in My Dreams" – 1924 – Gus Kahn and Isham Jones – Public Domain in the U.S.

Lonely days are long
Twilight sings a song
All the happiness that used to be

Soon my eyes will close
Soon I'll find repose
And in dreams
You're always near to me

I'll see you in my dreams
Hold you in my dreams
Someone took you right out of my arms
Still I feel the thrill of your charms

Smallpox Island

Lips that once were mine
Tender eyes that shine

They will light my way tonight
I'll see you in my dreams

Lips that once were mine
Tender eyes that shine
They will light my way tonight
I'll see you in my dreams

They will light my lonely way tonight
I'll see you in my dreams
(SONG'S ENDING)

As Will sang the tune, the skiff from *The Wiggins* left Smallpox Island behind. It floated down the river on a beautiful day assisted by the downstream currents. The bright yellow sun moved through the clouds in the afternoon sky, shining beams of light down upon the earth. One of the beams shined directly on the brothers and their little skiff. It was as if the great almighty had sanctified their journeys by placing the sun's beam of light directly upon them.

Both of the Logan brothers had navigated the twists and turns of their journeys. They had survived the Civil War and at the same time, they felt somehow enriched by what had happened to them. Their enrichment was not from the war, but from the people they had met along the way. They also felt enriched by their adventures on the river. They had learned much about life, about love, and about perseverance. They had become men.

As they rowed and coasted down the majestic river, Will's thoughts turned toward Belle and Jimmy's thoughts turned toward Patsy. The brothers were now ready to put Smallpox Island and the war behind them. They were now ready to put the rest of their lives in front of them. Jimmy and Will were cheerful, eager, and ready to open the next chapters of their lives.

Epilogue

July 10, 2020

One hundred and thirty-seven years later, most of Smallpox Island has been consumed by the Mississippi River. The Lincoln Tree with its carved initials has been largely gone for many years, taken by time and by the river. A small remnant of its stump still breaches the surface when the water levels are very low. Only the downstream southeastern end of Smallpox Island still exists above water and it is still possible to visit. No longer an island, it's now connected to land and is in a park appropriately named "Lincoln Shields Recreation Area." This remnant of the island is the actual location of the trenches that were dug between 1863 and 1865 to bury nearly three hundred Confederate prisoners who had died from smallpox.

In the 1930s, the burial trench was inadvertently disturbed by construction digging for a new lock and dam. The bones were left in place. A large granite monument was finally dedicated on April 27, 2002, to honor these Confederate soldiers and to mark their final resting place. On that special day, many grateful family members of the deceased attended the ceremony. This great granite monument displays the names of these soldiers. The names were derived from the best information that was available from official documents that were provided by the U.S. Army and Illinois state records.

One of the names listed on this monument is "PVT. WILLIAM G. LOGAN" from the "8th MISSOURI."

Smallpox Island

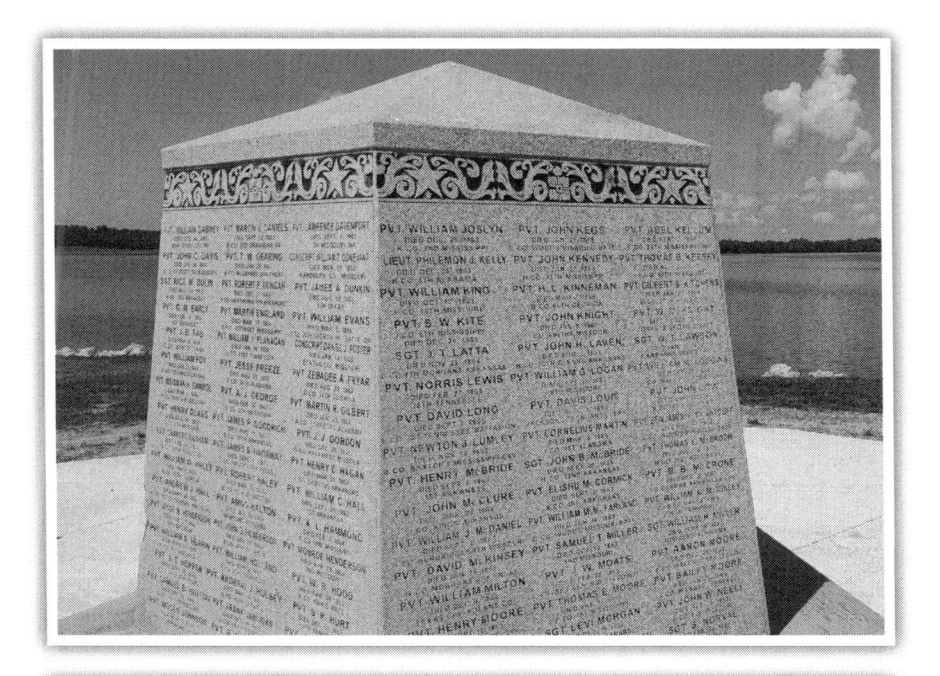

The End

Made in the USA
Middletown, DE
20 October 2022